## THE EARLY KINGDOMS

*The Stars, Like Dust* deals with a time before Trantor gained ascendancy and built its Empire. Mankind is spreading throughout the Galaxy, and many feudal star kingdoms are contending savagely for power, territory, and dominion. In such a time of treachery and high adventure, Biron Farril must face an impossible challenge.

## THE GALACTIC EMPIRE NOVELS

These three novels by Isaac Asimov show the development of the Galactic Empire, whose decay gave rise to the Foundation. They span the time from the first star kingdoms to the full flowering of the Empire that ruled all the Galaxy. Each is a complete, independent novel. Together they provide facts, history, and human developments that are often only hinted at in the Foundation Series. Much of the material in the bestselling *Foundation's Edge* derives directly from background material to be found in these marvelous precursor novels.

By Isaac Asimov
*Published by Ballantine Books:*

## THE CLASSIC FOUNDATION SERIES:
Foundation
Foundation and Empire
Second Foundation
Foundation's Edge

## THE GALACTIC EMPIRE NOVELS:
The Stars, Like Dust
The Currents of Space
Pebble in The Sky

## THE ROBOT NOVELS:
The Caves of Steel
The Naked Sun
The Robots of Dawn

I, ROBOT

THE GODS THEMSELVES

THE END OF ETERNITY

THE BICENTENNIAL MAN and Other Stories

NIGHTFALL and Other Stories

NINE TOMORROWS

THE MARTIAN WAY and Other Stories

THE WINDS OF CHANGE and Other Stories

THE EARLY ASIMOV—Book One

THE EARLY ASIMOV—Book Two

## THE LUCKY STARR ADVENTURES:
*Writing as Paul French:*
David Starr—Space Ranger
Lucky Starr and the Pirates of the Asteroids
Lucky Starr and the Oceans of Venus
Lucky Starr and the Big Sun of Mercury
Lucky Starr and the Moons of Jupiter
Lucky Starr and the Rings of Saturn

# ISAAC ASIMOV

# THE STARS, LIKE DUST

**A Galactic Empire Novel**

A DEL REY BOOK

BALLANTINE BOOKS • NEW YORK

# CONTENTS

# 1. THE BEDROOM MURMURED

The bedroom murmured to itself gently. It was almost below the limits of hearing — an irregular little sound, yet quite unmistakable, and quite deadly.

But it wasn't that which awakened Biron Farrill and dragged him out of a heavy, unrefreshing slumber. He turned his head restlessly from side to side in a futile struggle against the periodic burr-r-r on the end table.

He put out a clumsy hand without opening his eyes and closed contact.

"Hello," he mumbled.

Sound tumbled instantly out of the receiver. It was harsh and loud, but Biron lacked the ambition to reduce the volume.

It said, "May I speak to Biron Farrill?"

Biron said, fuzzily, "Speaking. What d'you want?"

"May I speak to Biron Farrill?" The voice was urgent.

Biron's eyes opened on the thick darkness. He became conscious of the dry unpleasantness of his tongue and the faint odor that remained in the room.

He said, "Speaking. Who is this?"

It went on, disregarding him, gathering tension, a loud voice in the night. "Is anyone there? I would like to speak to Biron Farrill."

Biron raised himself on one elbow and stared at the place where the visiphone sat. He jabbed at the vision control and the small screen was alive with light.

"Here I am," he said. He recognized the smooth, slightly asymmetric features of Sander Jonti. "Call me in the morning, Jonti."

He started to turn the instrument off once more, when Jonti said, "Hello, Hello. Is anyone there? Is this University Hall, Room 526? Hello."

Biron was suddenly aware that the tiny pilot light which would have indicated a live sending circuit was not on. He swore under his breath and pushed the switch. It stayed off. Then Jonti gave up, and the screen went blank, and was merely a small square of featureless light.

Biron turned it off. He hunched his shoulder and tried to burrow into the pillow again. He was annoyed. In the first place, no one had the right to yell at him in the middle of the night. He looked quickly at the gently luminous figures just over the headboard. Three-fifteen. House lights wouldn't go on for nearly four hours.

Besides, he didn't like having to wake to the complete darkness of his room. Four years' custom had not hardened him to the Earthman's habit of building structures of reinforced concrete, squat, thick, and windowless. It was a thousand-year-old tradition dating from the days when the primitive nuclear bomb had not yet been countered by the force-field defense.

But that was past. Nuclear warfare had done its worst to Earth. Most of it was hopelessly radioactive and useless. There was nothing left to lose, and yet architecture mirrored the old fears, so that when Biron woke, it was to pure darkness.

Biron rose on his elbow again. That was strange. He waited. It wasn't the fatal murmur of the bedroom he had become aware of. It was something perhaps even less noticeable and certainly infinitely less deadly.

He missed the gentle movement of air that one took so for granted, that trace of continuous renewal. He tried to swallow easily and failed. The atmosphere seemed to become oppressive even as he realized the situation. The ventilating system had stopped working, and now he really had a grievance. He couldn't even use the visiphone to report the matter.

He tried again, to make sure. The milky square of light sprang out and threw a faint, pearly luster on the bed. It was receiving, but it wouldn't send. Well, it didn't matter. Nothing would be done about it before day, anyway.

He yawned and groped for his slippers, rubbing his eyes with the heels of his palms. No ventilation, eh? That would account for the queer smell. He frowned and sniffed sharply two or three times. No use. It was familiar, but he couldn't place it.

He made his way to the bathroom, and reached automatically for the light switch, although he didn't really need it to draw himself a glass of water. It closed, but uselessly. He tried it several times, peevishly. Wasn't *anything* working? He shrugged, drank in the dark, and felt better. He yawned again on his way back to the bedroom where he tried the main switch. All the lights were out.

Biron sat on the bed, placed his large hands on his hard-muscled thighs and considered. Ordinarily, a thing like this would call for a terrific discussion with the service staff. No one expected hotel service in a college dormitory, but, by Space, there were certain minimum standards of efficiency one could demand. Not that it was of vital importance just now. Graduation was coming and he was through. In three days he'd be saying a last good-by to the room and to the University of Earth; to Earth itself, for that matter.

Still, he might report it anyway, without particular comment. He could go out and use the hall phone. They might bring in a self-powered light or even rig up a fan so he

could sleep without psychosomatic choking sensations. If
not, to Space with them! Two more nights.

In the light of the useless visiphone, he located a pair of
shorts. Over them he slipped a one-piece jumper, and decided that that would be enough for the purpose. He retained
his slippers. There was no danger of waking anybody even
if he clumped down the corridors in spiked shoes, considering the thick, nearly soundproof partitions of this concrete
pile, but he saw no point in changing.

He strode toward the door and pulled at the lever. It
descended smoothly and he heard the click that meant the
door release had been activated. Except that it wasn't. And
although his biceps tightened into lumps, nothing was accomplished.

He stepped away. This was ridiculous. Had there been
a general power failure? There couldn't have been. The
clock was going. The visiphone was still receiving properly.

Wait! It could have been the boys, bless their erratic
souls. It was done sometimes. Infantile, of course, but he'd
taken part in these foolish practical jokes himself. It wouldn't
have been difficult, for instance, for one of his buddies to
sneak in during the day and arrange matters. But, no, the
ventilation and lights were working when he had gone to
sleep.

Very well, then, during the night. The hall was an old,
outmoded structure. It wouldn't have taken an engineering
genius to hocus the lighting and ventilation circuits. Or to
jam the door, either. And now they would wait for morning
and see what would happen when good old Biron found he
couldn't get out. They would probably let him out toward
noon and laugh very hard.

"Ha, ha," said Biron grimly, under his breath. All right,
if that's the way it was. But he would have to do something
about it; turn the tables some way.

He turned away and his toe kicked something which
skidded metallically across the floor. He could barely make
out its shadow moving through the dim visiphone light. He
reached under the bed, patting the floor in a wide arc. He

brought it out and held it close to the light. (They weren't so smart. They should have put the visiphone entirely out of commission, instead of just yanking out the sending circuit.)

He found himself holding a small cylinder with a little hole in the blister on top. He put it close to his nose and sniffed at it. That explained the smell in the room, anyway. It was Hypnite. Of course, the boys would have had to use it to keep him from waking up while they were busy with the circuits.

Biron could reconstruct the proceedings step by step now. The door was jimmied open, a simple thing to do, and the only dangerous part, since he might have wakened then. The door might have been prepared during the day, for that matter, so that it would seem to close and not actually do so. He hadn't tested it. Anyway, once open, a can of Hypnite would be put just inside and the door would be closed again. The anesthetic would leak out slowly, building up to the one in ten thousand concentration necessary to put him definitely under. Then they could enter—masked, of course. Space! A wet handkerchief would keep out the Hypnite for fifteen minutes and that would be all the time needed.

It explained the ventilation system situation. That had to be eliminated to keep the Hypnite from dispersing too quickly. That would have gone first, in fact. The visiphone elimination kept him from getting help; the door jamming kept him from getting out; and the absence of lights induced panic. Nice kids!

Biron snorted. It was socially impossible to be thin-skinned about this. A joke was a joke and all that. Right now, he would have liked to break the door down and have done with it. The well-trained muscles of his torso tensed at the thought, but it would be useless. The door had been built with nuclear blasts in mind. *Damn* that tradition!

But there had to be some way out. He couldn't let them get away with it. First, he would need a light, a real one, not the immovable and unsatisfactory glow of the visiphone.

That was no problem. He had a self-powered flashlight in the clothes closet.

For a moment, as he fingered the closet-door controls, he wondered if they had jammed that too. But it moved open naturally, and slid smoothly into its wall socket. Biron nodded to himself. It made sense. There was no reason, particularly, to jam the closet, and they didn't have too much time, anyway.

And then, with the flashlight in his hand, as he was turning away, the entire structure of his theory collapsed in a horrible instant. He stiffened, his abdomen ridging with tension, and held his breath, listening.

For the first time since awakening, he heard the murmuring of the bedroom. He heard the quiet, irregular chuckling conversation it was holding with itself, and recognized the nature of the sound at once.

It was impossible not to recognize it. The sound was "Earth's death rattle." It was the sound that had been invented one thousand years before.

To be exact, it was the sound of a radiation counter, ticking off the charged particles and the hard gamma waves that came its way, the soft clicking electronic surges melting into a low murmur. It was the sound of a counter, counting the only thing it could count—death!

Softly, on tiptoe, Biron backed away. From a distance of six feet he threw the white beam into the recesses of the closet. The counter was there, in the far corner, but seeing it told him nothing.

It had been there ever since his freshman days. Most freshmen from the Outer Worlds bought a counter during their first week on Earth. They were very conscious of Earth's radioactivity then, and felt the need of protection. Usually they were sold again to the next class, but Biron had never disposed of his. He was thankful for that now.

He turned to the desk, where he kept his wrist watch while sleeping. It was there. His hand was shaking a little as he held it up to the flashlight's beam. The watch strap was an interwoven flexible plastic of an almost liquidly smooth whiteness. And it *was* white. He held it away and tried it at different angles. It *was* white.

That strap had been another freshman purchase. Hard radiation turned it blue, and blue on Earth was the color of death. It was easy to wander into a path of radiating soil during the day if you were lost or careless. The government fenced off as many patches as it could, and of course no one ever approached the huge areas of death that began several miles outside the city. But the strap was insurance.

If it should ever turn a faint blue, you would show up at the hospital for treatment. There was no argument about it. The compound of which it was made was precisely as sensitive to radiation as you were, and appropriate photoelectric instruments could be used to measure the intensity of the blueness so that the seriousness of the case might be determined quickly.

A bright royal blue was the finish. Just as the color would never change back, neither would you. There was no cure, no chance, no hope. You just waited anywhere from a day to a week, and all the hospital could do was to make final arrangements for cremation.

But at least it was still white, and some of the clamor in Biron's thoughts subsided.

There wasn't much radioactivity then. Could it be just another angle of the joke? Biron considered and decided that it couldn't. *Nobody* would do that to anyone else. Not on Earth, anyway, where illegal handling of radioactive material was a capital offense. They took radioactivity seriously here on Earth. They had to. So nobody would do this without overpowering reason.

He stated the thought to himself carefully and explicitly, facing it boldly. The overpowering reason, for instance, of a desire to murder. But why? There could be no motive. In his twenty-three years of life, he had never made a serious enemy. Not *this* serious. Not murder serious.

He clutched at his clipped hair. This was a ridiculous line of thought, but there was no escaping it. He stepped cautiously back to the closet. There had to be something there that was sending out radiation; something that had not been there four hours earlier. He saw it almost at once.

It was a little box not more than six inches in any direction. Biron recognized it and his lower lip trembled slightly. He had never seen one before, but he had heard of them. He lifted the counter and took it into the bedroom. The little murmur fell off, almost ceased. It started again when the thin mica partition, through which the radiation entered, pointed toward the box. There was no question in his mind. It was a radiation bomb.

The present radiations were not in themselves deadly; they were only a fuse. Somewhere inside the box a tiny nuclear bomb was constructed. Short-lived artificial isotopes heated it slowly, permeating it with the appropriate particles. When the threshold of heat and particle density was reached, the pile reacted. Not in an explosion, usually, although the heat of reaction would serve to fuse the box itself into a twist of metal, but in a tremendous burst of deadly radiation that would kill anything living within a radius of six feet to six miles, depending on the bomb's size.

There was no way of telling when the threshold would be reached. Perhaps not for hours, and perhaps the next moment. Biron remained standing helplessly, flashlight held loosely in his damp hands. Half an hour before, the visiphone had awakened him, and he had been at peace then. Now he knew he was going to die.

Biron didn't want to die, but he was penned in hopelessly, and there was no place to hide.

He knew the geography of the room. It was at the end of a corridor, so that there was another room only on one side, and, of course, above and below. He could do nothing about the room above. The room on the same floor was on the bathroom side, and it adjoined via its own bathroom. He doubted that he could make himself heard.

That left the room below.

There were a couple of folding chairs in the room, spare seats to accommodate company. He took one. It made a flat, slapping sound when it hit the floor. He turned it edgewise and the sound became harder and louder.

Between each blow, he waited; wondering if he could rouse the sleeper below and annoy him sufficiently to have him report the disturbance.

Abruptly, he caught a faint noise, and paused, the splintering chair raised above his head. The noise came again, like a faint shout. It was from the direction of the door.

He dropped the chair and yelled in return. He crushed his ear up against the crack where door joined wall, but the fit was good, and the sound even there was dim.

But he could make out his own name being called.

"Farrill! Farrill!" several times over, and something else. Maybe "Are you in there?" or "Are you all right?"

He roared back, "Get the door open." He shouted it three or four times. He was in a feverish sweat of impatience. The bomb might be on the point of letting loose even now.

He thought they heard him. At least, the muffled cry came back, "Watch out. Something, something, blaster." He knew what they meant and backed hurriedly away from the door.

There were a couple of sharp, cracking sounds, and he could actually feel the vibrations set up in the air of the room. Then there followed a splitting noise and the door was flung inward. Light poured in from the corridor.

Biron dashed out, arms flung wide. "Don't come in." he yelled. "For the love of Earth, don't come in. There's a radiation bomb in there."

He was facing two men. One was Jonti. The other was Esbak, the superintendent. He was only partly dressed.

"A radiation bomb?" he stuttered.

But Jonti said, "What size?" Jonti's blaster was still in his hand, and that alone jarred with the dandyish effect of his ensemble, even at this time of night.

Biron could only gesture with his hands.

"All right," said Jonti. He seemed quite cool about it, as he turned to the superintendent. "You'd better evacuate the rooms in this area, and if you have leadsheets anywhere on the university grounds, have them brought out here to line the corridor. And I wouldn't let anyone in there before morning."

He turned to Biron. "It probably has a twelve-to-eighteen-foot radius. How did it get there?"

"I don't know," said Biron. He wiped his forehead with the back of his hand. "If you don't mind, I've got to sit down somewhere." He threw a glance at his wrist, then realized his wrist watch was still in the room. He had a wild impulse to return after it.

There was action now. Students were being hustled out of their rooms.

"Come with me," said Jonti. "I think you had better sit down too."

Biron said, "What brought you out to my room? Not that I'm not thankful, you understand."

"I called you. There was no answer, and I had to see you."

"To see me?" He spoke carefully, trying to control his irregular breathing. "Why?"

"To warn you that your life was in danger."

Biron laughed raggedly. "I found out."

"That was only the first attempt. They'll try again."

"Who are 'they'?"

"Not here, Farrill," said Jonti. "We need privacy for this. You're a marked man, and I may already have endangered myself as well."

# 2. THE NET ACROSS SPACE

The student lounge was empty; it was dark as well. At four-thirty in the morning it could scarcely have been otherwise. Yet Jonti hesitated a moment as he held the door open, listening for occupants.

"No," he said softly, "leave the lights out. We won't need them to talk."

"I've had enough of the dark for one night," muttered Biron.

"We'll leave the door ajar."

Biron lacked the will to argue. He dropped into the nearest chair and watched the rectangle of light through the closing door narrow down to a thin line. Now that it was all over, he was getting the shakes.

Jonti steadied the door and rested his little swagger stick upon the crack of light on the floor. "Watch it. It will tell us if anyone passes, or if the door moves."

Biron said, "Please, I'm not in a conspiratorial mood. If you don't mind, I'd appreciate your telling me whatever it is you want to tell me. You've saved my life, I know, and

11

tomorrow I'll be properly thankful. Right now, I could do with a short drink and a long rest."

"I can imagine your feelings," Jonti said, "but the too-long rest you might have had has been avoided, momentarily. I would like to make it more than just momentarily. Do you know that I know your father?"

The question was an abrupt one, and Biron raised his eyebrows, a gesture lost in the dark. He said, "He has never mentioned knowing you."

"I would be surprised if he did. He doesn't know me by the name I use here. Have you heard from your father recently, by the way?"

"Why do you ask?"

"Because he is in great danger."

"*What?*"

Jonti's hand found the other's arm in the dimness and gripped it firmly. "Please! Keep your voice as it has been." Biron realized, for the first time, that they had been whispering.

Jonti resumed, "I'll be more specific. You father has been taken into custody. You understand the significance?"

"No, I certainly don't understand. *Who* has taken him into custody, and what are you getting at? Why are you bothering me?" Biron's temples were throbbing. The Hypnite and the near death had made it impossible to fence with the cool dandy sitting so close to him that his whispers were as plain as shouts.

"Surely," came the whisper. "you have some inkling of the work your father is doing?"

"If you know my father, you know he is Rancher of Widemos. That is his work."

Jonti said, "Well, there is no reason you should trust me, other than that I am risking my own life for you. But I already know all that you can tell me. As an example, I know that your father has been conspiring against the Tyranni."

"I deny that," said Biron tensely. "Your service to me

this night does not give you the right to make such statements about my father."

"You are foolishly evasive, young man, and you are wasting my time. Don't you see that the situation is beyond verbal fencing? I'll say it outright. Your father is in the custody of the Tyranni. He may be dead by now."

"I don't believe you." Biron half rose.

"I am in a position to know."

"Let's break this off, Jonti. I am in no mood for mystery, and I resent this attempt of yours to——"

"Well, to what?" Jonti's voice lost some of its refined edge. "What do I gain by telling you this? May I remind you that this knowledge of mine, which you will not accept, made it plain to me that an attempt might be made to kill you. Judge by what has happened, Farrill."

Biron said, "Start again and tell it straight. I'll listen."

"Very well. I imagine, Farrill, that you know me to be a fellow countryman from the Nebular Kingdoms, although I've been passing myself off as a Vegan."

"I judged that might be a possibility by your accent. It didn't seem important."

"It's important, my friend. I came here because, like your father, I didn't like the Tyranni. They've been oppressing our people for fifty years. That's a long time."

"I'm not a politician."

Again Jonti's voice had an irritated edge to it. "Oh, I'm not one of their agents trying to get you into trouble. I'm telling you the truth. They caught me a year ago as they have caught your father now. But I managed to get away, and came to Earth where I thought I might be safe until I was ready to return. That's all I need to tell you about myself."

"It is more than I have asked for, sir." Biron could not force the unfriendliness out of his voice. Jonti affected him unfavorably with his too-precise mannerisms.

"I know that. But it is necessary to tell you so much at least, for it was in this manner that I met your father. He worked with me, or, rather, I with him. He knew me but not in his official capacity as the greatest nobleman on the planet of Nephelos. You understand me?"

Biron nodded uselessly in the darkness and said, "Yes."

"It is not necessary to go into that further. My sources of information have been maintained even here, and I know that he has been imprisoned. It is *knowledge*. If it were merely suspicion, this attempt on your life would have been sufficient proof."

"In what way?"

"If the Tyranni have the father, would they leave the son at large?"

"Are you trying to tell me that the Tyranni set that radiation bomb in my room? That's impossible."

"Why is it impossible? Can't you understand their position? The Tyranni rule fifty worlds; they are outnumbered hundreds to one. In such a position, simple force is insufficient. Devious methods, intrigue, assassination are their specialties. The net they weave across space is a wide one, and close-meshed. I can well believe that it extends across five hundred light-years to Earth."

Biron was still in the grip of his nightmare. In the distance there were the faint sounds of the lead shields being moved into place. In his room the counter must still be murmuring.

He said, "It doesn't make sense. I am going back to Nephelos this week. They would know that. Why should they kill me here? If they'd wait, they'd have me." He was relieved to find the flaw, eager to believe his own logic.

Jonti leaned closer and his spiced breath stirred the hairs on Biron's temple. "Your father is popular. His death— and once imprisoned by the Tyranni, his execution becomes a probability you must face—will be resented even by the cowed slave race the Tyranni are trying to breed. You could rally that resentment as the new Rancher of Widemos, and to execute you as well would double the danger for them. To make martyrs is not their purpose. *But* if you were to die in a faraway world, by accident, it would be convenient for them."

"I don't believe you," said Biron. It had become his only defense.

Jonti rose, adjusting his thin gloves. He said, "You go too far, Farrill. Your role would be more convincing if you pretended to no such complete ignorance. Your father has been shielding you from reality for your own protection, presumably, yet I doubt that you could remain completely uninfluenced by his beliefs. Your hate for the Tyranni cannot help being a reflection of his own. You cannot help being ready to fight them."

Jonti said, "He may even recognize your new adulthood to the point of putting you to use. You are conveniently here on Earth and it is not unlikely you may be combining your education with a definite assignment. An assignment, perhaps, for the failure of which the Tyranni are ready to kill you."

"That's silly melodrama."

"Is it? Let it be so, then. If the truth will not persuade you now, events will later. There will be other attempts on your life, and the next one will succeed. From this moment on, Farrill, you are a dead man."

Biron looked up. "Wait! What's your own private interest in the matter?"

"I am a patriot. I would like to see the Kingdoms free again, with governments of their own choosing."

"No. Your *private* interest. I cannot accept idealism only, because I won't believe it of you. I am sorry if that offends you." Biron's words pounded doggedly.

Jonti seated himself again. He said, "My lands have been confiscated. Before my exile it was not comfortable to be forced to take orders from those dwarfs. And since then it has become more imperative than ever to become once again the man my grandfather had been before the Tyranni came. Is that enough of a practical reason for wanting a revolution? Your father would have been a leader of that revolution. Failing him, you!"

"I? I am twenty-three and know nothing of all this. You could find better men."

"Undoubtedly I could, but no one else is the son of your father. If your father is killed, you will be Rancher of Widemos, and as such you would be valuable to me if you were only twelve and an idiot besides. I need you for the same reason the Tyranni must be rid of you. And if my necessity is unconvincing to you, surely theirs cannot be. There *was* a radiation bomb in your room. It could only have been meant to kill you. Who else would want to kill you?"

Jonti waited patiently and picked up the other's whisper.

"No one," said Biron. "No one would want to kill me that I know of. Then it's true about my father!"

"It is true. View it as a casualty of war."

"You think that would make it better? They'll put up a monument to him someday, perhaps? One with a radiating inscription that you can see ten thousand miles out in space?" His voice was becoming a bit ragged. "Is that supposed to make me happy?"

Jonti waited, but Biron said nothing more.

Jonti said, "What do you intend doing?"

"I'm going home."

"You still don't understand your position, then."

"I said, I'm going home. What do you want me to do? If he's alive, I'll get him out of there. And if he's dead, I'll—I'll——"

"Quiet!" The older man's voice was coldly annoyed. "You rave like a child. You can't go to Nephelos. Don't you see that you can't? Am I talking to an infant or to a young man of sense?"

Biron muttered, "What do you suggest?"

"Do you know the Director of Rhodia?"

"The friend of the Tyranni? I know the man. I know who he is. Everyone in the Kingdoms knows who he is. Hinrik V, Director of Rhodia."

"Have you ever met him?"

"No."

"That is what I meant. If you haven't met him, you don't know him. He is an imbecile, Farrill. I mean it literally.

But when the Ranchy of Widemos is confiscated by the Tyranni—and it will be, as my lands were—it will be awarded to Hinrik. There the Tyranni will feel them to be safe, and there you must go."

"Why?"

"Because Hinrik, at least, has influence with the Tyranni; as much influence as a lickspittle puppet may have. He may arrange to have you reinstated."

"I don't see why. He's more likely to turn me over to them."

"So he is. But you'll be on your guard against it, and there is a fighting chance you may avoid it. Remember, the title you carry is valuable and important, but it is not all-sufficient. In this business of conspiracy, one must be practical above all. Men will rally about you out of sentiment and respect for your name, but to hold them, you will need money."

Biron considered. "I need time to decide."

"You have no time. Your time ran out when the radiation bomb was planted in your room. Let us take action. I can give you a letter of introduction to Hinrik of Rhodia."

"You know him so well, then?"

"Your suspicion never sleeps very soundly, does it? I once headed a mission to Hinrik's court on behalf of the Autarch of Lingane. His imbecile's mind will probably not remember me, but he will not dare to show he has forgotten. It will serve as introduction and you can improvise from there. I will have the letter for you in the morning. There is a ship leaving for Rhodia at noon. I have tickets for you. I am leaving myself, but by another route. Don't linger. You're all through here, aren't you?"

"There is the diploma presentation."

"A scrap of parchment. Does it matter to you?"

"Not now."

"Do you have money?"

"Enough."

"Very well. Too much would be suspicious." He spoke sharply. "Farrill!"

Biron stirred out of what was nearly a stupor. "What?"

"Get back to the others. Tell no one you are leaving. Let the act speak."

Biron nodded dumbly. Far away in the recesses of his mind there was the thought that his mission remained unaccomplished and that in this way, too, he failed his dying father. He was racked with a futile bitterness. He might have been told more. He might have shared the dangers. He should not have been allowed to act in ignorance.

And now that he knew the truth, or at least more of it, concerning the extent of his father's role in conspiracy, there was an added importance to the document he was to have obtained from Earth's archives. But there was no time any longer. No time to get the document. No time to wonder about it. No time to save his father. No time, perhaps, to live.

He said, "I'll do as you say, Jonti."

Sander Jonti looked briefly out over the university campus as he paused on the steps of the dormitory. Certainly there was no admiration in his glance.

As he stepped down the bricked walk that wound unsubtly through the pseudo-rustic atmosphere affected by all urban campuses since antiquity, he could see the lights of the city's single important street gleam just ahead. Past it, drowned in daytime, but visible now, was the eternal radioactive blue of the horizon, mute witness of prehistoric wars.

Jonti considered the sky for a moment. Over fifty years had passed since the Tyranni had come and put a sudden end to the separate lives of two dozen sprawling, brawling political units in the depths beyond the Nebula. Now, suddenly and prematurely, the peace of strangulation lay upon them.

The storm that had caught them in one vast thunderclap had been something from which they had not yet recovered. It had left only a sort of twitching that futilely agitated a world here and there, now and then. To organize those twitchings, to align them into a single well-timed heave would be a difficult task, and a long one. Well, he had been rusticating here on Earth long enough. It was time to go back.

The others, back home, were probably trying to get in touch with him at his rooms right now.

He lengthened his stride a bit.

He caught the beam as he entered his room. It was a personal beam, for whose security there were as yet no fears and in whose privacy there was no chink. No formal receiver was required; no thing of metal and wires to catch the faint, drifting surges of electrons, with their whispered impulses swimming through hyperspace from a world half a thousand light-years away.

Space itself was polarized in his room, and prepared for reception. Its fabric was smoothed out of randomness. There was no way of detecting that polarization, except by receiving. And in that particular volume of space, only his own mind could act as receiver; since only the electrical characteristics of his own particular nerve-cell system could resonate to the vibrations of the carrier beam that bore the message.

The message was as private as the unique characteristics of his own brain waves, and in all the universe, with its quadrillions of human beings, the odds against a duplication sufficiently close to allow one man to pick up another's personal wave was a twenty-figured number to one.

Jonti's brain tickled to the call as it whined through the endless empty incomprehensibility of hyperspace.

"...calling...calling...calling...calling..."

Sending was not quite so simple a job as receiving. A mechanical contrivance was needed to set up the highly specific carrier wave that would carry back to the contact beyond the Nebula. That was contained in the ornamental button that he carried on his right shoulder. It was automatically activated when he stepped into his volume of space polarization, and after that he had only to think purposefully and with concentration.

"Here I am!" No need for more specific identification.

The dull repetition of the calling signal halted and became words that took form within his mind. "We greet you, sir. Widemos has been executed. The news is, of course, not yet public."

"It does not surprise me. Was anyone else implicated?"

"No, sir. The Rancher made no statements at any time. A brave and loyal man."

"Yes. But it takes more than simply bravery and loyalty, or he would not have been caught. A little more cowardice might have been useful. No matter! I have spoken to his son, the new Rancher, who has already had his brush with death. He will be put to use."

"May one inquire in what manner, sir?"

"It is better to let events answer your question. Certainly I cannot foretell consequences at this early date. Tomorrow he will set off to see Hinrik of Rhodia."

"Hinrik! The young man will run a fearful risk. Is he aware that——"

"I have told him as much as I can," responded Jonti sharply. "We cannot trust him too far until he has proved himself. Under the circumstances as they exist, we can only view him as a man to be risked, like any other man. He is expendable, *quite* expendable. Do not call me here again, as I am leaving Earth."

And, with a gesture of finality, Jonti broke the connection mentally.

Quietly and thoughtfully, he went over the events of the day and the night, weighing each event. Slowly, he smiled. Everything had been arranged perfectly, and the comedy might now play itself out.

*Nothing* had been left to chance.

# 3. CHANCE AND
# THE WRIST WATCH

The first hour of a space-ship's rise from planetary thralldom is the most prosaic. There is the confusion of departure, which is much the same in essence as that which must have accompanied the shoving off of the first hollowed-out tree trunk on some primeval river.

You have your accommodations; your luggage is taken care of; there is the first stiff moment of strangeness and meaningless hustle surrounding you. The shouted last-moment intimacies, the quieting, the muted clang of the air locks, followed by the slow soughing of air as the locks screw inward automatically, like gigantic drills, becoming airtight.

Then the portentous silence and the red signs flicking in every room: "Adjust accelerations suits. . . . Adjust acceleration suits. . . . Adjust acceleration suits."

The stewards scour the corridors, knocking shortly on each door and jerking it open. "Beg pardon. Suits on."

You battle with the suits, cold, tight, uncomfortable, but

cradled in a hydraulic system which absorbs the sickening
pressures of the take-off.

There is the faraway rumble of the nuclear motors, on
low power for atmospheric maneuvering, followed instantly
by the giving back against the slow-yielding oil of the suit
cradle. You recede almost indefinitely back, then very slowly
forward again as the acceleration decreases. If you survive
nausea during this period, you are probably safe from space
sickness for duration.

The view-room was not open to the passengers for the
first three hours of the flight, and there was a long line
waiting when the atmosphere had been left behind and the
double doors were ready to separate. There were present
not only the usual hundred-per-cent turnout of all Planetaries
(those, in other words, who had never been in space before),
but a fair proportion of the more experienced travelers as
well.

The vision of Earth from space, after all, was one of the
tourist "musts."

The view-room was a bubble on the ship's "skin," a
bubble of curved two-foot-thick, steel-hard transparent plastic. The retractile iridium-steel lid which protected it against
the scouring of the atmosphere and its dust particles had
been sucked back. The lights were out and the gallery was
full. The faces peering over the bars were clear in the Earth-
shine.

For Earth was suspended there below, a gigantic and
gleaming orange-and-blue-and-white-patched balloon. The
hemisphere showing was almost entirely sunlit; the conti-
nents between the clouds, a desert orange, with thin, scattered lines of green. The seas were blue, standing out sharply
against the black of space where they met the horizon. And
all around in the black, undusted sky were the stars.

They waited patiently, those who watched.

It was not the sunlit hemisphere they wanted. The polar
cap, blinding bright, was shifting down into view as the
ship maintained the slight, unnoticed sidewise acceleration

that was lifting it out of the ecliptic. Slowly the shadow of night encroached upon the globe and the huge World-Island of Eurasia-Africa majestically took the stage, north side "down."

Its diseased, unliving soil hid its horror under a night-induced play of jewels. The radioactivity of the soil was a vast sea of iridescent blue, sparkling in strange festoons that spelled out the manner in which the nuclear bombs had once landed, a full generation before the force-field defense against nuclear explosions had been developed so that no other world could commit suicide in just that fashion again.

The eyes watched until, with the hours, Earth was a bright little half coin in the endless black.

Among the watchers was Biron Farrill. He sat by himself in the front row, arms upon the railing, eyes brooding and thoughtful. This was not the way he had expected to leave Earth. It was the wrong manner, the wrong ship, the wrong destination.

His tanned forearm rubbed against the stubble of his chin and he felt guilty about not having shaved that morning. He'd go back to his room after a while and correct that. Meanwhile, he hesitated to leave. There were people here. In his room he would be alone.

Or was that just the reason he should leave?

He did not like the new feeling he had, that of being hunted; that of being friendless.

All friendship had dropped from him. It had shriveled from the very moment he had been awakened by the phone call less than twenty-four hours earlier.

Even in the dormitory he had become an embarrassment. Old Esbak had pounced upon him when he had returned after his talk with Jonti in the student lounge. Esbak was in turmoil; his voice overshrill.

"Mr. Farrill, I've been looking for you. It has been a most unfortunate incident. I can't understand it. Do you have any explanation?"

"No," he half shouted. "I don't. When can I get into my room and get my stuff out?"

"In the morning, I am sure. We've just managed to get the equipment up here to test the room. There is no longer any trace of radioactivity above normal background level. It was a very fortunate escape for you. It must have missed you only by minutes."

"Yes, yes, but if you don't mind, I would like to rest."

"Please use my room till morning and then we'll get you relocated for the few days remaining you. Umm, by the way, Mr. Farrill, if you don't mind, there is another matter."

He was being overly polite. Biron could almost hear the egg-shells give slightly beneath his finicky feet.

"What other matter?" asked Biron wearily.

"Do you know of anyone who might have been interested in—er—hazing you?"

"Hazing me like *this*? Of course not."

"What are your plans, then? The school authorities would, of course, be most unhappy to have publicity arise as a result of this incident."

How he kept referring to it as an "incident"! Biron said dryly, "I understand you. But don't worry. I'm not interested in investigations or in the police. I'm leaving Earth soon, and I'd just as soon not have my own plans disrupted. I'm not bringing any charges. After all, I'm still alive."

Esbak had been almost indecently relieved. It was all they wanted from him. No unpleasantness. It was just an incident to be forgotten.

He got into his old room again at seven in the morning. It was quiet and there was no murmuring in the closet. The bomb was no longer there, nor was the counter. They had probably been taken away by Esbak and thrown into the lake. It came under the head of destroying evidence, but that was the school's worry. He threw his belongings into suitcases and then called the desk for assignment to another room. The lights were working again, he noticed, and so, of course, was the visiphone. The one remnant of last night was the twisted door, its lock melted away.

They gave him another room. That established his intention to stay for anyone that might be listening. Then, using the hall phone, he had called an air cab. He did not think anyone saw him. Let the school puzzle out his disappearance however they pleased.

For a moment he had caught sight of Jonti at the space port. They met in the fashion of a glancing blow. Jonti said nothing; gave no sign of recognition, but after he had passed by, there were in Biron's hand a featureless little black globe that was a personal capsule and a ticket for passage to Rhodia.

He spent a moment upon the personal capsule. It was not sealed. He read the message later in his room. It was a simple introduction with minimum wordage.

Biron's thoughts rested for a while upon Sander Jonti, as he watched Earth shrivel with time there in the viewroom. He had known the man very superficially until Jonti had whirled so devastatingly into his life, first to save it and then to set it upon a new and untried course. Biron had known his name; he had nodded when they passed; had exchanged polite formalities occasionally, but that was all. He had not liked the man, had not liked his coldness, his overdressed, overmannered personality. But all that had nothing to do with affairs now.

Biron rubbed his crew cut with a restless hand and sighed. He actually found himself hungering for Jonti's presence. The man was at least master of events. He had known what to do; he had known what Biron was to do; he had made Biron do it. And now Biron was alone and feeling very young, very helpless, very friendless, and almost frightened.

Through it all, he studiously avoided thinking of his father. It would not help.

"Mr. Malaine."

The name was repeated two or three times before Biron started at the respectful touch upon his shoulder and looked up.

The robot messenger said again, "Mr. Malaine," and for five seconds Biron stared blankly, until he remembered that that was his temporary name. It had been penciled lightly upon the ticket which Jonti had given him. A stateroom had been reserved in that name.

"Yes, what is it? I am Malaine."

The messenger's voice hissed very faintly as the spool within whirled off its message. "I have been asked to inform you that your stateroom has been changed, and that your baggage has already been shifted. If you will see the purser, you will be given your new key. We trust that this will cause no inconvenience for you."

"What's all this?" Biron whirled in his seat, and several of the thinning group of passengers, still watching, looked up at the explosive sound. "What's the idea?"

Of course, it was no use arguing with a machine that had merely fulfilled its function. The messenger had bowed its metal head respectfully, its gently fixed imitation of a human smile of ingratiation unchanging, and had left.

Biron strode out of the view-room and accosted the ship's officer at the door with somewhat more energy than he had planned.

"Look here. I want to see the captain."

The officer showed no surprise. "Is it important, sir?"

"It sure as Space is. I've just had my stateroom shifted without my permission and I'd like to know the meaning of it."

Even at the time, Biron felt his anger to be out of proportion to the cause, but it represented an accumulation of resentment. He had nearly been killed; he had been forced to leave Earth like a skulking criminal; he was going he knew not where to do he knew not what; and now they were pushing him around aboard ship. It was the end.

Yet, through it all, he had the uncomfortable feeling that Jonti, in his shoes, would have acted differently, perhaps more wisely. Well, he wasn't Jonti.

The officer said, "I will call the purser."

"I want the captain," insisted Biron.

"If you wish, then." And after a short conversation through the small ship's communicator suspended from his lapel, he said urbanely, "You will be called for. Please wait."

Captain Hirm Gordell was a rather short and thickset man, who rose politely and leaned over his desk to shake hands with Biron when the latter entered.

"Mr. Malaine," he said, "I am sorry we had to trouble you."

He had a rectangular face, iron-gray hair, a short, well-kept mustache of slightly darker hue, and a clipped smile.

"So am I," said Biron. "I had a stateroom reservation to which I was entitled and I feel that not even you, sir, had the right to change it without my permission."

"Granted, Mr. Malaine. But, you understand, it was rather an emergency. A last-minute arrival, an important man, insisted on being moved to a stateroom closer the gravitational center of the ship. He had a heart condition and it was important to keep ship's gravity as low as possible for him. We had no choice."

"All right, but why pick on me as the one to be shifted."

"It had to be someone. You were traveling alone; you are a young man who we felt would have no difficulty in taking a slightly higher gravity." His eyes traveled automatically up and down Biron's six-feet-two of hard musculature. "Besides, you will find your new room rather more elaborate than your old one. You have not lost by the exchange. No indeed."

The captain stepped from behind his desk. "May I show you your new quarters personally?"

Biron found it difficult to maintain his resentment. It seemed reasonable, this whole matter, and then again, not reasonable either.

The captain was saying as they left his quarters, "May I have your company at my table for tomorrow night's dinner? Our first Jump is scheduled for that time."

Biron heard himself saying, "Thank you. I will be honored."

Yet he thought the invitation strange. Granted that the captain was merely trying to soothe him, yet surely the method was stronger than necessary.

The captain's table was a long one, taking up an entire wall of the salon. Biron found himself near the center, taking an unsuitable precedence over others. Yet there was his place card before him. The steward had been quite firm; there was no mistake.

Biron was not particularly overmodest. As son of the Rancher of Widemos, there had never been any necessity for the development of any such characteristic. And yet as Biron Malaine, he was quite an ordinary citizen, and these things ought not to happen to ordinary citizens.

For one thing, the captain had been perfectly correct about his new stateroom. It *was* more elaborate. His original room had been what his ticket called for, a single, second class, while the replacement was a double room, first. There was a bathroom adjoining, private, of course, equipped with a stall shower and an air dryer.

It was near "officer's country," and the presence of uniforms was almost overpowering. Lunch had been brought to his room on silver service. A barber made a sudden appearance just before dinner. All this was perhaps to be expected when one traveled on a luxury space liner, first class, but it was too good for Biron Malaine.

It was far too good, for by the time the barber had arrived, Biron had just returned from an afternoon walk that had taken him through the corridors in a purposely devious path. There had been crewmen in his path wherever he had turned—polite, clinging. He shook them free somehow and reached 140 D, his first room, the one he had never slept in.

He stopped to light a cigarette and, in the interval spent thus, the only passenger in sight turned a corridor. Biron touched the signal light briefly and there was no answer.

Well, the old key had not been taken from him yet. An oversight, no doubt. He placed the thin oblong sliver of metal into its orifice and the unique pattern of leaden opacity within the aluminum sheath activated the tiny phototube. The door opened and he took one step inside.

It was all he needed. He left and the door closed automatically behind him. He had learned one thing immediately. His old room was not occupied; neither by an important personage with a weak heart nor by anyone else. The bed and furnishings were too neat; no trunks, no toilet articles were in sight; the very *air* of occupancy was missing.

So the luxury they were surrounding him with served only to prevent his taking further action to get back his original room. They were bribing him to stay quietly out of the old room. Why? Was it the room they were interested in, or was it himself?

And now he sat at the captain's table with the questions unanswered and rose politely with the rest as the captain entered, strode up the steps of the dais on which the long table was set, and took his place.

*Why* had they moved him?


There was music in the ship, and the walls that separated the salon from the view-room had been retracted. The lights were low and tinged with orange-red. The worst of such space sickness as there might have been after the original acceleration or as the result of the first exposure to the minor gravity variations between various parts of the ship had passed by now; the salon was full.

The captain leaned forward slightly and said to Biron, "Good evening, Mr. Malaine. How do you find your new room?"

"Almost too satisfactory, sir. A little rich for my way of life." He said it in a flat monotone, and it seemed to him that a faint dismay passed momentarily over the captain's face.

Over the dessert, the skin of the view-room's glass bubble slid smoothly back into its socket, and the lights dimmed to nearly nothing. Neither sun, earth, nor any planet was in view on that large, dark screen. They were facing the

Milky Way, that longwise view of the Galactic Lens, and it made a luminous diagonal track among the hard, bright stars.

Automatically the tide of conversation ebbed. Chairs shifted so that all faced the stars. The dinner guests had become an audience, the music a faint whisper.

The voice over the amplifiers was clear and well balanced in the gathered quiet.

"Ladies, gentlemen! We are ready for our first Jump. Most of you, I suppose, know, at least theoretically, what a Jump is. Many of you, however—more than half, in point of fact—have never experienced one. It is to those last I would like to speak in particular.

"The Jump is exactly what the name implies. In the fabric of space-time itself, it is impossible to travel faster than the speed of light. That is a natural law, first discovered by one of the ancients, the traditional Einstein, perhaps, except that so many things are credited to him. Even at the speed of light, of course, it would take years, in resting time, to reach the stars.

"Therefore one leaves the space-time fabric to enter the little-known realm of hyperspace, where time and distance have no meaning. It is like traveling across a narrow isthmus to pass from one ocean to another, rather than remaining at sea and circling a continent to accomplish the same distance.

"Great amounts of energy are required, of course, to enter this 'space within space' as some call it, and a great deal of ingenious calculation must be made to insure re-entry into ordinary space time at the proper point. The result of the expenditure of this energy and intelligence is that immense distances can be traversed in zero time. It is only the Jump which makes interstellar travel possible.

"The Jump we are about to make will take place in about ten minutes. You will be warned. There is never more than some momentary minor discomfort; therefore, I hope all of you will remain calm. Thank you."

The ship lights went out altogether, and there were only the stars left.

It seemed a long while before a crisp announcement filled the air momentarily: "The jump will take place in exactly one minute." And then the same voice counted the seconds backwards: "Fifty . . . forty . . . thirty . . . twenty . . . ten . . . five . . . three . . . two . . . one . . ."

It was as though there had been a momentary discontinuity in existence, a bump which joggled only the deep inside of a man's bones.

In that immeasurable fraction of a second, one hundred light-years had passed, and the ship, which had been on the outskirts of the solar system, was now in the depths of interstellar space.

Someone near Biron said shakily, "Look at the stars!"

In a moment the whisper had taken life through the large room and hissed itself across the tables: "The stars! See!"

In that same immeasurable fraction of a second the star view had changed radically. The center of the great Galaxy, which stretched thirty thousand light-years from tip to tip, was closer now, and the stars had thickened in number. They spread across the black velvet vacuum in a fine powder, back-dropping the occasional brightness of the nearby stars.

Biron, against his will, remembered the beginning of a poem he himself had once written at the sentimental age of nineteen, on the occasion of his first space flight; the one that had first taken him to the Earth he was now leaving. His lips moved silently:

> "The stars, like dust, encircle me
> In living mists of light;
> And all of space I seem to see
> In one vast burst of sight."

The lights went on then, and Biron's thoughts were snapped out of space as suddenly as they had entered it. He was in a space liner's salon again, with a dinner dragging to an end, and the hum of conversation rising to a prosaic level again.

He glanced at his wrist watch, half looked away, then, very slowly, brought the wrist watch into focus again. He stared at it for a long minute. It was the wrist watch he had left in his bedroom that night; it had withstood the killing radiation of the bomb, and he had collected it with the rest of his belongings the next morning. How many times had he looked at it since then? How many times had he stared at it, taken mental note of the time and no note at all of the other piece of information it shouted at him?

For the plastic wristband was *white*, not blue. *It was white!*

Slowly the events of that night, *all* of them, fell into place. Strange how one fact could shake all the confusion out of them.

He rose abruptly, murmuring, "Pardon me!" under his breath. It was a breach of etiquette to leave before the captain, but that was a matter of small importance to him then.

He hastened to his room, striding up the ramps rapidly, rather than waiting for the non-gravity elevators. He locked the door behind him and looked quickly through the bathroom and the built-in closets. He had no real hope of catching anyone. What they had had to do, they must have done hours ago.

Carefully, he went through his baggage. They had done a thorough job. With scarcely any sign to show that they had come and gone, they had carefully withdrawn his identification papers, a packet of letters from his father, and even his capsular introduction to Hinrik of Rhodia.

That was why they had moved him. It was neither the old room nor the new that they were interested in; merely the process of moving. For nearly an hour they must have legitimately—*legitimately*, by Space!—concerned themselves with his baggage, and served their own purposes thereby.

Biron sank down upon the double bed and thought furiously, but it didn't help. The trap had been perfect. *Everything* had been planned. Had it not been for the completely unpredictable chance of his leaving his wrist watch in the bedroom that night, he would not even now have realized how close-meshed the Tyranni's net through space was.

There was a soft burr as his door signal sounded.

"Come in," he said.

It was the steward, who said respectfully, "The captain wishes to know if there is anything he can do for you. You seemed ill as you left the table."

"I'm all right," he said.

How they watched him! And in that moment he knew that there was no escape, and that the ship was carrying him politely, but surely, to his death.

# 4. FREE?

Sander Jonti met the other's eyes coldly. He said, "Gone, you say?"

Rizzett passed a hand over his ruddy face. "*Something* is gone. I don't know its identity. It might have been the document we're after, certainly. All we know about it is that it had been dated somewhere in the fifteenth to twenty-first century of Earth's primitive calendar, and that it is dangerous."

"Is there any definite reason to believe that the missing one is *the* document?"

"Only circumstantial reasoning. It was guarded closely by the Earth government."

"Discount that. An Earthman will treat any document relating to the pre-Galactic past with veneration. It's their ridiculous worship of tradition."

"But this one was stolen and yet they never announced the fact. Why do they guard an empty case?"

"I can imagine their doing that rather than finding themselves forced to admit that a holy relic has been stolen. Yet

34

I cannot believe that young Farrill obtained it after all. I thought you had him under observation."

The other smiled. "He didn't get it."

"How do you know?"

Jonti's agent quickly exploded his land mine. "Because the document has been gone twenty years."

"What?"

"It has not been seen for twenty years."

"Then it can't be the right one. It was less than six months ago that the Rancher learned of its existence."

"Then somebody else beat him to it by nineteen and a half years."

Jonti considered. He said, "It does not matter. It cannot matter."

"Why so?"

"Because I have been here on Earth for months. Before I came, it was easy to believe that there might be information of value on the planet. But consider now. When Earth was the only inhabited planet in the Galaxy, it was a primitive place, militarily speaking. The only weapon they had ever invented worth mentioning was a crude and inefficient nuclear-reaction bomb for which they had not even developed the logical defense." He flung his arm outward in a delicate gesture to where the blue horizon gleamed its sickly radioactivity beyond the thick concrete of the room.

He went on. "All this is placed in sharp focus for me as a temporary resident here. It is ridiculous to assume that it is possible to learn anything from a society at that level of military technology. It is always very fashionable to assume that there are lost arts and lost sciences, and there are always these people who make a cult of primitivism and who make all sorts of ridiculous claims for the prehistoric civilizations on Earth."

Rizzett said, "Yet the Rancher was a wise man. He told us specifically that it was the most dangerous document he knew. You remember what he said. I can quote it. He said, 'The matter is death for the Tyranni, and death for us as well; but it would mean final life for the Galaxy.'"

"The Rancher, like all human beings, can be wrong."

"Consider, sir, that we have no idea as to the nature of the document. It could, for instance, be somebody's laboratory notes which had never been published. It might be something that could relate to a weapon the Earthmen had never recognized as a weapon; something which on the face of it might not be a weapon——"

"Nonsense. You are a military man and should know better. If there is one science into which man has probed continuously and successfully, it is that of military technology. No potential weapon would remain unrealized for ten thousand years. I think, Rizzett, we will return to Lingane."

Rizzett shrugged. He was not convinced.

Nor, a thousandfold, was Jonti. It had been stolen, and that was significant. It had been worth stealing! Anyone in the Galaxy might have it now.

Unwillingly the thought came to him that the Tyranni might have it. The Rancher had been most evasive on the matter. Even Jonti himself had not been trusted sufficiently. The Rancher had said it carried death; it could not be used without having it cut both ways. Jonti's lips clamped shut. The fool and his idiotic hintings! And now the Tyranni had him.

What if a man like Aratap were now in the possession of such a secret as this might be? Aratap! The one man, now that the Rancher was gone, who remained unpredictable; the most dangerous Tyrannian of them all.

Simok Aratap was a small man; a little bandy-legged, narrow-eyed fellow. He had the stumpy, thick-limbed appearance of the average Tyrannian, yet though he faced an exceptionally large and well-muscled specimen of the subject worlds, he was completely self-possessed. He was the confident heir (in the second generation) of those who had left their windy, infertile worlds and sparked across the emptiness to capture and enchain the rich and populous planets of the Nebular Regions.

His father had headed a squadron of small, flitting ships that had struck and vanished, then struck again, and made scrap of the lumbering titanic ships that had opposed them.

The worlds of the Nebula had fought in the old fashion, but the Tyranni had learned a new one. Where the huge, glittering vessels of the opposed navies attempted single combat, they found themselves flailing at emptiness and wasting their stores of energy. Instead, the Tyranni, abandoning power alone, stressed speed and co-operation, so that the opposed Kingdoms toppled one after the other, singly; each waiting (half joyfully at the discomfiture of its neighbors), fallaciously secure behind its steel-shipped ramparts, until its own turn came.

But those wars were fifty years earlier. Now the Nebular Regions were satrapies that required merely the acts of occupation and taxation. Previously there had been worlds to gain, Aratap thought wearily, and now there was little left to do but to contend with single men.

He looked at the young man who faced him. He was *quite* a young man. A tall fellow with very good shoulders indeed; an absorbed, intent face with the hair of his head cut ridiculously short in what was undoubtedly a collegiate affectation. In an unofficial sense, Aratap was sorry for him. He was obviously frightened.

Biron did not recognize the feeling inside him as "fright." If he had been asked to put a name to the emotion, he would have described it as "tension." All his life he had known the Tyranni to be the overlords. His father, strong and vital though he was, unquestioned on his own estate, respectfully heard on others, was quiet and almost humble in the presence of the Tyranni.

They came occasionally to Widemos on polite visits, with questions as to the annual tribute they called taxation. The Rancher of Widemos was responsible for the collection and delivery of these funds on behalf of the planet Nephelos and, perfunctorily, the Tyranni would check his books.

The Rancher himself would assist them out of their small vessels. They would sit at the head of the table at mealtimes, and they would be served first. When they spoke, all other conversation stopped instantly.

As a child, he wondered that such small, ugly men should be so carefully handled, but he learned as he grew up that they were to his father what his father was to a cow hand. He even learned to speak softly to them himself, and to address them as "Excellency."

He had learned so well that now that he faced one of the overlords, one of the Tyranni, he could feel himself shiver with tension.

The ship which he had considered his prison became officially one on the day of landing upon Rhodia. They had signaled at his door and two husky crewmen had entered and stood on either side of him. The captain, who followed, had said in a flat voice, "Biron Farrill, I take you into custody by the power vested in me as captain of this vessel, and hold you for questioning by the Commissioner of the Great King."

The Commissioner was this small Tyrannian who sat before him now, seemingly abstracted and uninterested. The "Great King" was the Khan of the Tyranni, who still lived in the legendary stone palace on the Tyrannian's home planet.

Biron looked furtively about him. He was not physically constrained in any way, but four guards in the slate blue of the Tyrannian Outer Police flanked him, two and two. They were armed. A fifth, with a major's insignia, sat beside the Commissioner's desk.

The Commissioner spoke to him for the first time. "As you may know"—his voice was high-pitched, thin—"the old Rancher of Widemos, your father, has been executed for treason."

His faded eyes were fixed on Biron's. There seemed nothing beyond mildness in them.

Biron remained stolid. It bothered him that he could do nothing. It would have been so much more satisfying to howl at them, to flail madly at them, but that would not make his father less dead. He thought he knew the reason for this initial statement. It was intended to break him down, to make him give himself away. Well, it wouldn't.

He said evenly, "I am Biron Malaine of Earth. If you are questioning my identity, I would like to communicate with the Terrestrial Consul."

"Ah yes, but we are at a purely informal stage just now. You are Biron Malaine, you say, of Earth. And yet"—Aratap indicated the papers before him—"there are letters here which were written by Widemos to his son. There is a college registration receipt and tickets to commencement exercises made out to a Biron Farrill. They were found in your baggage."

Biron felt desperate but he did not let it show. "My baggage was searched illegally, so that I deny that those can be admitted as evidence."

"We are not in a court of law, Mr. Farrill or Malaine. How do you explain them?"

"If they were found in my baggage, they were placed there by someone else."

The Commissioner passed it by, and Biron felt amazed. His statements sounded so thin, so patently foolish. Yet the Commissioner did not remark upon them, but only tapped the black capsule with his forefinger. "And this introduction to the Director of Rhodia? Also not yours?"

"No, that is mine." Biron had planned that. The introduction did not mention his name. He said, "There is a plot to assassinate the Director——"

He stopped, appalled. It sounded so completely unconvincing when he finally put the beginning of his carefully prepared speech into actual sound. Surely the Commissioner was smiling cynically at him?

But Aratap was not. He merely sighed a little and with quick, practiced gestures removed contact lenses from his eyes and placed them carefully in a glass of saline solution that stood on the desk before him. His naked eyeballs were a little watery.

He said, "And you know of it? Even back on Earth, five

hundred light-years away? Our own police here on Rhodia have not heard of it."

"The police are here. The plot is being developed on Earth."

"I see. And are you their agent? Or are you going to warn Hinrik against them?"

"The latter, of course."

"Indeed? And why do you intend to warn him?"

"For the substantial reward which I expect to get."

Aratap smiled. "That, at least, rings true and lends a certain truthful gloss to your previous statements. What are the details of the plot you speak of?"

"That is for the Director only."

A momentary hesitation, then a shrug. "Very well. The Tyranni are not interested and do not concern themselves with local politics. We will arrange an interview between yourself and the Director and that will be our contribution to his safety. My men will hold you until your baggage can be collected, and then you will be free to go. Remove him."

The last was to the armed men, who left with Biron. Aratap replaced his contact lenses, an action which removed instantly that look of vague incompetence their absence had seemed to induce.

He said to the major, who had remained, "We will keep an eye, I think, on this young Farrill."

The officer nodded shortly. "Good! For a moment I thought you might have been taken in. To me, his story was quite incoherent."

"It was. It's just that which makes him maneuverable for the while. All young fools who get their notions of interstellar intrigue from the video spy thrillers are easily handled. He *is*, of course, the son of the ex-Rancher."

And now the major hesitated. "Are you sure? It's a vague and unsatisfactory accusation we have against him."

"You mean that it might be arranged evidence after all? For what purpose?"

"It could mean that he is a decoy, sacrificed to divert our attention from a real Biron Farrill elsewhere."

"No. Improbably theatrical, that. Besides, we have a photocube."

"What? Of the boy?"

"Of the Rancher's son. Would you like to see it?"

"I certainly would."

Aratap lifted the paperweight upon his desk. It was a simple glass cube, three inches on each side, black and opaque. He said, "I meant to confront him with it if it had seemed best. It is a cute process, this one, Major. I don't know if you're acquainted with it. It's been developed recently among the inner worlds. Outwardly, it seems an ordinary photocube, but when it is turned upside down, there's an automatic molecular re-arrangement which renders it totally opaque. It is a pleasant conceit."

He turned the cube right side up. The opacity shimmered for a moment, then cleared slowly like a black fog wisping and feathering before the wind. Aratap watched it calmly, hands folded across his chest.

And then it was water-clear, and a young face smiled brightly out of it, accurate and alive, trapped and solidified in mid-breath forever.

"An item," said Aratap, "in the ex-Rancher's possessions. What do you think?"

"It is the young man, without question."

"Yes." The Tyrannian official regarded the photocube thoughtfully. "You know, using this same process, I don't see why six photographs could not be taken in the same cube. It has six faces, and by resting the cube on each of them in turn, a series of new molecular orientations might be induced. Six connected photographs, flowing one into another as you turned, a static phenomenon turned dynamic and taking on new breadth and vision. Major, it would be a new art form." A mounting enthusiasm had crept into his voice.

But the silent major looked faintly scornful, and Aratap left his artistic reflections to say, abruptly, "Then you will watch Farrill?"

"Certainly."

"Watch Hinrik as well."

*"Hinrik?"*

"Of course. It is the whole purpose of freeing the boy. I want some questions answered. Why is Farrill seeing Hinrik? What is the connection between them? The dead Rancher did not play a lone hand. There was—there *must* have been—a well-organized conspiracy behind them. And we have not yet located the workings of that conspiracy."

"But surely Hinrik could not be involved. He lacks the intelligence, even if he had the courage."

"Granted. But it is just because he is half an idiot that he may serve them as a tool. If so, he represents a weakness in our scheme of things. We obviously cannot afford to neglect the possibility."

He gestured absently; the major saluted, turned on his heel, and left.

Aratap sighed, thoughtfully turned the photocube in his hand, and watched the blackness wash back like a tide of ink.

Life was simpler in his father's time. To smash a planet had a cruel grandeur about it; while this careful maneuvering of an ignorant young man was simply cruel.

And yet necessary.

# 5. UNEASY LIES THE HEAD

The directorship of Rhodia is not ancient, when compared with Earth, as a habitat for *Homo sapiens*. It is not ancient even when compared with the Centaurian or Sirian worlds. The planets of Arcturus, for instance, had been settled for two hundred years when the first space ships circled the Horsehead Nebula to find the nest of hundreds of oxygen-water planets behind. They clustered thickly and it was a real find, for although planets infest space, few can satisfy the chemical necessities of the human organism.

There are between one and two hundred billion radiant stars in the Galaxy. Among them are some five hundred billion planets. Of these, some have gravities more than 120 per cent that of Earth, or less than 60 per cent, and are therefore unbearable in the long run. Some are too hot, some too cold. Some have poisonous atmospheres. Planetary atmospheres consisting largely or entirely of neon, methane, ammonia, chlorine—even silicon tetrafluoride—have been recorded. Some planets lack water, one with oceans of almost pure sulphur dioxide having been described. Others lack carbon.

Any one of these failings is sufficient, so that not one world in a hundred thousand can be lived on. Yet this still leaves an estimated four million habitable worlds.

The exact number of these which are actually occupied is disputable. According to the *Galactic Almanac*, admittedly dependent on imperfect records, Rhodia was the 1098th world settled by man.

Ironically enough, Tyrann, eventually Rhodia's conqueror, was the 1099th.

The pattern of history in the Trans-Nebular Region was distressingly similar to that elsewhere during the period of development and expansion. Planet republics were set up in rapid succession, each government confined to its own world. With expanding economy, neighboring planets were colonized and integrated with the home society. Small "empires" were established and these inevitably clashed.

Hegemony over sizable regions were established by first one, then another of these governments, depending upon the fluctuations of the fortunes of war and of leadership.

Only Rhodia maintained a lengthy stability, under the able dynasty of the Hinriads. It was perhaps well on the road to establishing finally a universal Trans-Nebular Empire in a stolid century or two, when the Tyranni came and did the job in ten years.

Ironical that it should be the men of Tyrann. Until then, during the seven hundred years of its existence, Tyrann had done little better than maintain a precarious autonomy, thanks largely to the undesirability of its barren landscape, which, because of a planetary water dearth, was largely desert.

But even after the Tyranni came, the Directorship of Rhodia continued. It had even grown. The Hinriads were popular with the people, so their existence served as a means of easy control. The Tyranni did not care who got the cheers as long as they themselves received the taxes.

To be sure, the Directors were no longer the Hinriads of old. The Directorship had always been elective within the family so that the ablest might be chosen. Adoptions into the family had been encouraged for the same purpose.

But now the Tyranni could influence the elections for other reasons, and twenty years earlier, for instance, Hinrik (fifth of that name) had been chosen Director. To the Tyranni, it had seemed a useful choice.

Hinrik had been a handsome man at the time of his election, and he still made an impressive appearance when he addressed the Rhodian Council. His hair had grayed smoothly, and his thick mustache remained, startlingly enough, as black as his daughter's eyes.

At the moment he faced his daughter, and she was furious. She lacked only two inches of his height, and the Director lacked less than an inch of six feet. She was a smoldering girl, dark of hair and of eyes, and, at the moment, loweringly dark of complexion.

She said again, "I can't do it! I *won't* do it!"

Hinrik said, "But, Arta, Arta, this is unreasonable. What am I to do? What *can* I do? In my position, what choice have I?"

"If Mother were alive, *she* would find a way out." And she stamped her foot. Her full name was Artemisia, a royal name that had been borne by at least one female of the Hinriads in every generation.

"Yes, yes, no doubt. Bless my soul! what a way your mother had with her! There are times when you seem all of her and none of me. But surely, Arta, you haven't given him a chance. Have you observed his—ah—better points?"

"Which are those?"

"The ones which..." He gestured vaguely, thought a while and gave it up. He approached her and would have put a consoling hand upon her shoulder, but she squirmed away from him, her scarlet gown shimmering in the air.

"I have spent an evening with him," she said bitterly, "and he tried to kiss me. It was disgusting!"

"But everyone kisses, dear. It's not as though this were your grandmother's time—of respected memory. Kisses are nothing—less than nothing. Young blood, Arta, young blood!"

"Young blood, my foot. The only time that horrible little

man has had young blood in him these fifteen years has been immediately after a transfusion. He's four inches shorter than I am, Father. How can I be seen in public with a pygmy?"

"He's an important man. Very important!"

"That doesn't add a single inch to his height. He is bowlegged, as they all are, and his breath smells."

"His breath smells?"

Artemisia wrinkled her nose at her father. "That's right; it smells. It has an unpleasant odor. I didn't like it and I let him know it."

Hinrik dropped his jaw wordlessly for a moment, then said in a hoarse half whisper, "You let him know it? You implied that a high official of the Royal Court of Tyrann could have an unpleasant personal characteristic?"

"He did! I have a nose, you know! So when he got too close, I just held it and pushed. A figure of man to admire, that one is. He went flat on his back, with his legs sticking up." She gestured with her fingers in illustration, but it was lost on Hinrik, who, with a moan, hunched his shoulders and put his hands over his face.

He peered miserably from between two fingers. "What will happen now? How can you act so?"

"It didn't do me any good. Do you know what he said? *Do you know what he said?* It was the last straw. It was absolutely the limit. I made up my mind then that I couldn't stand that man if he were ten feet tall."

"But—but—what did he say?"

"He said—straight out of a video, Father—he said, 'Ha! A spirited wench! I like her all the better for that!' and two servants helped him stagger to his feet. But he didn't try to breathe in my face again."

Hinrik doubled into a chair, leaned forward and regarded Artemisia earnestly. "You could go through the motions of marrying him, couldn't you? You needn't be in earnest. Why not merely, for the sake of political expedience——"

"How do you mean, not in earnest, Father? Shall I cross

the fingers of my left hand while signing the contract with my right?"

Hinrik looked confused. "No, of course not. What good would that do? How would crossing fingers alter the validity of the contract? Really, Arta, I'm surprised at your stupidity."

Artemisia sighed. "What *do* you mean, then?"

"Mean by what? You see, you've disrupted things. I can't keep my mind on matters properly when you argue with me. What was I saying?"

"I was merely to pretend I was getting married, or something. Remember?"

"Oh yes. I mean, you needn't take it too seriously, you see."

"I can have lovers, I suppose."

Hinrik stiffened and frowned. "Arta! I brought you up to be a modest, self-respecting girl. So did your mother. How can you say such things? It's shameful."

"But isn't that what you mean?"

"*I* can say it. I am a man, a mature man. A girl like you ought not to repeat it."

"Well, I have repeated it and it's out in the open. I don't mind lovers. I'll probably *have* to have them if I'm forced to marry for reasons of state, but there are limits." She placed her hands upon her hips, and the cape-like sleeves of her gown slithered away from her tanned and dimpled shoulders. "What will I do between lovers? He'll still be my husband and I just can't bear that particular thought."

"But he's an old man, my dear. Life with him would be short."

"Not short enough, thank you. Five minutes ago he had young blood. Remember?"

Hinrik spread his hands wide and let them drop. "Arta, the man is a *Tyrannian*, and a powerful one. He is in good odor at the Khan's court."

"The Khan might think it's a good odor. He probably would. He probably stinks himself."

Hinrik's mouth was an O of horror. Automatically, he

looked over his shoulder. Then he said hoarsely, "Don't ever say anything like that again."

"I will if I feel like it. Besides, the man has had three wives already." She forestalled him. "Not the Khan, the man you want me to marry."

"But they're dead," Henrik explained earnestly. "Arta, they're not alive. Don't think that. How can you imagine I would let my daughter marry a bigamist? We'll have him produce documents. He married them consecutively, not simultaneously, and they're dead now, entirely dead, all of them."

"It's no wonder."

"Oh, bless my soul, what shall I do?" He made a last effort at dignity. "Arta, it is the price of being a Hinriad and a Director's daughter."

"I didn't ask to be a Hinriad and a Director's daughter."

"That has nothing to do with it. It is just that the history of all the Galaxy, Arta, shows that there are occasions when reasons of state, the safety of planets, the best interests of people require that, uh——"

"That some poor girl prostitute herself."

"Oh, this vulgarity! Someday, you'll see—someday you'll say something of the sort in public."

"Well, that's what it is, and I won't do it. I'd rather die. I'd rather do *anything*. And I will."

The Director got to his feet and held out his arms to her. His lips trembled and he said nothing. She ran to him in a sudden agony of tears and clung desperately to him. "I can't, Daddy. I can't. Don't make me."

He patted her awkwardly. "But if you don't, what will happen? If the Tyranni are displeased, they will remove me, imprison me, maybe even exec——" He gagged on the word. "These are very unhappy times, Arta—very unhappy. The Rancher of Widemos was condemned last week and I believe he has been executed. You remember him, Arta? He was at court half a year ago. A big man, with a round head and deep-set eyes. You were frightened of him at first.

"I remember."

"Well, he is probably dead. And who knows? Myself next, perhaps. Your poor, harmless old father next. It is a bad time. He was at our court and that's very suspicious."

She suddenly held herself out at arm's length. "Why should it be suspicious? You weren't involved with him, were you?"

"I? Indeed not. But if we openly insult the Khan of Tyrann by refusing an alliance with one of his favorites, they may choose to think even that."

Hinrik's hand wringing was interrupted by the muted buzz of the extension. He started uneasily.

"I'll take it in my own room. You just rest. You'll feel better after a nap. You'll see, you'll see. It's just that you're a little on edge now."

Artemisia looked after him and frowned. Her face was intensely thoughtful, and for minutes only the gentle tide of her breasts betrayed life.

There was the sound of stumbling feet at the door, and she turned.

"What is it?" The tone was sharper than she had intended.

It was Hinrik, his face sallow with fear. "Major Andros was calling."

"Of the Outer Police?"

Hinrik could only nod.

Artemisia cried, "Surely, he's not——" She paused reluctantly at the threshold of putting the horrible thought into words, but waited in vain for enlightenment.

"There is a young man who wants an audience. I don't know him. Why should he come here? He's from Earth." He was gasping for breath and staggered as he spoke, as though his mind were on a turntable and he had to follow it in its gyrations.

The girl ran to him and seized his elbow. She said sharply, "Sit down, Father. Tell me what has happened." She took him and some of the panic drained out of his face.

"I don't know exactly," he whispered. "There's a young

man coming here with details concerning a plot on my life. On *my* life. And *they* tell me I ought to listen to him."

He smiled foolishly. "I'm loved by the people. No one would want to kill me. Would they? Would they?"

He was watching her eagerly, and relaxed when she said, "Of course no one would want to kill you."

Then he was tense again. "Do you think it might be *they*?"

"Who?"

He leaned over to whisper. "The Tyranni. The Rancher of Widemos was here yesterday, and they killed him." His voice ascended the scale. "And now they're sending someone over to kill me."

Artemisia gripped his shoulder with such force that his mind turned to the present pain.

She said, "Father! Sit quietly! Not a word! Listen to me. No one will kill you. Do you hear me? No one will kill you. It was six months ago that the Rancher was here. Do you remember? Wasn't it six months ago? Think!"

"So long?" whispered the Director. "Yes, yes, it must have been so."

"Now you stay here and rest. You're overwrought. I'll see the young man myself and then I'll bring him to you if it's safe."

"Will you, Arta? Will you? He won't hurt a woman. Surely he wouldn't hurt a woman."

She bent suddenly and kissed his cheek.

"Be careful," he murmured, and closed his eyes wearily.

# 6. THAT WEARS A CROWN

Biron Farrill waited uneasily in one of the outer buildings on the Palace Grounds. For the first time in his life he experienced the deflating sensation of being a provincial.

Widemos Hall, where he had grown up, had been beautiful in his eyes, and now his memory endowed it with merely barbaric glitter. Its curved lines, its filigree work, its curiously wrought turrets, its elaborate "false windows"——He winced at the thought of them.

But this—this was different.

The Palace Grounds of Rhodia were no mere lump of ostentation built by the petty lords of a cattle kingdom; nor were they the childlike expression of a fading and dying world. They were the culmination, in stone, of the Hinriad dynasty.

The buildings were strong and quiet. Their lines were straight and vertical, lengthening toward the center of each structure, yet avoiding anything as effeminate as a spire effect. They held a bluntness about them, yet lifted into a climax that affected the onlooker without revealing their method of doing so at a casual glance. They were reserved, self-contained, proud.

And as each building was, so was the group as a whole, the huge Palace Central becoming a crescendo. One by one, even the few artificialities remaining in the masculine Rhodian style had dropped away. The very "false windows," so valued as decoration and so useless in a building of artificial light and ventilation, were done away with. And that, somehow, without loss.

It was only line and plane, a geometrical abstraction that led the eye upward to the sky.

The Tyrannian major stopped briefly at his side as he left the inner room.

"You will be received now," he said.

Biron nodded, and after a while a larger man in a uniform of scarlet and tan clicked heels before him. It struck Biron with sudden force that those who had the real power did not need the outward show and could be satisfied with slate blue. He recalled the garish formality of a Rancher's life and bit his lip at the thought of its futility.

"Biron Malaine?" asked the Rhodian guard, and Biron rose to follow.

There was a little gleaming monorail carriage that was suspended delicately by diamagnetic forces upon a single ruddy shaft of metal. Biron had never seen one before. He paused before entering.

The little carriage, big enough for five or six at the most, swayed with the wind, a graceful teardrop returning the gleam of Rhodia's splendid sun. The single rail was slender, scarcely more than a cable, and ran the length of the carriage's underside without touching. Biron bent and saw blue sky all the length between them. For a moment, as he watched, a lifting gust of wind raised it, so that it hovered a full inch above the rail, as though impatient for flight and tearing at the invisible force field that held it. Then it fluttered back to the rail, closer and still closer, but never touching.

"Get in," said the guard behind him impatiently, and Biron climbed two steps into the carriage.

The steps remained long enough for the guard to follow, then lifted quietly and smoothly into place, forming no break in the carriage's even exterior.

Biron became aware that the outer opacity of the carriage was an illusion. Once within, he found himself sitting in a transparent bubble. At the motion of a small control, the carriage lifted upward. It climbed the heights easily, buffeting the atmosphere which whistled past. For one moment, Biron caught the panorama of the Palace Grounds from the apex of the arc.

The structures became a gorgeous whole (could they have been originally conceived other than as an air view?) laced by the shining copper threads, along one or two of which the graceful carriage bubbles skimmed.

He felt himself pressed forward, and the carriage came to a dancing halt. The entire run had lasted less than two minutes.

A door stood open before him. He entered and it closed behind him. There was no one in the room, which was small and bare. For the moment, no one was pushing him, but he felt no comfort because of it. He was under no illusions. Ever since that damned night, others had forced his moves.

Jonti had placed him on the ship. The Tyrannian Commissioner had placed him here. And each move had increased the measure of his desperation.

It was obvious to Biron that the Tyrannian had not been fooled. It had been too easy to get away from him. The Commissioner might have called the Terrestrial Consul. He might have hyper-waved Earth, or taken his retinal patterns. These things were routine; they could not have been omitted accidentally.

He remembered Jonti's analysis of affairs. Some of it might still be valid. The Tyranni would not kill him outright to create another martyr. But Hinrik was their puppet, and he was as capable as they of ordering an execution. And then he would have been killed by one of his own, and the Tyranni would merely be disdainful onlookers.

Biron clenched his fists tightly. He was tall and strong, but he was unarmed. The men who would come for him would have blasters and neuronic whips. He found himself backing against the wall.

He whirled quickly at the small sound of the opening door to his left. The man who entered was armed and uniformed but there was a girl with him. He relaxed a bit. It was only a girl with him. At another time he might have observed the girl closely, since she was worth observation and approval, but at the moment she was only a girl.

They approached together, stopping some six feet away. He kept his eye on the guard's blaster.

The girl said to the guard, "I'll speak to him first, Lieutenant."

There was a little vertical line between her eyes as she turned to him. She said, "Are you the man who has this story of an assassination plot against the Director?"

Biron said, "I was told I would see the Director."

"That is impossible. If you have anything to say, say it to me. If your information is truthful and useful, you will be well treated."

"May I ask you who you are? How do I know you are authorized to speak for the Director?"

The girl seemed annoyed. "I am his daughter. Please answer my questions. Are you from outside the System?"

"I am from Earth." Biron paused, then added, "Your Grace."

The addition pleased her. "Where is that?"

"It is a small planet of the Sirian Sector, Your Grace."

"And what is your name?"

"Biron Malaine, Your Grace."

She stared at him thoughtfully. "From Earth? Can you pilot a space ship?"

Biron almost smiled. She was testing him. She knew very well that space navigation was one of the forbidden sciences in the Tyranni-controlled worlds.

He said, "Yes, Your Grace." He could prove that when the performance test came, *if* they let him live that long. Space navigation was not a forbidden science on Earth, and in four years one could learn much.

She said, "Very well. And your story?"

He made his decision suddenly. To the guard alone, he would not have dared. But this was a girl, and if she were not lying, if she really *were* the Director's daughter, she might be a persuasive factor on his behalf.

He said, "There is no assassination plot, Your Grace."

The girl was startled. She turned impatiently to her companion. "Would you take over, Lieutenant? Get the truth out of him."

Biron took a step forward and met the cold thrust of the guard's blaster. He said urgently, "Wait, Your Grace. Listen to me! It was the only way to see the Director. Don't you understand?"

He raised his voice and sent it after her retreating form. "Will you tell His Excellency, at least, that I am Biron Farrill and claim my sanctuary right?"

It was a feeble straw at which to clutch. The old feudal customs had been losing their force with the generations even before the Tyranni came. Now they were archaisms. But there was nothing else. Nothing.

She turned, and her eyebrows were arched. "Are you claiming now to be of the aristocratic order? A moment ago your name was Malaine."

A new voice sounded unexpectedly. "So it was, but it is the second name which is correct. You are Biron Farrill indeed, my good sir. Of course you are. The resemblance is unmistakable."

A small, smiling man stood in the doorway. His eyes, widely spaced and brilliant, were taking in all of Biron with an amused sharpness. He cocked his narrow face upward at Biron's height and said to the girl, "Don't you recognize him, too, Artemisia?"

Artemisia hurried to him, her voice troubled. "Uncle Gil, what are you doing here?"

"Taking care of my interests, Artemisia. Remember that if there were an assassination, I would be the closet of the Hinriads to the possible succession." Gillbret oth Hinriad winked elaborately, then added, "Oh, get the lieutenant out of here. There isn't any danger."

She ignored that and said, "Have you been tapping the communicator again?"

"But yes. Would you deprive me of an amusement? It is pleasant to eavesdrop on them."

"Not if they catch you."

"The danger is part of the game, my dear. The amusing part. After all, the Tyranni do not hesitate to tap the Palace. We can't do much without *their* knowing. Well, turnabout, you know. Aren't you going to introduce me?"

"No, I'm not," she said shortly. "This is none of your business."

"Then I'll introduce you. When I heard his name, I stopped listening and came in." He moved past Artemisia, stepped up to Biron, inspected him with an impersonal smile, and said, "This is Biron Farrill."

"I have said so myself," said Biron. More than half his attention was upon the lieutenant, who still held his blaster in firing position.

"But you have not added that you are the son of the Rancher of Widemos."

"I would have but for your interruption. In any case, you've got the story now. Obviously, I had to get away from the Tyranni, and that without giving them my real name." Biron waited. This was it, he felt. If the next move was not an immediate arrest, there was still a trifling chance.

Artemisia said, "I see. This *is* a matter for the Director. You are sure there is no plot of any sort, then."

"None, Your Grace."

"Good. Uncle Gil, will you remain with Mr. Farrill? Lieutenant, will you come with me?"

Biron felt weak. He would have liked to sit down, but no suggestion to that effect was made by Gillbret, who still inspected him with an almost clinical interest.

"The Rancher's son! Amusing!"

Biron brought his attention downward. He was tired of cautious monosyllables and careful phrases. He said abruptly, "Yes, the Rancher's son. It is a congenital situation. Can I help you in any other way?"

Gillbret showed no offense. His thin face merely creased further as his smile widened. He said, "You might satisfy my curiosity. You really came for Sanctuary? Here?"

"I'd rather discuss that with the Director, sir."

"Oh, get off it, young man. You'll find that very little business can be done with the Director. Why do you suppose you had to deal with his daughter just now? That's an amusing thought, if you'll consider it."

"Do you find everything amusing?"

"Why not? As an attitude toward life, it's an amusing one. It's the only adjective that will fit. Observe the universe, young man. If you can't force amusement out of it, you might as well cut your throat, since there's damned little good in it. I haven't introduced myself, by the way. I'm the Director's cousin."

Biron said coldly, "Congratulations!"

Gillbret shrugged. "You're right. It's not impressive. And I'm likely to remain just that indefinitely since there is no assassination to be expected, after all."

"Unless you whip one up for yourself."

"My dear sir, your sense of humor! You'll have to get used to the fact that nobody takes *me* seriously. My remark was only an expression of cynicism. You don't suppose the Directorship is worth anything these days, do you? Surely you cannot believe that Hinrik was always like this? He was never a great brain, but with every year he becomes more impossible. I forget! You haven't seen him yet. But you will! I hear him coming. When he speaks to you, remember that he is the ruler of the largest of the Trans-Nebular Kingdoms. It will be an amusing thought."

Hinrik bore his dignity with the ease of experience. He acknowledged Biron's painstakingly ceremonious bow with

the proper degree of condescension. He said, with a trace
of abruptness, "And your business with us, sir?"

Artemisia was standing at her father's side, and Biron
noticed, with some surprise, that she was quite pretty. He
said, "Your Excellency, I have come on behalf of my father's good name. You must know his execution was unjust."

Hinrik looked away. "I knew your father slightly. He
was in Rhodia once or twice." He paused, and his voice
quavered a bit. "You are very like him. Very. But he was
tried, you know. At least I imagine he was. And according
to law. Really, I don't know the details."

"Exactly, Your Excellancy. But I would like to learn
those details. I am sure that my father was no traitor."

Hinrik broke in hurriedly. "As his son, of course, it is
understandable that you should defend your father, but,
really, it is difficult to discuss such matters of state now.
Highly irregular, in fact. Why don't you see Aratap?"

"I do not know him, Excellency."

"Aratap! The Commissioner! The Tyrannian Commissioner!"

"I have seen him and he sent me here. Surely, you understand that I dare not let the Tyranni——"

But Hinrik had grown stiff. His hand had wandered to
his lips, as though to keep them from trembling, and his
words were consequently muffled. "Aratap sent you here,
you say?"

"I found it necessary to tell him——"

"Don't repeat what you told him. I know," said Hinrik.
"I can do nothing for you, Rancher—uh—Mr. Farrill. It
is not in my jurisdiction alone. The Executive Council—
stop pulling at me, Arta. How can I pay attention to matters
when you distract me?—must be consulted. Gillbret! Will
you see that Mr. Farrill is taken care of? I will see what
can be done. Yes, I will consult the Executive Council. The
forms of law, you know. Very important. Very important."

He turned on his heel, mumbling.

Artemisia lingered for a moment and touched Biron's

sleeve. "A moment. Was it true, your statement that you could pilot a space ship?"

"Quite true," said Biron. He smiled at her, and after a moment's hesitation, she dimpled briefly in return.

"Gillbret," she said, "I want to speak to you later."

She hurried off. Biron looked after her till Gillbret tweaked at his sleeve.

"I presume you are hungry, perhaps thirsty, would like a wash?" asked Gillbret. "The ordinary amenities of life continue, I take it?"

"Thank you, yes," said Biron. The tension had almost entirely washed out of him. For a moment he was relaxed and felt wonderful. She *was* pretty. *Very* pretty.

But Hinrik was not relaxed. In his own chambers his thoughts whirled at a feverish pace. Try as he might, he could not wriggle out of the inevitable conclusion. It was a trap! Aratap had sent him and it was a trap!

He buried his head in his hands to quiet and deaden the pounding, and then he knew what he *had* to do.

# 7. MUSICIAN OF THE MIND

Night settles in time on all habitable planets. Not always, perhaps, at respectable intervals, since recorded periods of rotation vary from fifteen to fifty-two hours. That fact requires the most strenuous psychological adjustment from those traveling from planet to planet.

On many planets such adjustments are made, and the waking-sleeping periods are tailored to fit. On many more the almost universal use of conditioned atmospheres and artificial lighting make the day-night question secondary except in so far as it modifies agriculture. On a few planets (those of the extremes) arbitrary divisions are made which ignore the trivial facts of light and dark.

But always, whatever the social conventions, the coming of night has a deep and abiding psychological significance, dating back to man's pre-human arboreal existence. Night will always be a time of fear and insecurity, and the heart will sink with the sun.

Inside Palace Central there was no sensory mechanism by which one could tell the coming of night, yet Biron felt that coming through some indefinite instinct hidden in the unknown corridors of the human brain. He knew that out-doors the night's blackness was scarcely relieved by the futile sparks of the stars. He knew that, if it were the right time of year, the jagged "hole in space" known as the Horse-head Nebula (so familiar to all the Trans-Nebular Kingdoms) inked out half the stars that might otherwise have been visible.

And he was depressed again.

He had not seen Artemisia since the little talk with the Director, and he found himself resenting that. He had looked forward to dinner; he might have spoken to her. Instead, he had eaten alone, with two guards lounging discontentedly just outside the door. Even Gillbret had left him, presumably to eat a less lonely meal in the company one would expect in a palace of the Hinriads.

So that when Gillbret returned and said, "Artemisia and I have been discussing you," he obtained a prompt and interested reaction.

It merely amused him and he said so. "First I want to show you my laboratory," he had said then. He gestured and the two guards moved off.

"What kind of a laboratory?" asked Biron with a definite loss of interest.

"I build gadgets," was the vague response.

It was not a laboratory to the eye. It was more nearly a library, with an ornate desk in the corner.

Biron looked it over slowly. "And you build gadgets here? What kind of gadgets?"

"Well, special tapping devices to spy out the Tyrannian spy beams in a brand-new way. Nothing *they* can detect. That's how I found out about you, when the first word came through from Aratap. And I have other amusing trinkets. My visisonor, for instance. Do you like music?"

"Some kinds."

"Good. I invented an instrument, only I don't know if you can properly call it music." A shelf of book films slid out and aside at a touch. "This is not really much of a hiding place, but nobody takes *me* seriously, so they don't look. Amusing, don't you think? But I forget, you're the un-amused one."

It was a clumsy, boxlike affair, with that singular lack of gloss and polish that marks the homemade object. One side of it was studded with little gleaming knobs. He put it down with that side upward.

"It isn't pretty," Gillbret said, "but who in Time cares? Put the lights out. No, no! No switches or contacts. Just wish the lights were out. Wish hard! Decide you want them out."

And the lights dimmed, with the exception of the faint pearly luster of the ceiling that made them two ghostly faces in the dark. Gillbret laughed lightly at Biron's exclamation.

"Just one of the tricks of my visisonor. It's keyed to the mind like personal capsules are. Do you know what I mean?"

"No, I don't, if you want a plain answer."

"Well," he said, "look at it this way. The electric field of your brain cells sets up an induced one in the instrument. Mathematically, it's fairly simple, but as far as I know, no one has ever jammed all the necessary circuits into a box this size before. Usually, it takes a five-story generating plant to do it. It works the other way too. I can close circuits here and impress them directly upon your brain, so that you'll see and hear without any intervention of eyes and ears. Watch!"

There was nothing to watch, at first. And then something fuzzy scratched faintly at the corner of Biron's eyes. It became a faint blue-violet ball hovering in mid-air. It followed him as he turned away, remained unchanged when he closed his eyes. And a clear, musical tone accompanied it, was part of it, *was* it.

It was growing and expanding and Biron became disturbingly aware that it existed inside his skull. It wasn't really a color, but rather a colored sound, though without noise. It was tactile, yet without feeling.

It spun and took on an iridescence while the musical tone rose in pitch till it hovered above him like falling silk. Then it exploded so that gouts of color splattered at him in touches that burned momentarily and left no pain.

Bubbles of rain-drenched green rose again with a quiet, soft moaning. Biron thrust at them in confusion and became aware that he could not see his hands nor feel them move. There was nothing, only the little bubbles filling his mind to the exclusion of all else.

He cried out soundlessly and the fantasy ceased. Gillbret was standing before him once again in a lighted room, laughing. Biron felt an acute dizziness and wiped shakily at a chilled, moist forehead. He sat down abruptly.

"What happened?" he demanded, in as stiff a tone as he could manage.

Gillbret said, "I don't know. I stayed out of it. You don't understand? It was something your brain had lacked previous experience with. Your brain was sensing directly and it had no method of interpretation for such a phenomenon. So as long as you concentrated on the sensation, your brain could only attempt, futilely, to force the effect into the old, familiar pathways. It attempts separately and simultaneously to interpret it as sight and sound and touch. Were you conscious of an odor, by the way? Sometimes it seemed to me that I smelled the stuff. With dogs I imagine the sensation would be forced almost entirely into odor. I'd like to try it on animals someday.

"On the other hand, if you ignore it, make no attack upon it, it fades away. It's what I do, when I want to observe its effects on others, and it isn't difficult."

He placed a little veined hand upon the instrument, fingering the knobs aimlessly. "Sometimes I think that if one could really study this thing, one could compose symphonies in a new medium; do things one could never do with simple sound or sight. I lack the capacity for it, I'm afraid."

Biron said abruptly, "I'd like to ask you a question."

"By all means."

"Why don't you put your scientific ability to worth-while use instead of——"

"Wasting it on useless toys? I don't know. It may not be entirely useless. This is against the law, you know."

"What is?"

"The visisonor. Also my spy devices. If the Tyranni knew, it could easily mean a death sentence."

"Surely, you're joking."

"Not at all. It is obvious that you were brought up on a cattle ranch. The young people cannot remember what it was like in the old days, I see." Suddenly his head was to one side and his eyes were narrowed to slits. He asked, "Are you opposed to Tyrannian rule? Speak freely. I tell you frankly that *I* am. I tell you also that your father was."

Biron said calmly, "Yes, I am."

"Why?"

"They are strangers, outlanders. What right have they to rule in Nephelos or in Rhodia?"

"Have you always thought that?"

Biron did not answer.

Gillbret sniffed. "In other words, you decided they were strangers and outlanders only after they executed your father, which, after all, was their simple right. Oh, look, don't fire up. Consider it reasonably. Believe me, I'm on your side. But think! You father was Rancher. What rights did his herdsmen have? If one of them had stolen cattle for his own use or to sell to others, what would have been his punishment? Imprisonment as a thief. If he had plotted the death of your father, for whatever reason, for perhaps a worthy reason in his own eyes, what would have been the result? Execution, undoubtedly. And what right has your father to make laws and visit punishment upon his fellow human beings? *He* was *their* Tyranni.

"Your father, in his own eyes and in mine, was a patriot. But what of that? To the Tyranni, he was a traitor, and they removed him. Can you ignore the necessity of self-defense? The Hinriads have been a bloody lot in their time. Read your history, young man. All governments kill as part of the nature of things.

"So find a better reason to hate the Tyranni. Don't think

it is enough to replace one set of rulers by another; that the simple change brings freedom."

Biron pounded a fist into his cupped palm. "All this objective philosophy is fine. It is very soothing to the man who lives apart. But what if it had been your father who was murdered?"

"Well, wasn't it? My father was Director before Hinrik, and he was killed. Oh, not outright, but subtly. They broke his spirit, as they are breaking Hinrik's now. They wouldn't have *me* as Director when my father died; I was just a little too unpredictable. Hinrik was tall, handsome, and, above all, pliant. Yet not pliant enough, apparently. They hound him continuously, grind him into a pitiful puppet, make sure he cannot even itch without permission. You've seen him. He's deteriorating by the month now. His continual state of fear is pathetically psychopathic. But that—all that—is not why I want to destroy Tyrannian rule."

"No?" said Biron. "You have invented an entirely new reason?"

"An entirely old one, rather. The Tyranni are destroying the right of twenty billion human beings to take part in the development of the race. You've been to school. You've learned the economic cycle. A new planet is settled"—he was ticking the points off on his fingers—"and its first care is to feed itself. It becomes an agricultural world, a herding world. It begins to dig in the ground for crude ore to export, and sends it agricultural surplus abroad to buy luxuries and machinery. That is the second step. Then, as population increases and foreign investments grow, an industrial civilization begins to bud, which is the third step. Eventually, the world becomes mechanized, importing food, exporting machinery, investing in the development of more primitive worlds, and so on. The fourth step.

"Always the mechanized worlds are the most thickly populated, the most powerful, militarily—since war is a function of machines—and they are usually surrounded by a fringe of agricultural, dependent worlds.

"But what has happened to us? We were at the third

step, with a growing industry. And now? That growth has been stopped, frozen, forced to recede. It would interfere with Tyrannian control of our industrial necessities. It is a short-term investment on their part, because eventually we'll become unprofitable as we become impoverished. But meanwhile, they skim the cream.

"Besides, if we industrialized ourselves, we might develop weapons of war. So industrialization is stopped; scientific research is forbidden. And eventually the people become so used to that, they lack the realization even that anything is missing. So that you are surprised when I tell you that I could be executed for building a visisonor.

"Of course, someday we will beat the Tyranni. It is fairly inevitable. They can't rule forever. No one can. They'll grow soft and lazy. They will intermarry and lose much of their separate traditions. They will become corrupt. But it may take centuries, because history doesn't hurry. And when those centuries have passed, we will still all be agricultural worlds with no industrial or scientific heritage to speak of, while our neighbors on all sides, those not under Tyrannian control, will be strong and urbanized. The Kingdoms will be semicolonial areas forever. They will *never* catch up, and we will be merely observers in the great drama of human advance."

Biron said, "What you say is not completely unfamiliar."

"Naturally, if you were educated on Earth. Earth occupies a very peculiar position in social development."

"Indeed?"

"Consider! All the Galaxy has been in a continuous state of expansion since the first discovery of interstellar travel. We have always been a growing society, therefore, an immature society. It is obvious that human society reached maturity in only one place and at only one time and that this was on Earth immediately prior to its catastrophe. There we had a society which had temporarily lost all possibility for geographical expansion and was therefore faced with such problems as over-population, depletion of resources, and so on; problems that have never faced any other portion of the Galaxy.

"They were *forced* to study the social sciences intensively. We have lost much or all of that and it is a pity. Now here's an amusing thing. When Hinrik was a young man, he was a great Primitivist. He had a library on things Earthly that was unparalleled in the Galaxy. Since he became Director, that's gone by the board along with everything else. But in a way, I've inherited it. Their literature, such scraps as survive, is fascinating. It has a peculiarly introspective flavor to it that we don't have in our extraverted Galactic civilization. It is *most* amusing."

Biron said, "You relieve me. You have been serious for so long that I began to wonder if you had lost your sense of humor."

Gillbret shrugged. "I am relaxing and it is wonderful. First time in months, I think. Do you know what it is to play a part? To split your personality deliberately for twenty-four hours a day? Even when with friends? Even when alone, so that you will never forget inadvertently? To be a dilettante? To be eternally amused? To be of no account? To be so effete and faintly ridiculous that you have convinced all who know you of your own worthlessness? All so that your life may be safe even though it means it has become barely worth living. But, even so, once in a while I can fight them."

He looked up, and his voice was earnest, almost pleading. "You can pilot a ship. I cannot. Isn't that strange? You talk about my scientific ability, yet I cannot pilot a simple one-man space gig. But you can, and it follows then that you must leave Rhodia."

There was no mistaking the pleading, but Biron frowned coldly. "Why?"

Gillbret continued, speaking rapidly: "As I said, Artemisia and I have discussed you and arranged this. When you leave here, proceed directly to her room, where she is waiting for you. I have drawn a diagram for you, so that you won't have to ask your way through the corridors." He was forcing a small sheet of metallene upon Biron. "If anyone does stop you, say that you have been summoned by the Director, and proceed. There will be no trouble if you show no uncertainty——"

"Hold on!" said Biron. He was not going to do it again. Jonti had chevied him to Rhodia and, consequently, succeeded in bringing him before the Tyranni. The Tyrannian Commissioner had then chevied him to Palace Central before he could feel his own secret way there and, consequently, subjected him, nakedly unprepared, to the whims of an unsteady puppet. But that was all! His moves, henceforward, might be severely limited, but, by Space and Time, they would be his own. He felt very stubborn about it.

He said, "I'm here on what is important business to me, sir. I'm not leaving."

"What! Don't be a young idiot." For a moment the old Gillbret was showing through. "Do you think you will accomplish anything here? Do you think you will get out of the Palace alive if you let the morning sun rise? Why, Hinrik will call in the Tyranni and you will be imprisoned within twenty-four hours. He is only waiting this while because it takes him so long to make up his mind to do anything. He is my cousin. I know him, I tell you."

Biron said, "And if so, what is that to you? Why should you be so concerned about me?" He was *not* going to be chevied. He would never again be another man's fleeing marionette.

But Gillbret was standing, staring at him. "I want you to take me with you. I'm concerned about myself. I cannot endure life under the Tyranni any longer. It is only that neither Artemisia nor I can handle a ship or we would have left long ago. It's our lives too."

Biron felt a certain weakening of his resolve. "The Director's daughter? What has she to do with this?"

"I believe that she is the most desperate of us. There is a special death for women. What should be ahead of a Director's daughter who is young, personable, and unmarried, but to become young, personable, and married? And who, in these days, should be the delightful groom? Why, an old, lecherous Tyrannian court functionary who has buried three wives and wishes to revive the fires of his youth in the arms of a girl."

"Surely the Director would never allow such a thing!"

"The Director will allow anything. Nobody waits upon his permission."

Biron thought of Artemisia as he had last seen her. Her hair had been combed back from her forehead and allowed to fall in simple straightness, with a single inward wave at shoulder level. Clear, fair skin, black eyes, red lips! Tall, young, smiling! Probably the description of a hundred million girls throughout the Galaxy. It would be ridiculous to let that sway him.

Yet he said, "Is there a ship ready?"

Gillbret's face wrinkled under the impact of a sudden smile. But, before he could say a word, there came a pounding at the door. It was no gentle interruption of the photobeam, no tender of the weapon of authority.

It was repeated, and Gillbret said, "You'd better open the door."

Biron did so, and two uniforms were in the room. The foremost saluted Gillbret with abrupt efficiency, then turned to Biron. "Biron Farrill, in the name of the Resident Commissioner of Tyrann and of the Director of Rhodia, I place you under arrest."

"On what charge?" demanded Biron.

"On that of high treason."

A look of infinite loss twisted Gillbret's face momentarily. He looked away. "Hinrik was quick this once; quicker than I had ever expected. An amusing thought!"

He was the old Gillbret, smiling and indifferent, eyebrows a little raised, as though inspecting a distasteful fact with a faint tinge of regret.

"Please follow me," said the guard, and Biron was aware of the neuronic whip resting easily in the other's hand.

# 8. A LADY'S SKIRTS

Biron's throat was growing dry. He could have beaten either of the guards in fair fight. He knew that, and he itched for the chance. He might even have made a satisfactory showing against both together. But they had the whips, and he couldn't have lifted an arm without having them demonstrate the fact. Inside his mind he surrendered. There was no other way.

But Gillbret said, "Let him take his cloak, men."

Biron, startled, looked quickly toward the little man and retracted that same surrender. He knew he had no cloak.

The guard whose weapon was out clicked his heels as a gesture of respect. He motioned his whip at Biron. "You heard milord. Get your cloak and snap it up!"

Biron stepped back as slowly as he dared. He retreated to the bookcase and squatted, groping behind the chair for his nonexistent cloak. And as his fingers clawed at the empty space behind the chair, he waited tensely for Gillbret.

The visisonor was just a queer knobbed object to the guards. It would mean nothing to them that Gillbret fingered and stroked the knobs gently. Biron watched the muzzle of the whip intensely and allowed it to fill his mind. Certainly nothing else he saw or heard (*thought* he saw or heard) must enter.

But how much longer?

The armed guard said, "Is your cloak behind that chair? Stand up!" He took an impatient step forward, and then stopped. His eyes narrowed in deep amazement and he looked sharply to his left.

That was it! Biron straightened and threw himself forward and down. He clasped the guard's knees and jerked. The guard was down with a jarring thud, and Biron's large fist closed over the other's hand, grasping for the neuronic whip it contained.

The other guard had his weapon out, but for the moment it was useless. With his free hand, he was brushing wildly at the space before his eyes.

Gillbret's high-pitched laugh sounded. "Anything bothering you, Farrill?"

"Don't see a thing," he grunted, and then, "except this whip I've got now."

"All right, then leave. They can't do anything to stop you. Their minds are full of sights and sounds that don't exist." Gillbret skipped out of the way of the writhing tangle of bodies.

Biron wrenched his arms free and heaved upward. He brought his arm down solidly just below the other's ribs. The guard's face twisted in agony and his body doubled convulsively. Biron rose, whip in hand.

"Careful," cried Gillbret.

But Biron did not turn quickly enough. The second guard was upon him, bearing him down again. It was a blind attack. What it was that the guard thought he was grasping, it was impossible to tell. That he knew nothing of Biron at the moment was certain. His breath rasped in Biron's ear and there was a continuous incoherent gurgle bubbling in his throat.

Biron twisted in an attempt to bring his captured weapon into play and was frighteningly aware of the blank and empty eyes that must be aware of some horror invisible to anyone else.

Biron braced his legs and shifted weight in an effort to break loose, quite uselessly. Three times he felt the guard's whip flung hard against his hip, and flinched at the contact.

And then the guard's gurgle dissolved into words. He yelled, "I'll get you all!" and the very pale, almost invisible shimmer of the ionized air in the path of the whip's energy beam made its appearance. It swept wide through the air, and the path of the beam intersected Biron's foot.

It was as though he had stepped into a bath of boiling lead. Or as if a granite block had toppled upon it. Or as if it had been crunched off by a shark. Actually, nothing had happened to it physically. It was only that the nerve endings that governed the sensation of pain had been universally and maximally stimulated. Boiling lead could have done no more.

Biron's yell tore his throat raw, and he collapsed. It did not even occur to him that the fight was over. Nothing mattered but the ballooning pain.

Yet, though Biron did not know it, the guard's grip had relaxed, and minutes later, when the young man could force his eyes open and blink away the tears, he found the guard backed against the wall, pushing feebly at nothing with both hands and giggling to himself. The first guard was still on his back, arms and legs spread-eagled now. He was conscious, but silent. His eyes were following something in an erratic path, and his body quivered a little. There was froth on his lips.

Biron forced himself to his feet. He limped badly as he made his way to the wall. He used the butt of the whip and the guard slumped. Then back to the first, who made no defense either, his eyes moving silently to the very moment of unconsciousness.

Biron sat down again, nursing his foot. He stripped shoe and stocking from it, and stared in surprise at the unbroken skin. He chafed it and grunted at the burning sensation. He looked up at Gillbret, who had put down his visisonor and was now rubbing one lean cheek with the back of his hand.

"Thank you," said Biron, "for the help of your instrument."

Gillbret shrugged. He said, "There'll be more here soon. Get to Artemisia's room. Please! Quickly!"

Biron realized the sense of that. His foot had subsided to a quiet quiver of pain, but it felt swollen and puffy. He put on a stocking and tucked the shoe under his elbow. He already had one whip, and he relieved the second guard of the other. He stuffed it precariously within his belt.

He turned at the door and asked, with a sense of crawling revulsion, "What did you make them see, sir?"

"I don't know. I can't control it. I just gave them all the power I could and the rest depended on their own complexes. Please don't stand there talking. Do you have the map to Artemisia's room?"

Biron nodded and set off down the corridor. It was quite empty. He could not walk quickly, since trying to do so made his walk a hobble.

He looked at his watch, then remembered that he had somehow never had the time to adjust it to Rhodian local chronometry. It still ran on Standard Interstellar Time as used aboard ship, where one hundred minutes made an hour and a thousand a day. So the figure 876 which gleamed pinkly on the cool metal face of the watch meant nothing now.

Still, it had to be well into the night, or into the planetary sleeping period, at any rate (supposing that the two did not coincide), as otherwise the halls would not be so empty and the bas-reliefs on the wall would not phosphoresce unwatched. He touched one idly as he passed, a coronation scene, and found it to be two-dimensional. Yet it gave the perfect illusion of standing out from the wall.

It was sufficiently unusual for him to stop momentarily in order to examine the effect. Then he remembered and hurried on.

The emptiness of the corridor struck him as another sign

of the decadence of Rhodia. He had grown very conscious of all these symbols of decline now that he had become a rebel. As the center of an independent power, the Palace would always have had it sentries and its quiet wardens of the night.

He consulted Gillbret's crude map and turned to the right, moving up a wide, curving ramp. There might have been processions here once, but nothing of that would be left now.

He leaned against the proper door and touched the photo-signal. The door moved ajar a bit, then opened wide.

"Come in, young man."

It was Artemisia. Biron slipped inside, and the door closed swiftly and silently. He looked at the girl and said nothing. He was gloomily conscious of the fact that his shirt was torn at the shoulder so that one sleeve flapped loosely, that his clothes were grimy and his face welted. He remembered the shoe he was still carrying, dropped it and wriggled his foot into it.

Then he said, "Mind if I sit down?"

She followed him to the chair, and stood before him, a little annoyed. "What happened? What's wrong with your foot?"

"I hurt it," he said shortly. "Are you ready to leave?"

She brightened. "You'll take us, then?"

But Biron was in no mood to be sweet about it. His foot still twinged and he cradled it. He said, "Look, get me out to a ship. I'm leaving this damn planet. If you want to come along, I'll take you."

She frowned. "You might be more pleasant about it. Were you in a fight?"

"Yes, I was. With your father's guards, who wanted to arrest me for treason. So much for my Sanctuary Right."

"Oh! I'm sorry."

"I'm sorry too. It's no wonder the Tyranni can lord it over fifty worlds with a handful of men. We help them. Men like your father would do anything to keep in power; they would forget the basic duties of a simple gentle-man——Oh, never mind!"

"I said I was sorry, Lord Rancher." She used the title with a cold pride. "Please don't set yourself up as judge of my father. You don't know all the facts."

"I'm not interested in discussing it. We'll have to leave in a hurry, before more of your father's precious guards come. Well, I don't mean to hurt your feelings. It's all right." Biron's surliness canceled out any meaning to his apology, but, damn it, he had never been hit by a neuronic whip before and it *wasn't* fun. And, by Space, they had *owed* him Sanctuary. At least that much.

Artemisia felt angry. Not at her father, of course, but at the stupid young man. He was *so* young. Practically a child, she decided, scarcely older than herself, if that.

The communicator sounded and she said sharply, "Please wait a minute and we'll go."

It was Gillbret's voice, sounding faintly. "Arta? All right at your end?"

"He's here," she whispered back.

"All right. Don't say anything. Just listen. Don't leave your room. Keep him there. There's going to be a search of the Palace, which there's no way of stopping. I'll try to think of something, but, meanwhile, *don't move*." He waited for no reply. Contact was broken.

"So that's that," said Biron. He had heard also. "Shall I stay and get you into trouble, or shall I go out and give myself up? There's no reason to expect Sanctuary anywhere on Rhodia, I suppose."

She faced him in a rage, crying in a choked whisper, "Oh, shut up, you big, ugly fool."

They glared at each other. Biron's feelings were hurt. In a way, he was trying to help her too. There was no reason for her to be insulting.

She said, "I'm sorry," and looked away.

"That's all right," he said coldly, without meaning it. "You're entitled to your opinion."

"You don't have to say the things you do about my father.

You don't know what being Director is like. He's working for his people, whatever you may think."

"Oh, sure. He has to sell me to the Tyranni for the sake of the people. That makes sense."

"In a way, it does. He has to show them he's loyal. Otherwise, they might depose him and take over the direct rule of Rhodia. Would that be better?"

"If a nobleman can't find Sanctuary——"

"Oh, you think only of yourself. That's what's wrong with you."

"I don't think it's particularly selfish not to want to die. At least for nothing. I've got some fighting to do before I go. *My* father fought them." He knew he was beginning to sound melodramatic, but she affected him that way.

She said, "And what good did it do your father?"

"None, I suppose. He was killed."

Artemisia felt unhappy. "I keep saying I'm sorry, and this time I really mean it. I'm all upset." Then, in defense, "I'm in trouble, too, you know."

Biron remembered. "I know. All right, let's start all over." He tried to smile. His foot was feeling better anyway.

She said, in an attempt at lightness, "You're not *really* ugly."

Biron felt foolish. "Oh well——"

Then he stopped, and Artemisia's hand flew to her mouth. Abruptly, their heads turned to the door.

There was the sudden, soft sound of many ordered feet on the semi-elastic plastic mosaic that floored the corridor outside. Most passed by, but there was a faint, disciplined heel-clicking just outside the door, and the night signal purred.

Gillbret had to work quickly. First, he had to hide his visisonor. For the first time he wished he had a better hiding place. *Damn* Hinrik for making up his mind so quickly this once, for not waiting till morning. He *had* to get away; he might never have another chance.

Then he called the captain of the guard. He couldn't very well neglect a little matter of two unconscious guards and an escaped prisoner.

The captain of the guard was grim about it. He had the two unconscious men cleared out, and then faced Gillbret.

"My lord, I am not quite clear from your message exactly what happened," he said.

"Just what you see," said Gillbret. "They came to make their arrest, and the young man did not submit. He is gone, Space knows where."

"That is of little moment, my lord," said the captain. "The Palace is honored tonight with the presence of a personage, so it is well guarded despite the hour. He cannot get out and we will draw the net through the interior. But *how* did he escape? My men were armed. He was not."

"He fought like a tiger. From that chair, behind which I hid——"

"I am sorry, my lord, that you did not think to aid my men against an accused traitor."

Gillbret looked scornful. "What an amusing thought, Captain. When your men, with doubled advantage in numbers and weapons, need help from myself, it is time you recruited yourself other men."

"Very well! We will search the Palace, find him, and see if he can repeat the performance."

"I shall accompany you, Captain."

It was the captain's turn to raise his eyebrows. He said, "I would not advise it, my lord. There would be some danger."

It was the kind of remark that one did not make to a Hinriad. Gillbret knew that, but he only smiled and let the wrinkles fill his lean face. "I know that," he said, "but occasionally I find even danger amusing."

It took five minutes for the company of guards to assemble. Gillbret, alone in his room during that time, called Artemisia.

*  *  *

Biron and Artemisia had frozen at the purring of the little signal. It sounded a second time and then there was the cautious rap upon the door, and Gillbret's voice was heard.

"Do let me try, Captain," it said. Then, more loudly, "Artemisia!"

Biron grinnned his relief and took a step forward, but the girl put a sudden hand upon his mouth. She called out, "One moment, Uncle Gil," and pointed desperately toward the wall.

Biron could only stare stupidly. The wall was quite blank. Artemisia made a face and stepped quickly past him. Her hand on the wall caused a portion of it to slide noiselessly aside, revealing a dressing room. Her lips motioned a "Get inside!" and her hands were fumbling at the ornamental pin at her right shoulder. The unclasping of that pin broke the tiny force field that held an invisible seam tightly closed down the length of the dress. She stepped out of it.

Biron turned around after stepping across what had been the wall, and its closing endured just long enough for him to see her throwing a white-furred dressing gown across her shoulders. The scarlet dress lay crumpled upon the chair.

He looked about him and wondered if they would search Artemisia's room. He would be quite helpless if a search took place. There was no way out of the dressing room but the way he had entered, and there was nothing in it that could serve as a still more confined hiding place.

Along one wall there hung a row of gowns, and the air shimmered very faintly before it. His hand passed easily through the shimmer, with only a faint tingling where it crossed his wrist, but then it was meant to repel only dust so that the space behind it could be kept aseptically clean.

He might hide behind the skirts. It was what he was doing, really. He had manhandled two guards, with Gillbret's help, to get here, but, now that he was here, he was hiding behind a lady's skirts. A lady's skirts, in fact.

Incongruously, he found himself wishing he had turned a bit sooner before the wall had closed behind him. She had quite a remarkable figure. It was ridiculous of him to have been so childishly nasty awhile back. Of course she was not to blame for the faults of her father.

And now he could only wait, staring at the blank wall; waiting for the sound of feet within the room, for the wall to pull back once more, for the muzzles facing him again, this time without a visisonor to help him.

He waited, holding a neuronic whip in each hand.

# 9. AND AN OVERLORD'S TROUSERS

"What's the matter?" Artemisia did not have to feign uneasiness. She spoke to Gillbret, who, with the captain of the guard, was at the door. Half a dozen uniformed men hovered discreetly in the background. Then, quickly, "Has anything happened to Father?"

"No, no," Gillbret assured her, "nothing has happened that need concern you at all. Were you asleep?"

"Just about," she replied, "and my girls have been about their own affairs for hours. There was no one to answer but myself and you nearly frightened me to death."

She turned to the captain suddenly, with a stiffening attitude. "What is wanted of me, Captain? Quickly, please. This is not the time of day for a proper audience."

Gillbret broke in before the other could more than open his mouth. "A most amusing thing, Arta. The young man, whatsisname—you know—has dashed off, breaking two heads on his way. We're hunting him on even terms now. One platoon of soldiers to one fugitive. And here I am myself, hot on the trail, delighting our good captain with my zeal and courage."

Artemisia managed to look completely bewildered.

Under his breath the captain muttered a monosyllabic imprecation. His lips scarcely moved. He said then, "If you please, my lord, you are not quite plain, and we are delaying matters insufferably. My Lady, the man who calls himself the son of the ex-Rancher of Widemos has been arrested for treason. He has managed to escape and is now at large. We must search the Palace for him, room by room."

Artemisia stepped back, frowning. "Including my room?"

"If Your Ladyship permits."

"Ah, but I do not. I would certainly know if there was a strange man in my room. And the suggestion that I might be having dealings with such a man, or any strange man, at this time of night is highly improper. Please observe due respect for my position, Captain."

It worked quite well. The captain could only bow and say, "No such implication was intended, my lady. Your pardon for annoying you at this time of night. Your statement that you have not seen the fugitive is, of course, sufficient. Under the circumstances, it was necessary to assure ourselves of your safety. He is a dangerous man."

"Surely not so dangerous that he cannot be handled by you and your company."

Gillbret's high-pitched voice interposed again. "Captain, come—come. While you exchange courtly sentiments with my niece, our man has had time to rifle the armory. I would suggest that you leave a guard at the Lady Artemisia's door, so that what remains of her sleep will not be further disturbed. Unless, my dear"—and he twinkled his fingers at Artemisia—"you would care to join us."

"I shall satisfy myself," said Artemisia coldly, "in locking my door and retiring, thank you."

"Pick a large one," cried Gillbret. "Take that one. A fine uniform our guards have, Artemisia. You can recognize a guard as far as you can see him by his uniform alone."

"My lord," said the captain impatiently, "there is no time. You delay matters."

At a gesture from him, a guard fell out of the platoon,

saluted Artemisia through the closing door, then the captain. The sound of ordered footsteps fell away in both directions.

Artemisia waited, then slid the door quietly open an inch or two. The guard was there, legs apart, back rigid, right hand armed, left hand at his alarm button. He was the guard suggested by Gillbret, a tall one. As tall as Biron of Widemos, though without his breadth of shoulders.

It occurred to her, at that moment, that Biron, though young and, therefore, rather unreasonable in some of his viewpoints, was at least large and well muscled, which was convenient. It had been foolish of her to snap at him. Quite pleasant looking too.

She closed the door, and stepped toward the dressing room.

Biron tensed as the door slid away again. He held his breath and his fingers stiffened.

Artemisia stared at his whips. "Be *careful*!"

He puffed out his breath in relief and stuffed each into a pocket. They were very uncomfortable there, but he had no proper holsters. He said, "That was just in case it was somebody looking for me."

"Come out. And speak in a whisper."

She was still in her night robe, woven out of a smooth fabric with which Biron was unfamiliar, adorned with little tufts of silvery fur, and clinging to the body through some faint static attraction inherent in the material, so that neither buttons, clasps, loops, or seam fields were necessary. Nor, as a consequence, did it do more than merely faintly dim the outlines of Artemisia's figure.

Biron felt his ears reddening, and liked the sensation very much.

Artemisia waited, then made a little whirling gesture with her forefinger and said, "Do you mind?"

Biron looked up at her face. "What? Oh, I'm sorry."

He turned his back to her and remained stiffly attentive to the faint rustling of the change of outer garments. It did not occur to him to wonder why she did not use the dressing room, or why, better still, she had not changed before opening the door. There are depths in feminine psychology, which, without experience, defy analysis.

She was in black when he turned, a two-piece suit which did not reach below the knee. It had that more substantial appearance that went with clothing meant for the outdoors rather than for the ballroom.

Biron said, automatically, "Are we leaving, then?"

She shook her head. "You'll have to do your part first. You'll need other clothes yourself. Get to one side of the door, and I'll have the guard in."

"What guard?"

She smiled briefly. "They left a guard at the door, at Uncle Gil's suggestion."

The door to the corridor ran smoothly along its runners an inch or two. The guard was still there, stiffly immobile.

"Guard," she whispered. "In here, quickly."

There was no reason for a common soldier to hesitate in his obedience to the Director's daughter. He entered the widening door, with a respectful, "At your service, my l——" and then his knees buckled under the weight which came down upon his shoulders, while his words were cut off, without even an interrupting squawk, by the forearm which slammed against his larynx.

Artemisia closed the door hurriedly and watched with sensations that amounted almost to nausea. The life in the Palace of the Hinriads was mild almost to decadence, and she had never before seen a man's face congest with blood and his mouth yawn and puff futilely under the influence of asphyxia. She looked away.

Biron bared his teeth with effort as he tightened the circle of bone and muscle about the other's throat. For a minute the guard's weakening hands ripped futilely at Biron's arm, while his feet groped in aimless kicks. Biron heaved him clear of the floor without relaxing his grip.

And then the guard's hands fell to his sides, his legs hung loosely, and the convulsive and useless heavings of the chest began to subside. Biron lowered him gently to the floor. The guard sprawled out limply, as though he were a sack which had been emptied.

"Is he dead?" asked Artemisia, in a horrified whisper.

"I doubt it," said Biron. "It takes four or five minutes of it to kill a man. But he'll be out of things for a while. Do you have anything to tie him up with?"

She shook her head. For the moment, she felt quite helpless.

Biron said, "You must have some Cellite stockings. They would do fine." He had already stripped the guard of weapons and outer clothing. "And I'd like to wash up too. In fact, I have to."

It was pleasant to step through the detergent mist in Artemisia's bathroom. It left him perhaps a trifle over-scented, but the open air would take care of the fragrance, he hoped. At least he was clean, and it had required merely the momentary passage through the fine, suspended droplets that shot past him forcefully in a warm air stream. No special drying chamber was required, since he stepped out dry as well as clean. They didn't have this on Widemos, or on Earth.

The guard's uniform was a bit tight, and Biron did not like the way the somewhat ugly, conical military cap fit over his brachycephalic head. He stared at his reflection with some dissatisfaction. "How do I look?"

"Quite like a soldier," she said.

He said, "You'll have to carry one of these whips. I can't handle three."

She took it between two fingers and dropped it into her bag, which was then suspended from her wide belt by another microforce, so that her hands remained free.

"We had better go now. Don't say a word if we meet anyone, but let me do the talking. Your accent isn't right, and it would be impolite to talk in my presence unless you were directly addressed, anyway. Remember! You're a common soldier."

The guard on the floor was beginning to wriggle a bit and roll his eyes. His wrists and ankles were securely tied in a clump at the small of his back with stockings that had the tensile strength of more than an equal amount of steel. His tongue worked futilely at his gag.

He had been shoved out of the way, so that it was not necessary to step over him to get to the door.

"This way," breathed Artemisia.

At the first turning there was a footstep behind them, and a light hand came down on Biron's shoulder.

Biron stepped to one side quickly and turned, one hand catching the other's arm, while his other snatched at his whip.

But it was Gillbret who said, "Easy, man!"

Biron loosened his grip.

Gillbret rubbed his arm. "I've been waiting for you, but that's no reason to break my bones. Let me stare admiringly at you, Farrill. Your clothes seem to have shrunk on you, but not bad—not bad at all. Nobody would look twice at you in that getup. It's the advantage of a uniform. It's taken for granted that a soldier's uniform holds a soldier and nothing else."

"Uncle Gil," whispered Artemisia urgently, "don't talk so much. Where are the other guards?"

"Everyone objects to a few words," he said pettishly. "The other guards are working their way up the tower. They've decided that our friend is on none of the lower levels, so they've just left some men at the main exits and at the ramps, with the general alarm system in operation as well. We can get past it."

"Won't they miss you, sir?" asked Biron.

"Me? Hah. The captain was glad to see me go, for all his toe scraping. They won't look for me, I assure you."

They were speaking in whispers, but now even those died away. A guard stood at the bottom of the ramp, while two others flanked the large, carved double door that led to the open air.

Gillbret called out, "Any word of the escaped prisoner, men?"

"No, my lord," said the nearest. He clicked his heels together and saluted.

"Well, keep your eyes open," and they walked past them and out, one of the guards at the door carefully neutralizing that section of the alarm as they left.

It was nighttime outside. The sky was clear and starry, the ragged mass of the Dark Nebula blotting out the specks of light near the horizon. Palace Central was a dark mass behind them, and the Palace Field was less than half a mile away.

But after five minutes of walking along the quiet path, Gillbret grew restless.

"There's something wrong," he said.

Artemisia said, "Uncle Gill, you haven't forgotten to arrange to have the ship ready?"

"Of course not," he snapped at her, as nearly as one could snap in a whisper, "but why is the Field Tower lit up? It should be dark."

He pointed up through the trees, to where the tower was a honeycomb of white light. Ordinarily, that would indicate business at the field: ships leaving for space or arriving from it.

Gillbret muttered, "*Nothing* was scheduled for tonight. That was definite."

They saw the answer at a distance, or Gillbret did. He stopped suddenly and spread his arms wide to hold back the others.

"That's all," he said, and giggled almost hysterically. "This time Hinrik has really messed things properly, the idiot. They're here! The Tyranni! Don't you understand? That's Aratap's private armored cruiser."

Biron saw it, gleaming faintly under the lights, standing out among the other undistinguished ships. It was smoother, thinner, more feline than the Rhodian vessels.

Gillbret said, "The captain *said* a 'personage' was being entertained today, and I paid no attention. There's nothing to do now. We can't fight Tyranni."

Biron felt something suddenly snap. "Why not?" he said

savagely. "Why can't we fight them? They have no reason to suspect trouble, and we're armed. Let's take the Commissioner's own ship. Let's leave him with his trousers down."

He stepped forward, out of the relative obscurity of the trees and onto the bare field. The others followed. There was no reason to hide. They were two memebers of the royal family and an escorting soldier.

But it was the Tyranni they were fighting now.

Simok Aratap of Tyrann had been impressed the first time he had ever seen the Palace Grounds at Rhodia years earlier, but it had turned out to be only a shell that had impressed him. The interior was nothing but a musty relic. Two generations earlier Rhodia's legislative chambers had met on these grounds and most of the administrative offices had been quartered there. Palace Central had been the heartbeat of a dozen worlds.

But now the legislative chambers (still existing, for the Khan never interfered with local legalisms) met once a year to ratify the executive orders of the past twelve months. It was quite a formality. The Executive Council was still, nominally, in continuous session, but it consisted of a dozen men who remained on their estates nine weeks in ten. The various executive bureaus were still active, since one could not govern without them, whether the Director of the Khan ruled, but they were now scattered over the planet; made less dependent upon the Director, more conscious of their new masters, the Tyranni.

Which left the Palace as majestic as it had always been in stone and metal, and that only. It housed the Directorial family, a scarcely adequate corps of servants, and an entirely inadequate corps of native guards.

Aratap felt uncomfortable in the shell and was unhappy. It was late, he was tired, his eyes burned so that he longed to remove his contact lenses, and, most of all, he was disappointed.

There was no pattern! He glanced occasionally at his

military aide, but the major was listening to the Director with expressionless stolidity. As for Aratap himself, he paid little attention.

"Widemos's son! Indeed?" he would say, in abstraction. Then, later, "And so you arrested him? Quite right!"

But it meant little to him, since events lacked a design. Aratap had a neat and tidy mind which could not bear the thought of individual facts loosely clumped together with no decent arrangement.

Widemos had been a traitor, and Widemos's son had attempted a meeting with the Director of Rhodia. He had attempted it first in secret, and when that had failed, such was the urgency, he had attempted it openly with his ridiculous story of an assassination plot. Surely that must have been the beginning of a pattern.

And now it fell apart. Hinrik was giving up the boy with indecent haste. He could not even wait the night, it seemed. And that did not fit at all. Or else Aratap had not yet learned all the facts.

He focused his attention on the Director again. Hinrik was beginning to repeat himself. Aratap felt a twinge of compassion. The man had been made into such a coward that even the Tyranni themselves grew impatient with him. And yet it was the only way. Only fear could insure absolute loyalty. That and nothing else.

Widemos had not been afraid, and despite the fact that his self-interest had been bound at every point with the maintenance of Tyrannian rule, he had rebelled. Hinrik *was* afraid and that made the difference.

And because Hinrik was afraid, he sat there, lapsing into incoherence as he struggled to obtain some gesture of approval. The major would give none, of course, Aratap knew. The man had no imagination. He sighed and wished he had none either. Politics was a filthy business.

So he said, with some air of animation, "Quite so. I commend your quick decision and your zeal in the service of the Khan. You may be sure he will hear of it."

Hinrik brightened visibly, his relief obvious.

Aratap said, "Have him brought in, then, and let us hear what our cockerel has to say." He suppressed a desire to yawn. He had absolutely no interest in what the "cockerel" had to say.

It was Hinrik's intention at this point to signal for the captain of the guard, but there was no necessity for that, as the captain stood in the doorway, unannounced.

"Excellency," he cried and strode in without waiting for permission.

Hinrik stared hard at his hand, still inches from the signal, as though wondering whether his intention had somehow developed sufficient force to substitute for the act.

He said uncertainly, "What is it, Captain?"

The captain said, "Excellency, the prisoner has escaped."

Aratap felt some of the weariness disappear. What was this? "The details, Captain!" he ordered, and straightened in his chair.

The captain gave them with a blunt economy of words. He concluded, "I ask your permission, Excellency, to proclaim a general alarm. They are yet but minutes away."

"Yes, by all means," stuttered Hinrik, "by all means. A general alarm, indeed. Just the thing. Quickly! Quickly! Commissioner, I cannot understand how it could have happened. Captain, put every man to work. There will be an investigation, Commissioner. If necessary, every man on the guards will be broken. Broken! Broken!"

He repeated the word in near hysteria but the captain remained standing. It was obvious that he had more to say.

Aratap said, "Why do you wait?"

"May I speak to Your Excellency in private?" said the captain abruptly.

Hinrik cast a quick, frightened look at the bland, unperturbed Commissioner. He mustered a feeble indignation. "There are no secrets from the soldiers of the Khan, our friends, our——"

"Say your say, Captain," interposed Aratap gently.

The captain brought his heels together sharply and said, "Since I am ordered to speak, Your Excellency, I regret to inform you that my Lady Artemisia and my Lord Gillbret accompanied the prisoner in his escape."

"He dared to kidnap them?" Hinrik was on his feet. "And my guards allowed it?"

"They were not kidnaped, Excellency. They accompanied him voluntarily."

"How do you know?" Aratap was delighted, and thoroughly awake. It formed a pattern now, after all. A better pattern than he could have anticipated.

The captain said, "We have the testimony of the guard they overpowered, and the guards who, unwittingly, allowed them to leave the building." He hesitated, then added grimly, "When I interviewed my Lady Artemisia at the door of her private chambers, she told me she had been on the point of sleep. It was only later that I realized that when she told me that, her face was elaborately made-up. When I returned, it was too late. I accept the blame for the mismanagement of this affair. After tonight I will request Your Excellency to accept my resignation, but first have I still your permission to sound the general alarm? Without your authority I could not interfere with members of the royal family."

But Hinrik was swaying on his feet and could only stare at him vacantly.

Aratap said, "Captain, you would do better to look to the health of your Director. I would suggest you call his physician."

"The general alarm!" repeated the captain.

"There will be no general alarm," said Aratap. "Do you understand me? No general alarm! No recapture of the prisoner! The incident is closed! Return your men to their quarters and ordinary duties and look to your Director. Come, Major."

The Tyrannian major spoke tensely once they had left the mass of Palace Central behind them.

"Aratap," he said, "I presume you know what you're

doing. I kept my mouth shut in there on the basis of that presumption."

"Thank you, Major." Aratap liked the night air of a planet full of green and growing things. Tyrann was more beautiful in its way, but it was a terrible beauty of rocks and mountains. It was dry, dry!

He went on: "You cannot handle Hinrik, Major Andros. In your hands he would wilt and break. He is useful, but requires gentle treatment if he is to remain so."

The major brushed that aside. "I'm not referring to that. Why not the general alarm? Don't you want them?"

"Do you?" Aratap stopped. "Let us sit here for a moment, Andros. A bench on a pathway along a lawn. What more beautiful, and what place is safer from spy beams? Why do you want the young man, Major?"

"Why do I want any traitor and conspirator?"

"Why do you, indeed, if you only catch a few tools while leaving the source of the poison untouched? Whom would you have? A cub, a silly girl, a senile idiot?"

There was a faint splashing of an artificial waterfall nearby. A small one, but decorative. Now that was a real wonder to Aratap. Imagine water, spilling out, running to waste, pouring indefinitely down the rocks and along the ground. He had never educated himself out of a certain indignation over it.

"As it is," said the major, "we have nothing."

"We have a pattern. When the young man first arrived, we connected him with Hinrik, and that bothered us, because Hinrik is—what he is. But it was the best we could do. Now we see it was not Hinrik at all; that Hinrik was a misdirection. It was Hinrik's daughter and cousin he was after, and that makes more sense."

"Why didn't he call us sooner? He waited for the middle of the night."

"Because he is the tool of whoever is the first to reach him, and Gillbret, I am sure, suggested this night meeting as a sign of great zeal on his part."

"You mean we were called here on purpose? To *witness* their escape?"

"No, not for that reason. Ask yourself. Where do these people intend on going?"

The major shrugged. "Rhodia is big."

"Yes, if it were the young Farrill alone who was concerned. But where on Rhodia would two members of the royal family go unrecognized? Particularly the girl."

"They would have to leave the planet, then? Yes, I agree."

"And from where? They can reach the Palace Field in a fifteen-minute walk. Now do you see the purpose of our being here?"

The major said, *"Our ship?"*

"Of course. A Tyrannian ship would seem ideal to them. Otherwise, they would have to choose among freighters. Farrill has been educated on Earth, and, I'm sure, can fly a cruiser."

"Now there's a point. Why do we allow the nobility to send out their sons in all directions? What business has a subject to know more about travel than will suffice him for local trade? We bring up soldiers against us."

"Nevertheless," said Aratap, with polite indifference, "at the moment Farrill has a foreign education, and let us take that into account objectively, without growing angry about it. The fact remains that I am certain they have taken our cruiser."

"I can't believe it."

"You have your wrist caller. Make contact with the ship, if you can."

The major tried, futilely.

Aratap said, "Try the Field Tower."

The major did so, and the small voice came out of the tiny receiver, in minute agitation: "But, Excellency, I don't understand—— There is some mistake. Your pilot took off ten minutes ago."

Aratap was smiling. "You see? Work out the pattern and each little event becomes inevitable. And now do you see the consequences?"

The major did. He slapped his thigh, and laughed briefly. "Of course!" he said.

"Well," said Aratap, "they couldn't know, of course, but they have ruined themselves. Had they been satisfied with the clumsiest Rhodian freighter on the field, they would surely have escaped and—what's the expression?—I would have been caught with my trousers down this night. As it is, my trousers are firmly belted, and nothing can save *them*. And when I pluck them back, in my own good time"—he emphasized the words with satisfaction—"I will have the rest of the conspiracy in my hands as well."

He sighed and found himself beginning to feel sleepy once more. "Well, we have been lucky, and now there is no hurry. Call Central Base, and have them send another ship after us."

# 10. MAYBE!

Biron Farrill's training in spationautics back on Earth had been largely academic. There had been the university courses in the various phases of spatial engineering, which, though half a semester was spent on the theory of the hyperatomic motor, offered little when it came to the actual manipulation of ships in space. The best and most skilled pilots learned their art in space and not in schoolrooms.

He had managed to take off without actual accident, though that was more luck than design. The *Remorseless* answered the controls far more quickly than Biron had anticipated. He had manipulated several ships on Earth out into space and back to the planet, but those had been aged and sedate models, maintained for the use of students. They had been gentle, and very, very tired, and had lifted with an effort and spiraled slowly upward through the atmosphere and into space.

The *Remorseless*, on the other hand, had lifted effortlessly, springing upward and whistling through the air, so that Biron had fallen backward out of his chair and all but dislocated his shoulder. Artemisia and Gillbret, who, with

94

the greater caution of the inexperienced, had strapped themselves in, were bruised against the padded webbing. The Tyrannian prisoner had lain pressed against the wall, tearing heavily at his bonds and cursing in a monotone.

Biron had risen shakily to his feet, kicked the Tyrannian into a brooding silence, and made his way along the wall rail, hand over hand against the acceleration, back to his seat. Forward blasts of power quivered the ship and reduced the rate of increasing velocity to a bearable quantity.

They were in the upper reaches of the Rhodian atmosphere by then. The sky was a deep violet and the hull of the ship was hot with air friction, so that warmth could be felt within.

It took hours thereafter to set the ship into an orbit about Rhodia. Biron could find no way of readily calculating the velocity necessary to overcome Rhodia's gravity. He had to work it by hit and miss, varying the velocity with puffs of power forward and backward, watching the massometer, which indicated their distance from the planet's surface by measuring the intensity of the gravitational field. Fortunately, the massometer was already calibrated for Rhodia's mass and radius. Without considerable experimentation, Biron could not have adjusted the calibration himself.

Eventually, the massometer held steady and over a period of two hours showed no appreciable drift. Biron allowed himself to relax, and the others climbed out of their belts.

Artemisia said, "You don't have a very light touch, my Lord Rancher."

"I'm flying, my lady," Biron replied curtly. "If you can do better, you're welcome to try, but only after I myself disembark."

"Quiet, quiet, quiet," said Gillbret. "The ship is too cramped for pettishness, and, in addition, since we *are* to be crushed into an inconvenient familiarity in this leaping prison pen, I suggest we discard the many 'lords' and 'ladies' which will otherwise encrust our conversation to an unbearable degree. I am Gillbret, you are Biron, she is Artemisia. I suggest we memorize those terms of address, or any variation we care to use. And as for piloting the ship, why not use the help of our Tyrannian friend here?"

The Tyrannian glared, and Biron said, "No. There is no way we could trust him. And my own piloting will improve as I get the hang of this ship. I haven't cracked you up yet, have I?"

His shoulder still hurt as a result of the first lurch and, as usual, pain made him peevish.

"Well," said Gillbret, "what *do* we do with him?"

"I don't like to kill him in cold blood," said Biron, "and that won't help us. It would just make the Tyranni doubly excited. Killing one of the master race is really the unforgivable sin."

"But what is the alternative?"

"We'll land him."

"All right. But where?"

"On Rhodia."

"What!"

"It's the one place they won't be looking for us. Besides which, we've got to go down pretty soon, anyway."

"Why?"

"Look, this is the Commissioner's ship, and he's been using it for hopping about the surface of the planet. It isn't provisioned for space voyages. Before we go anywhere, we'll have to take complete inventory aboard ship, and at least make sure that we have enough food and water."

Artemisia was nodding vigorously. "That's right. Good! I wouldn't have thought of that myself. That's very clever, Biron."

Biron made a deprecating gesture, but warmed with pleasure, nevertheless. It was the first time she had used his first name. She could be quite pleasant, when she tried.

Gillbret said, "But he'll radio our whereabouts instantly."

"I don't think so," said Biron. "In the first place, Rhodia has its desolate areas, I imagine. We don't have to drop him into the business section of a city, or into the middle of one of the Tyrannian garrisons. Besides, he may not be so anxious to contact his superiors as you might think. . . . Say,

Private, what would happen to a soldier who allowed the Commissioner of the Khan to have his private cruiser stolen from him?"

The prisoner did not answer, but his lip line became pale and thin.

Biron would not have wanted to be in the soldier's place. To be sure, he could scarcely be blamed. There was no reason why he should have suspected trouble resulting from mere politeness to members of the Rhodian royal family. Sticking to the letter of the Tyrannian military code, he had refused to allow them aboard ship without the permission of his commanding officer. If the Director himself had demanded permission to enter, he insisted, he would have to deny it. But, in the meantime, they had closed in upon him, and by the time he realized he should have followed the military code still more closely and had his weapon ready, it was too late. A neuronic whip was practically touching his chest.

Nor had he given in tamely, even then. It had taken a whip blast at his chest to stop him. And, even so, he could face only court-martial and conviction. No one doubted that, least of all the soldier.

They had landed two days later at the outskirts of the city of Southwark. It had been chosen deliberately because it lay far from the main centers of Rhodian population. The Tyrannian soldier had been strapped into a repulsion unit and allowed to flutter downward some fifty miles from the nearest sizable town.

The landing, on an empty beach, was only mildly jerky, and Biron, as the one least likely to be recognized, made the necessary purchases. Such Rhodian currency as Gillbret had had the presence of mind to bring with him had scarcely sufficed for elementary needs, since much of it went for a little biwheel and tow cart, on which he could carry the supplies away piecemeal.

"You might have stretched the money farther," said Artemisia, "if you hadn't wasted so much of it on the Tyrannian mush you bought."

"I think there was nothing else to do," said Biron hotly. "It may be Tyrannian mush to you, but it's a well-balanced food, and will see us through better than anything else I could have gotten."

He was annoyed. It had been stevedore's work, getting all that out of the city and then aboard ship. And it had meant a considerable risk, buying it at one of the Tyrannian-run commissaries in the city. He had expected appreciation.

And there was no alternative anyway. The Tyrannian forces had evolved an entire technique of supply adapted strictly to the fact that they used tiny ships. They couldn't afford the huge storage spaces of other fleets which were stacked with the carcasses of whole animals, neatly hung in rows. They had had to develop a standard food concentrate containing what was necessary in the way of calories and food factors and let it go at that. It took up only one twentieth of the space that an equivalent supply of natural animal food would take, and it could be piled up in the low-temperature storeroom like packaged bricks.

"Well, it tastes awful," said Artemisia.

"Well, you'll get used to it," retorted Biron, mimicking her petulance so that she flushed and turned away angrily.

What was bothering her, Biron knew, was simply the lack of space and all that accompanied the lack. It wasn't just a question of using a monotonous food stock because in that way more calories could be packed to the cubic inch. It was that there were no separate sleeping rooms, for instance. There were the engine rooms and the control room, which took up most of the ship's space. (After all, Biron thought, this is a warship, not a pleasure yacht.) Then there was the storeroom, and one small cabin, with two tiers of three bunks on either side. The plumbing was located in a little niche just outside the cabin.

It meant crowding; it meant a complete absence of privacy; and it meant that Artemisia would have to adjust herself to the fact that there were no women's clothes aboard, no mirrors, no washing facilities.

Well, she would have to get used to it. Biron felt that he had done enough for her, gone sufficiently out of his way. Why couldn't she be pleasant about it and smile once in a while? She had a nice smile, and he had to admit that she wasn't bad, except for her temper. But oh, that temper!

Well, why waste his time thinking about her?

The water situation was the worst. Tyrann was a desert planet, in the first place, where water was at a premium and men knew its value, so none was included on board ship for washing purposes. Soldiers could wash themselves and their personal effects once they had landed on a planet. During trips a little grime and sweat would not hurt them. Even for drinking purposes, water was barely sufficient for the longer trips. After all, water could be neither concentrated nor dehydrated, but had to be carried in bulk; and the problem was aggravated by the fact that the water content of the food concentrates was quite low.

There were distilling devices to re-use water lost by the body, but Biron, when he realized their function, felt sick and arranged for the disposal of waste products without attempt at water recovery. Chemically, cycling was a sensible procedure, but one has to be educated into that sort of thing.

The second take-off was, comparatively, a model of smoothness, and Biron spent time playing with the controls afterward. The control board resembled only in the dimmest fashion those of the ships he had handled on Earth. It had been compressed and compacted frightfully. As Biron puzzled out the action of a contact or the purpose of a dial, he wrote out minute directions on paper and pasted them appropriately on the board.

Gillbret entered the pilot room.

Biron looked over his shoulder. "Artemisia's in the cabin, I suppose?"

"There isn't anyplace else she could be and stay inside the ship."

Biron said, "When you see her, tell her I'll make up a bunk here in the pilot room. I'd advise you to do the same, and let her have the cabin to herself." He muttered the addition, "Now there's one childish girl."

"You have your moments, too, Biron," said Gillbret. "You'll have to remember the sort of life she's used to."

"All right. I do remember it, and so what? What sort of life do you think I'm used to? I wasn't born in the mine fields of some asteroidal belt, you know. I was born on the biggest Ranch of Nephelos. But if you're caught in a situation, you've got to make the best of it. Damn it, I can't stretch the hull of the ship. It will hold just so much food and water, and I can't do anything about the fact that there isn't any shower bath. She picks on me as if I personally manufactured this ship." It was a relief to shout at Gillbret. It was a relief to shout at anybody.

But the door opened again, and Artemisia stood there. She said, freezingly, "I would refrain, Mr. Farrill, from shouting, if I were you. You can be distincly heard all over the ship."

"That," said Biron, "does not bother me. And if the ship bothers *you*, just remember that if your father hadn't tried to kill me off and marry you off, neither one of us would be here."

"Don't talk about my father."

"I'll talk about anyone I please."

Gillbret put his hands over his ears. *"Please!"*

It brought the argument to a momentary halt. Gillbret said, "Shall we discuss the matter of our destination now? It's obvious at this point that the sooner we're somewhere else and out of this ship, the more comfortable we'll be."

"I agree with you there, Gil," said Biron. "Just let's go somewhere where I don't have to listen to her clacking. Talk about women on space ships!"

Artemisia ignored him and addressed Gillbret exclusively. "Why don't we get out of the Nebular area altogether?"

"I don't know about you," said Biron at once, "but I've

got to get my Ranch back and do a little something about my father's murder. I'll stay in the Kingdoms."

"I did not mean," said Artemisia, "that we were to leave forever; only till the worst of the search was over. I don't see what you intend doing about your Ranch, anyway. You can't get it back unless the Tyrannian Empire is broken to pieces, and I don't see you doing that."

"You never mind what I intend doing. It's my business."

"Might I make a suggestion?" asked Gillbret mildly.

He took silence for consent, and went on, "Then suppose I tell you where we ought to go, and exactly what we ought to do to help break the Empire to pieces, just as Arta said."

"Oh? How do you propose doing that?" said Biron.

Gillbret smiled. "My dear boy, you're taking a very amusing attitude. Don't you trust me? You look at me as though you think that any enterprise I might be interested in was bound to be a foolish one. I got you out of the Palace."

"I know that. I'm perfectly willing to listen to you."

"Do so, then. I've been waiting for over twenty years for my chance to get away from them. If I had been a private citizen, I could have done it long since; but through the curse of birth, I've been in the public eye. And yet if it hadn't been for the fact that I was born a Hinriad, I would not have attended the coronation of the present Khan of Tyrann, and in that case I would never have stumbled on the secret which will someday destroy that same Khan."

"Go on," said Biron.

"The trip from Rhodia to Tyrann was by Tyrannian warship, of course, as was the trip back. A ship like this, I might say, but rather larger. The trip there was uneventful. The stay on Tyrann had its points of amusements, but, for our purposes now, was likewise uneventful. On the trip back, however, a meteor hit us."

"What?"

Gillbret held up a hand. "I know quite well it's an unlikely accident. The incidence of meteors in space—especially in interstellar space—is low enough to make the chances of collision with a ship completely insignificant, but it does happen, as you know. And it did happen in this case. Of course any meteor that does hit, even when it is the size of a pinhead, as most of them are, can penetrate the hull of any but the most heavily armored ship."

"I know," said Biron. "It's a question of their momentum, which is a product of their mass and velocity. The velocity more than makes up for their lack of mass." He recided it glumly, like a school lesson, and caught himself watching Artemisia furtively.

She had seated herself to listen to Gillbret, and she was so close to him that they were almost touching. It occurred to Biron that her profile was beautiful as she sat there, even if her hair was becoming a little bedraggled. She wasn't wearing her little jacket, and the fluffy whiteness of her blouse was still smooth and unwrinkled after forty-eight hours. He wondered how she managed that.

The trip, he decided, could be quite wonderful if she would only learn to behave herself. The trouble was that no one had ever controlled her properly, that was all. Certainly not her father. She'd become too used to having her own way. If she'd been born a commoner, she would be a very lovely creature.

He was just beginning to slip into a tiny daydream in which *he* controlled her properly and brought her to a state of proper appreciation of himself, when she turned her head and met his eye calmly. Biron looked away and fastened his attention instantly on Gillbret. He had missed a few sentences.

"I haven't the slightest idea why the ship's screen had failed. It was just one of those things to which no one will ever know the answer, but it had failed. Anyway, the meteor struck amidships. It was pebble-sized and piercing the hull slowed it just sufficiently so that it couldn't blaze its way out again through the other side. If it had done that, there would have been little harm to it, since the hull could have been temporarily patched in no time.

"As it was, however, it plunged into the control room, ricocheted off the far wall and slammed back and forth till it came to a halt. It couldn't have taken more than a fraction of a minute to come to a halt, but at an original velocity of a hundred miles a minute, it must have criss-crossed the room a hundred times. Both crewmen were cut to pieces, and I escaped only because I was in the cabin at the time.

"I heard the thin clang of the meteor when it originally penetrated the hull, then the click-clack of its bouncing, and the terrifying short screams of the two crewmen. When I jumped into the control room, there was only the blood everywhere and the torn flesh. The things that happened next I remember only vaguely, although for years I lived it over step by step in my nightmares.

"The cold sound of escaping air led me to the meteor hole. I slapped a disk of metal over it and air pressure made a decent seal of it. I found the little battered space pebble on the floor. It was warm to the touch, but I hit it with a spanner and split it in two. The exposed interior frosted over instantly. It was still at the temperature of space.

"I tied a cord to the wrist of each corpse and then tied each cord to a towing magnet. I dumped them through the air lock, heard the magnets clank against the hold, and knew that the hard-frozen bodies would follow the ship now wherever it went. You see, once we returned to Rhodia, I knew I would need the evidence of their bodies to show that it had been the meteor that had killed them and not I.

"But how was I to return? I was quite helpless. There was no way *I* could run the ship, and there was nothing I dared try there in the depths of interstellar space. I didn't even know how to use the sub-etheric communication system, so that I couldn't SOS. I could only let the ship travel on its own course."

"But you couldn't very well do that, could you?" Biron said. He wondered if Gillbret were inventing this, either out of simple romantic imaginings or for some severely practical reason of his own. "What about the Jumps through hyperspace? You must have managed those, or you wouldn't be here."

"A Tyrannian ship," said Gillbret, "once the controls are

properly set, will make any number of Jumps quite auto-matically."

Biron stared his disbelief. Did Gillbret take him for a fool? "You're making that up," he said.

"I am not. It's one of the damned military advances which won their wars for them. They didn't defeat fifty planetary systems outnumbering Tyrann by hundreds of times in popu-lation and resources, just by playing mumbletypeg, you know. Sure they tackled us one at a time, and utilized our traitors very skillfully, but they had a definite military edge as well. Everyone knows that their tactics were superior to ours, and part of that was due to the automatic Jump. It meant a great increase in the maneuverability of their ships and made possible much more elaborate battle plans than any we could set up.

"I'll admit it's one of their best-kept secrets, this tech-nique of theirs. I never learned it until I was trapped alone on the *Bloodsucker*—the Tyranni have the most annoying custom of naming their ships unpleasantly, though I suppose it's good psychology—and watched it happen. I *watched* it make the Jumps without a hand on the controls."

"And you mean to say that this ship can do that too?"

"I don't know. I wouldn't be surprised."

Biron turned to the control board. There were still dozens of contacts he had not determined the slightest use for. Well, later!

He turned to Gillbret again. "And the ship took you home?"

"No, it didn't. When that meteor wove its pattern through the control room, it didn't leave the board untouched. It would have been most amazing if it had. Dials were smashed, the casing battered and dented. There was no way of telling how the previous set of the controls had been altered, but it must have been somehow, because it never took me back to Rhodia.

"Eventually, of course, it began deceleration, and I knew the trip was theoretically over. I couldn't tell where I was, but I managed to maneuver the visiplate so that I could tell there was a planet close enough to show a disk in the ship telescope. It was blind luck, because the disk was increasing in size. The ship was heading for the planet.

"Oh, not directly. That would have been too impossible to hope for. If I had just drifted, the ship would have missed the planet by a million miles, at least, but at that distance I could use ordinary etheric radio. I knew how to do that. It was after this was all over that I began educating myself in electronics. I made up my mind that I would never be quite so helpless again. Being helpless is one of the things that isn't altogether amusing."

Biron prompted, "So you used the radio."

Gillbret went on: "Exactly, and they came and got me."

"Who?"

"The men of the planet. It was inhabited."

"Well, the luck piles up. What planet was it?"

"I don't know."

"You mean they didn't tell you?"

"Amusing, isn't it? They didn't. But it was somewhere among the Nebular Kingdoms!"

"How did you know that?"

"Because they knew the ship I was in was a Tyrannian vessel. They knew that by sight, and almost blasted it before I could convince them I was the only one on board alive."

Biron put his large hands on his knees and kneaded them. "Now hold on and pull back. I don't get this. If they knew it was a Tyrannian vessel and intending blasting it, isn't that the best proof that the world was *not* in the Nebular Kingdoms? that it was anywhere but there?"

"*No*, by the Galaxy." Gillbret's eyes were shining, and his voice climbed in enthusiasm. "It *was* in the Kingdoms. They took me to the surface, and what a world it was! There were men there from all over the Kingdoms. I could tell by the accents. And *they* had no fear of the Tyranni. The place was an arsenal. You couldn't tell from space. It might have been a rundown farming world, but the life of the planet was underground. Somewhere in the Kingdoms, my boy, *somewhere* there is that planet still, and it is *not* afraid of the Tyranni, and it is going to destroy the Tyranni as it would have destroyed the ship I was on then, if the crewmen had been still alive."

Biron felt his heart bound. For a moment he wanted to believe.

After all, maybe. Maybe!

# 11. AND MAYBE NOT!

And then again, maybe not!

Biron said, "How did you learn all this about its being an arsenal? How long did you stay? What did you see?"

Gillbret grew impatient. "It wasn't exactly what I saw at all. They didn't conduct me on any tours, or anything like that." He forced himself to relax. "Well, look, this is what happened. By the time they got me off the ship, I was in more or less of a bad state. I had been too frightened to eat much—it's a terrible thing, being marooned in space—and I must have looked worse than I really was.

"I identified myself, more or less, and they took me underground. With the ship, of course. I suppose they were more interested in the ship than in myself. It gave them a chance to study Tyrannian spatio-engineering. They took me to what must have been a hospital."

"But what did you see, Uncle?" asked Artemisia.

Biron interrupted, "Hasn't he ever told *you* this before?"

Artemisia said, "No."

And Gillbret added, "I've never told anyone till now. I was taken to a hospital, as I said. I passed research laboratories in that hospital that must have been better than anything we have in Rhodia. On the way to the hospital I passed factories in which some sort of metalwork was going on. The ships that had captured me were certainly like none I've ever heard about.

"It was all so apparent to me at the time that I have never questioned it in the years since. I think of it as my 'rebellion world,' and I know that someday swarms of ships will leave it to attack the Tyranni, and that the subject worlds will be called upon to rally round the rebel leaders. From year to year I've waited for it to happen. Each new year I've thought to myself: This may be the one. And, each time, I half hoped it wouldn't be, because I was longing to get away first, to join them so that I might be part of the great attack. I didn't want them to start without me."

He laughed shakily. "I suppose it would have amused most people to know what was going on in my mind. In *my* mind. Nobody thought much of me, you know."

Biron said, "All this happened over twenty years ago, and they haven't attacked? There's been no sign of them? No strange ships have been reported? No incidents? And you still think——"

Gillbret fired at him, "Yes, I do. Twenty years isn't too long to organize a rebellion against a planet that rules fifty systems. I was there just at the beginning of the rebellion. I know that too. Slowly, since then, they must have been honeycombing the planet with their underground preparations, developing newer ships and weapons, training more men, organizing the attack.

"It's only in the video thrillers that men spring to arms at a moment's notice; that a new weapon is needed one day, invented the next, mass-produced the third, and used the fourth. These things take time, Biron, and the men of the rebellion world must know they will have to be completely ready before beginning. They won't be able to strike twice.

"And what do you call 'incidents'? Tyrannian ships have disappeared and never been found. Space is big, you might say, and they might simply be lost, but what if they were captured by the rebels? There was the case of the *Tireless* two years back. It reported a strange object close enough to stimulate the massometer, and then was never heard from again. It could have been a meteor, I suppose, but *was it*?

"The search lasted months. They never found it. *I* think the rebels have it. The *Tireless* was a new ship, an experimental model. It would be just what they would want."

Biron said, "Once having landed there, why didn't you stay?"

"Don't you suppose I wanted to? I had no chance. I listened to them when they thought I was unconscious, and I learned a bit more then. They were just starting, out there, at that time. They couldn't afford to be found out then. They knew I was Gillbret oth Hinriad. There was enough identification on the ship, even if I hadn't told them myself, which I had. They knew that if I didn't return to Rhodia there would be a full-scale search that would not readily come to a halt.

"They couldn't risk such a search, so they had to see to it that I was returned to Rhodia. And that's where they took me."

"What!" cried Biron. "But that must have been an even greater risk. How did they do that?"

"I don't know." Gillbret passed his thin fingers through his graying hair, and his eyes seemed to be probing uselessly into the backward stretches of his memory. "They anesthetized me, I suppose. That part all blanks out. Past a certain point there is nothing. I can only remember that I opened my eyes and was back in the *Bloodsucker*; I was in space, just off Rhodia."

"The two dead crewmen were still attached by the tow magnets? They hadn't been removed on the rebellion world?" asked Biron.

"They were still there."

"Was there any evidence at all to indicate that you had been on the rebellion world?"

"None; except for what I remembered."

"How did you know you were off Rhodia?"

"I didn't. I knew I was near a planet; the massometer said so. I used the radio again, and this time it was Rhodian ships that came for me. I told my story to the Tyrannian Commissioner of that day, with appropriate modifications. I made no mention of the rebellion world, of course. And I said the meteor had hit just after the last Jump. I didn't want them to think I knew that a Tyrannian ship could make the Jumps automatically."

"Do you think the rebellion world found out that little fact? Did you tell them?"

"I didn't tell them. I had no chance. I wasn't there long enough. Conscious, that is. But I don't know how long I was unconscious and what they managed to find out for themselves."

Biron stared at the visiplate. Judging from the rigidity of the picture it presented, the ship they were on might have been nailed in space. The *Remorseless* was traveling at the rate of ten thousand miles an hour, but what was that to the immense distances of space. The stars were hard, bright, and motionless. They had a hypnotic quality about them.

He said, "Then where are we going? I take it you still don't know where the rebellion world is?"

"I don't. But I have an idea who would. I am almost sure I know." Gillbret was eager about it.

"Who?"

"The Autarch of Lingane."

"Lingane?" Biron frowned. He had heard the name some time back, it seemed to him, but he had forgotten the connection. "Why he?"

"Lingane was the last Kingdom captured by the Tyranni. It is not, shall we say, as pacified as the rest. Doesn't that make sense?"

"As far as it goes. But how far is that?"

"If you want another reason, there is your father."

"My father?" For a moment Biron forgot that his father was dead. He saw him standing before his mind's eye, large and alive, but then he remembered and there was that same cold wrench inside him. "How does my father come into this?"

"He was at court six months ago. I gained certain notions as to what he wanted. Some of his talks with my cousin, Hinrik, I overheard."

"Oh, Uncle," said Artemisia impatiently.

"My dear?"

"You had no right to eavesdrop on Father's private discussions."

Gillbret shrugged. "Of course not, but it was amusing, and useful as well."

Biron interrupted, "Now, wait. You say it was six months ago that my father was at Rhodia?" He felt excitement mount.

"Yes."

"Tell me. While there, did he have access to the Director's collection of Primitivism? You told me once that the Director had a large library of matters concerning Earth."

"I imagine so. The library is quite famous and it is usually made available to distinguished visitors, if they're interested. They usually aren't, but your father was. Yes, I remember that very well. He spent nearly a day there."

That checked. It had been half a year ago that his father had first asked his help. Biron said, "You yourself know the library well, I imagine."

"Of course."

"Is there anything in the library that would suggest that there exists a document on Earth of great military value?"

Gillbret was blank of face and, obviously, blank of mind.

Biron said, "Somewhere in the last centuries of prehistoric Earth there must have been such a document. I can only tell you that my father thought it to be the most valuable single item in the Galaxy, and the deadliest. I was to have gotten it for him, but I left Earth too soon, and in any case"—his voice faltered—"he died too soon."

But Gillbret was still blank. "I don't know what you're talking about."

"You don't understand. My father mentioned it to me

first six months ago. He must have learned of it in the library on Rhodia. If you've been through it yourself, can't you tell me what it was he must have learned?"

But Gillbret could only shake his head.

Biron said, "Well, continue with your story."

Gillbret said, "They spoke of the Autarch of Lingane, your father and my cousin. Despite your father's cautious phraseology, Biron, it was obvious that the Autarch was the fount and head of the conspiracy.

"And then"—he hesitated—"there was a mission from Lingane and the Autarch himself was at its head. I—I told him of the rebellion world."

"You said a while ago you told nobody," said Biron.

"Except the Autarch. I *had* to know the truth."

"What did he tell you?"

"Practically nothing. But then, he had to be cautious too. Could he trust me? I might have been working for the Tyranni. How could he know? But he didn't close the door altogether. It's our only lead."

"Is it?" Biron said. "Then we'll go to Lingane. One place, I suppose, is like another."

Mention of his father had depressed him, and, for the moment, nothing mattered much. Let it be Lingane.

Let it be Lingane! That was easy to say. But how does one go about pointing the ship at a tiny speck of light thirty-five light-years away. Two hundred trillion miles. A two with fourteen zeros after it. At ten thousand miles an hour (current cruising speed of the *Remorseless*) it would take well over two million years to get there.

Biron leafed through the *Standard Galactic Ephemeris* with something like despair. Tens of thousands of stars were listed in detail, with their positions crammed into three figures. There were hundreds of pages of these figures, symbolized by the Greek letters $\rho$ (rho), $\Theta$ (theta), and $\phi$ (phi).

$\rho$ was the distance from the Galactic Center in parsecs; $\Theta$, the angular separation, along the plane of the Galactic

Lens from the Standard Galactic Baseline (the line, that is, which connects the Galactic Center and the sun of the planet, Earth); $\phi$, the angular separation from the Baseline in the plane perpendicular to that of the Galactic Lens, the two latter measurements being expressed in radians. Given those three figures, one could locate any star accurately in all the vast immensity of space.

That is, on a given date. In addition to the star's position on the standard day for which all the data were calculated, one had to know the star's proper motion, both speed and direction. It was a small correction, comparatively, but necessary. A million miles is virtually nothing compared with stellar distances, but it is a long way with a ship.

There was, of course, the question of the ship's own position. One could calculate the distance from Rhodia by the reading of the massometer, or, more correctly, the distance from Rhodia's sun, since this far out in space the sun's gravitational field drowned out that of any of its planets. The direction they were traveling with reference to the Galactic Baseline was more difficult to determine. Biron had to locate two known stars other than Rhodia's sun. From their apparent positions and the known distance from Rhodia's sun, he could plot their actual position.

It was roughly done but, he felt sure, accurately enough. Knowing his own position and that of Lingane's sun, he had only to adjust the controls for the proper direction and strength of the hyperatomic thrust.

Biron felt lonely and tense. Not frightened! He rejected the word. But tense, definitely. He was deliberately calculating the elements of the Jump for a time six hours later. He wanted plenty of time to check his figures. And perhaps there might be the chance for a nap. He had dragged the bed makings out of the cabin and it was ready for him now.

The other two were, presumably, sleeping in the cabin. He told himself that that was a good thing and that he wanted nobody around bothering him, yet when he heard the small sound of bare feet outside, he looked up with a certain eagerness.

"Hello," he said, "why aren't you sleeping?"

Artemisia stood in the doorway, hesitating. She said, in a small voice, "Do you mind if I come in? Will I be bothering you?"

"It depends on what you do."

"I'll try to do the right things."

She seemed *too* humble, Biron thought suspiciously, and then the reason for it came out.

"I'm awfully frightened," she said. "Aren't you?"

He wanted to say no, not at all, but it didn't come out that way. He smiled sheepishly, and said, "Sort of."

Oddly enough, that comforted her. She knelt down on the floor beside him and looked at the thick volumes opened before him and at the sheets of calculations.

"They had all these books here?"

"You bet. They couldn't pilot a ship without them."

"And you understand all that?"

"Not *all* that. I wish I did. I hope I understand enough. We'll have to Jump to Lingane, you know."

"Is that hard to do?"

"No, not if you know the figures, which are all here, and have the controls, which are all there, *and* if you have experience, which I haven't. For instance, it should be done in several Jumps, but I'm going to try it in one because there'll be less chance of trouble, even though it means a wasteful use of energy."

He shouldn't tell her; there was no point in telling her; it would be cowardly to frighten her; and she'd be hard to handle if she got really frightened, panicky frightened. He kept telling himself all that and it did no good. He wanted to share it with somebody. He wanted part of it off his own mind.

He said, "There are some things I should know that I don't. Things like the mass density between here and Lingane affect the course of the Jump, because that mass density is what controls the curvature of this part of the universe. The *Ephemeris*—that's this big book here—mentions the curvature corrections that must be made in certain standard

Jumps, and from those you're supposed to be able to calculate your own particular corrections. But then if you happen to have a super giant within ten light-years, all bets are off. I'm not even sure if I used the computer correctly."

"But what would happen if you were wrong?"

"We *could* re-enter space too close to Lingane's sun."

She considered that, then said, "You have no idea how much better I feel."

"After what I've just said?"

"Of course. In my bunk I simply felt helpless and lost with so much emptiness in all directions. Now I know that we're going somewhere and that the emptiness is under our control."

Biron was pleased. How different she was. "I don't know about its being under our control."

She stopped him. "It is. I *know* you can handle the ship."

And Biron decided that maybe he could at that.

Artemisia had tucked her long unclad legs under her and sat facing him. She had only her filmy underclothes for cover, but seemed unconscious of the fact, though Biron was definitely not.

She said, "You know, I had an awfully queer sensation in the bunk, almost as if I were floating. That was one of the things that frightened me. Every time I'd turn, I'd give a queer little jump into the air and then flop back slowly as if there were springs in the air holding me back."

"You weren't sleeping in a top bunk, were you?"

"Yes, I was. The bottom ones give me claustrophobia, with another mattress six inches over your head."

Biron laughed. "Then that explains it. The ship's gravitational force is directed toward its base, and falls off as we move away from it. In the top bunk you were probably twenty or thirty pounds lighter than on the floor. Were you ever on a passenger liner? A really big one?"

"Once. When Father and I visited Tyrann last year."

"Well, on the liners they have the gravitation in all parts of the ship directed toward the outer hull, so that the long axis of the ship is always 'up,' no matter where you are.

That's why the motors of one of those big babies are always lined up in a cylinder running right along the long axis. No gravity there."

"It must take an awful lot of power to keep an artificial gravity going."

"Enough to power a small town."

"There isn't any danger of our running short of fuel, is there?"

"Don't worry about that. Ships are fueled by the total conversion of mass to energy. Fuel is the last thing we'll run out of. The outer hull will wear away first."

She was facing him. He noted that her face had been cleaned of its make-up and wondered how that had been done; probably with a handkerchief and as little of the drinking water as she could manage. She didn't suffer as a result, for her clear white skin was the more startlingly perfect against the black of her hair and eyes. Her eyes were very warm, thought Biron.

The silence had lasted a little too long. He said hurriedly, "You don't travel very much, do you? I mean, you were on a liner only once?"

She nodded. "Once too often. If we hadn't gone to Tyrann, that filthy chamberlain wouldn't have seen me and—I don't want to talk about that."

Biron let it go. He said, "Is that usual? I mean, not traveling."

"I'm afraid so. Father is always hopping around on state visits, opening agricultural expositions, dedicating buildings. He usually just makes some speech that Aratap writes for him. As for the rest of us, however, the more we stay in the Palace, the better the Tyranni like it. Poor Gillbret! The one and only time he left Rhodia was to attend the Khan's coronation as Father's representative. They've never let him get into a ship again."

Her eyes were downcast and, absently, she pleated the material of Biron's sleeve where it ended at the wrist. She said, "Biron."

"Yes—Arta?" He stumbled a bit, but it came out.

"Do you think Uncle Gil's story can be true? Do you suppose it could be his imagination? He's been brooding about the Tyranni for years, and he's never been able to do anything, of course, except to rig up spy beams, which is only childish, and he knows it. He may have built himself a daydream and, over the years, gradually come to believe in it. I *know* him, you see."

"Could be, but let's follow it up a little. We can travel to Lingane, anyway."

They were closer to one another. He could have reached out and touched her, held her in his arms, kissed her.

And he did so.

It was a complete *non sequitur*. Nothing, it seemed to Biron, had led to it. One moment they were discussing Jumps and gravity and Gillbret, and the next she was soft and silky in his arms and soft and silky on his lips.

His first impulse was to say he was sorry, to go through all the silly motions of apology, but when he drew away and would have spoken, she still made no attempt at escape but rested her head on the crook of his left arm. Her eyes remained closed.

So he said nothing at all but kissed her again, slowly and thoroughly. It was the best thing he could have done, and at the time he knew it.

Finally she said, a bit dreamily, "Aren't you hungry? I'll bring you some of the concentrate and warm it for you. Then, if you want to sleep, I can keep an eye on things for you. And—and I'd better put on more of my clothes."

She turned as she was about to go out the door. "The food concentrate tastes very nice after you get used to it. Thank you for getting it."

Somehow *that*, rather than the kisses, was the treaty of peace between them.

When Gillbret entered the control room, hours later, he showed no surprise at finding Biron and Artemisia lost in a foolish kind of conversation. He made no remarks about the fact that Biron's arm was about his niece's waist.

He said, "When are we Jumping, Biron?"

"In half an hour," said Biron.

The half hour passed; the controls were set; conversation languished and died.

At zero time Biron drew a deep breath and yanked a lever the full length of its arc, from left to right.

It was not as it had been on the liner. The *Remorseless* was smaller and the Jump was consequently less smooth. Biron staggered, and for a split second things wavered.

And then they were smooth and solid again.

The stars in the visiplate had changed. Biron rotated the ship, so that the star field lifted, each star moving in a stately arc. One star appeared finally, brilliantly white and more than a point. It was a tiny sphere, a burning speck of sand. Biron caught it, steadied the ship before it was lost again, and turned the telescope upon it, throwing in the spectroscopic attachment.

He turned again to the *Ephemeris*, and checked under the column headed "Spectral Characteristics." Then he got out of the pilot's chair and said, "It's still too far. I'll have to nudge up to it. But, anyway, that's Lingane right ahead."

It was the first Jump he had ever made, and it was successful.

# 12. THE AUTARCH COMES

The Autarch of Lingane pondered the matter, but his cool, well-trained features scarcely creased under the impact of thought.

"And you waited forty-eight hours to tell me," he said.

Rizzett said boldly, "There was no reason to tell you earlier. If we bombarded you with all matters, life would be a burden to you. We tell you now because we still make nothing of it. It is queer, and in our position we can afford nothing queer."

"Repeat this business. Let me hear it again."

The Autarch threw a leg upon the flaring window sill and looked outward thoughtfully. The window itself represented perhaps the greatest single oddity of Linganian architecture. It was moderate in size and set at the end of a five-foot recess that narrowed gently toward it. It was extremely clear, immensely thick, and precisely curved; not so much a window as a lens, funneling the light inward from all directions, so that, looking outward, one eyed a miniature panorama.

From any window in the Autarch's Manor a sweep of

vision embracing half the horizon from zenith to nadir could be seen. At the edges there was increasing minuteness and distortion, but that itself lent a certain flavor to what one saw: the tiny flattened motions of the city; the creeping, curved orbits of the crescent-shaped stratospherics, climbing from the airport. One grew so used to it that unhinging the window to allow the flat tameness of reality to enter would seem unnatural. When the position of the sun made the lenslike windows a focus for impossible heat and light, they were blanked out automatically, rather than opened, rendered opaque by a shift in the polarization characteristics of the glass.

And certainly the theory that a planet's architecture is the reflection of a planet's place in the Galaxy would seem to be borne out by the case of Lingane and its windows.

Like the windows, Lingane was small yet commanded a panoramic view. It was a "planet state" in a Galaxy, which, at the time, had passed beyond that stage of enconomic and political development. Where most political units were conglomerations of stellar systems, Lingane remained what it had been for centuries—a single inhabited world. This did not prevent it from being wealthy. In fact, it was almost inconceivable that Lingane could be anything else.

It is difficult to tell in advance when a world is so located that many Jump routes may use it as a pivotal intermediate point; or even *must* use it in the interests of optimal economy. A great deal depends on the pattern of development of that region of space, There is the question of the distribution of the naturally habitable planets; the order in which they are colonized and developed; the types of economy they possess.

Lingane discovered its own values early, which was the great turning point of its history. Next to the actual possession of a strategic position, the capacity to appreciate and exploit that position is most important. Lingane had proceeded to occupy small planetoids with neither resources nor capacity for supporting an independent population, choosing them only because they would help maintain Lingane's trade monopoly. They built servicing stations on those rocks. All that ships would need, from hyperatomic replacements to new book reels, could be found there. The stations grew to huge trading posts. From all the Nebular Kingdoms fur, minerals, grain, beef, timber poured in; from the Inner Kingdoms, machinery, appliances, medicinals; finished products of all sorts formed a similar flood.

So that, like its windows, Lingane's minuteness looked out on all the Galaxy. It was a planet alone, but it did well.

The Autarch said, without turning from the window, "Start with the mail ship, Rizzett. Where did it meet this cruiser in the first place?"

"Less than one hundred thousand miles off Lingane. The exact coordinates don't matter. They've been watched ever since. The point is that, even then, the Tyrannian cruiser was in an orbit about the planet."

"As though it had no intention of landing, but, rather, was waiting for something?"

"Yes."

"No way of telling how long they'd been waiting?"

"Impossible, I'm afraid. They were sighted by no one else. We checked thoroughly."

"Very well," said the Autarch. "We'll abandon that for the moment. They stopped the mail ship, which is, of course, interference with the mails and a violation of our Articles of Association with Tyrann."

"I doubt that they were Tyranni. Their unsure actions are more those of outlaws, of prisoners in flight."

"You mean the men on the Tyrannian cruiser? It may be what they want us to believe, of course. At any rate, their only overt action was to ask that a message be delivered directly to me."

"Directly to the Autarch, that is right."

"Nothing else?"

"Nothing else."

"They at no time entered the mail ship?"

"All communications were by visiplate. The mail capsule

was shot across two miles of empty space and caught by the ship's net."

"Was it vision communication or sound only?"

"Full vision. That's the point. The speaker was described by several as being a young man of 'aristocratic bearing,' whatever that means."

The Autarch's fist clenched slowly. "Really? And no photo-impression was taken of his face? That was a mistake."

"Unfortunately there was no reason for the mail captain to have anticipated the importance of doing so. If any importance exists! Does all this mean anything to you, sir?"

The Autarch did not answer the question. "And this is the message?"

"Exactly. A tremendous message of one word that we were supposed to bring directly to you; a thing we did not do, of course. It might have been a fission capsule, for instance. Men have been killed that way before."

"Yes, and Autarchs too," said the Autarch. "Just the word 'Gillbret.' One word, 'Gillbret.'"

The Autarch maintained his indifferent calm, but a certain lack of certainty was gathering, and he did not like to experience a lack of certainty. He liked nothing which made him aware of limitations. An Autarch should have no limitations, and on Lingane he had none that natural law did not impose.

There had not always been an Autarch. In its earlier days Lingane had been ruled by dynasties of merchant princes. The families who had first established the subplanetary service stations were the aristocrats of the state. They were not rich in land, hence could not compete in social position with the Ranchers and Grangers of the neighboring worlds. But they were rich in negotiable currency and so could buy and sell those same Ranchers and Grangers; and, by way of high finance, they sometimes did.

And Lingane suffered the usual fate of a planet ruled (or misruled) under such circumstances. The balance of power oscillated from one family to another. The various groups alternated in exile. Intrigues and palace revolutions were chronic, so that if the Directorship of Rhodia was the Sector's prime example of stability and orderly development, Lingane was the example of restlessness and disorder. "As fickle as Lingane," people said.

The outcome was inevitable, if one judges by hindsight. As the neighboring planet states consolidated into group states and became powerful, civil struggles on Lingane became increasingly expensive and dangerous to the planet. The general population was quite willing, finally, to barter anything for general calm. So they exchanged a plutocracy for an autocracy, and lost little liberty in the exchange. The power of several was concentrated in one, but that one, frequently enough, was deliberately friendly to the populace he sought to use as a make-weight against the never-reconciled merchants.

Under the Autarchy, Lingane increased its wealth and strength. Even the Tyranni, attacking thirty years earlier at the height of their power, had been fought to a standstill. They had not been defeated, but they had been stopped. The shock, even of that, had been permanent. Not a planet had been conquered by the Tyranni since the year they had attacked Lingane.

Other planets of the Nebular Kingdoms were outright vassals of the Tyranni. Lingane, however, was an Associated State, theoretically the equal "ally" of Tyrann, with its rights guarded by the Articles of Association.

The Autarch was not fooled by the situation. The chauvinistic of the planet might allow themselves the luxury of considering themselves free, but the Autarch knew that the Tryannian danger had been held at arm's length this past generation. Only that far. No farther.

And now it might be moving in quickly for the final, long-delayed bear hug. Certainly, he had given it the opportunity it was waiting for. The organization he had built up, ineffectual though it was, was sufficient grounds for punitive action of any type the Tyranni might care to undertake. Legally, Lingane would be in the wrong.

Was the cruiser the first reaching out for the final bear hug?

The Autarch said, "Has a guard been placed on that ship?"

"I said they were watched. Two of our *freighters*"—he smiled one-sidedly, "keep in massometer range."

"Well, what do you make of it?"

"I don't know. The only Gillbret I know whose name by itself would mean anything is Gillbret oth Hinriad of Rhodia. Have you had dealings with him?"

The Autarch said, "I saw him on my last visit to Rhodia."

"You told him nothing, of course."

"Of course."

Rizzett's eyes narrowed. "I thought there might have been a certain lack of caution on your part; that the Tyranni had been the recipients of an equal lack of caution on the part of this Gillbret—the Hinriads are notable weaklings these days—and that this now was a device to trap you into final self-betrayal."

"I doubt it. It comes at a queer time, this business. I have been away from Lingane for a year or more. I arrived last week and I shall leave in a matter of days again. A message such as this reaches me just when I am in a position *to* be reached."

"You don't think it is a coincidence?"

"I don't believe in coincidence. And there is *one* way in which all this would not be coincidence. I will therefore visit that ship. Alone."

"Impossible, sir." Rizzet was startled. He had a small, uneven scar just above his right temple and it suddenly showed red.

"You forbid me?" asked the Autarch dryly.

And he was Autarch, after all, since Rizzett's face fell, and he said, "As you please, sir."

Aboard the *Remorseless*, the wait was proving increasingly unpleasant. For two days they hadn't budged from their orbit.

Gillbret watched the controls with relentless concentration. His voice had an edge to it. "Wouldn't you say they were moving?"

Biron looked up briefly. He was shaving, and handling the Tyranni erosive spray with finicky care.

"No," he said, "they're not moving. Why should they? They're watching us, and they'll keep on watching us."

He concentrated upon the difficult area of the upper lip, and frowned impatiently as he felt the slightly sour taste of the spray upon his tongue. A Tyrannian could handle the spray with a grace that was almost poetic. It was undoubtedly the quickest and closest non-permanent shaving method in existence, in the hands of an expert. In essence, it was an extremely fine air-blown abrasive that scoured off the hairs without harming the skin. Certainly the skin felt like nothing more than the gentle pressure of what might have been an air stream.

However, Biron felt queasy about it. There was the well-known legend, or story, or fact (whatever it was), about the incidence of face cancer being higher among the Tyranni than among other cultural groups, and some attributed this to the Tyranni shave spray. Biron wondered for the first time if it might not be better to have his face completely depilated. It was done in some parts of the Galaxy, as a matter of course. He rejected the thought. Depilation was permanent. The fashion might always shift to mustaches or cheek curls.

Biron was surveying his face in the mirror, wondering how he would look in sideburns down to the angle of the jaw, when Artemisia said from the doorway, "I thought you were going to sleep."

"I did," he said. "Then I woke up." He looked up at her and smiled.

She patted his cheek, then stroked it gently with her fingers. "It's smooth. You look about eighteen."

He carried her hand to his lips. "Don't let that fool you," he said.

She said, "They're still watching?"

"Still watching. Isn't it annoying, these dull interludes that give you time to sit and worry?"

"I don't find this interlude dull."

"You're talking about other aspects of it now, Arta."

She said, "Why don't we cross them up and land on Lingane?"

"We've thought of it. I don't think we're ready for that kind of risk. We can afford to wait till the water supply gets a bit lower."

Gillbret said loudly, "I tell you they *are* moving."

Biron crossed over to the control panel and considered the massometer readings. He looked at Gillbret and said, "You may be right."

He pecked away at the calculator for a moment or two and stared at its dials.

"No, the two ships haven't moved relative to us, Gillbret. What's changed the massometer is that a third ship has joined them. As near as I can tell, it's five thousand miles off, about 46 degrees $\rho$ and 192 degrees $\phi$ from the ship-planet line, if I've got the clockwise and counterclockwise conventions straight. If I haven't, the figures are, respectively, 314 and 168 degrees."

He paused to take another reading. "I think they're approaching. It's a small ship. Do you think you can get in touch with them, Gillbret?"

"I can try," said Gillbret.

"All right. No vision. Let's leave it at sound, till we get some notion of what's coming."

It was amazing to watch Gillbret at the controls of the etheric radio. He was obviously the possessor of a native talent. Contacting an isolated point in space with a tight radio beam remains, after all, a task in which the ship's control-panel information can participate only slightly. He had a notion of the distance of the ship which might be off by a hundred miles plus or minus. He had two angles, either or both of which might easily be wrong by five or six degrees in any direction.

This left a volume of about ten million cubic miles within

which the ship might be. The rest was left to the human operator, and a radio beam which was a probing finger not half a mile in cross section at the widest point of its receivable range. It was said that a skilled operator could tell by the feel of the controls how closely the beam missed the target. Scientifically, that theory was nonsense, of course, but it often seemed that no other explanation was possible.

In less than ten minutes the activity gauge of the radio was jumping and the *Remorseless* was both sending and receiving.

In another ten minutes Biron was able to lean back and say, "They're going to send a man aboard."

"Ought we let them?" asked Artemisia.

"Why not? One man? We're armed."

"But if we let their ship get too close?"

"We're a Tyrannian cruiser, Arta. We've got three to five times their power, even if they were the best warship Lingane had. They're not allowed too much by their precious Articles of Association, and we've got five high-caliber blasters."

Artemisia said, "Do you know how to use the Tyrannian blasters? I didn't know you did."

Biron hated to turn the admiration off, but he said, "Unfortunately, I don't. At least, not yet. But then, the Linganian ship won't allow that, you see."

Half an hour later the visiplate showed a visible ship. It was a stubby little craft, fitted with two sets of four fins, as though it were frequently called upon to double for stratospheric flight.

At its first appearance in the telescope, Gillbret shouted in delight. "That's the Autarch's yacht," he cried, and his face wrinkled into a grin. "It's his private yacht. I'm sure of it. I told you that the bare mention of my name was the surest way to get his attention."

There was the period of deceleration and adjustment of velocity on the part of the Linganian ship, until it hung motionless in the plate.

A thin voice came from the receiver. "Ready for boarding?"

"Ready!" clipped Biron. "One person only."

"One person," came the response.

It was like a snake uncoiling. The metal-mesh rope looped outward from the Linganian ship, shooting at them harpoon-fashion. Its thickness expanded in the visiplate, and the magnetized cylinder that ended it approached and grew in size. As it grew closer, it edged toward the rim of the cone of vision, then veered off completely.

The sound of its contact was hollow and reverberant. The magnetized weight was anchored, and the line was a spider thread that did not sag in a normal weighted curve but retained whatever kinks and loops it had possessed at the moment of contact, these moving slowly forward as units under the influence of inertia.

Easily and carefully, the Linganian ship edged away and the line straightened. It hung there then, taut and fine, thinning into space until it was an almost invisible thing, glancing with incredible daintiness in the light of Lingane's sun.

Biron threw in the telescopic attachment, which bloated the ship monstrously in the field of vision, so that one could see the origin of the half-mile length of connecting line and the little figure that was beginning to swing hand over hand along it.

It was not the usual form of boarding. Ordinarily, two ships would maneuver to near-contact, so that extensible air locks could meet and merge under intense magnetic fields. A tunnel through space would connect the ships, and a man could travel from one to the other with no further protection than he needed to wear aboard ship. Naturally, this form of boarding required mutual trust.

By space line, one was dependent upon his space suit. The approaching Linganian was bloated in his, a fat thing of air-extended metal mesh, the joints of which required no small muscular effort to work. Even at the distance at which he was, Biron could see his arms flex with a snap as the joint gave and came to rest in a new groove.

And the mutual velocities of the two ships had to be carefully adjusted. An inadvertent acceleration on the part of either would tear the line loose and send the traveler tumbling through space under the easy grip of the faraway sun and of the initial impulse of the snapping line—with nothing, neither friction nor obstruction, to stop him this side of eternity.

The approaching Linganian moved on confidently and quickly. When he came closer it was easy to see that it was not a simple hand-over-hand procedure. Each time the forward hand flexed, pulling him on, he would let go and float onward some dozen feet before his other hand had reached forward for a new hold.

It was a brachiation through space. The spaceman was a gleaming metal gibbon.

Artemisia said, "What if he misses?"

"He looks too expert to do that," said Biron, "but if he does, he'd still shine in the sun. We'd pick him up again."

The Linganian was close now. He had passed out of the field of the visiplate. In another five seconds there was the clatter of feet on the ship's hull.

Biron yanked the lever that lit the signals which outlined the ship's air lock. A moment later, in answer to an imperative series of raps, the outer door was opened. There was a thump just beyond a blank section of the pilot-room's wall. The outer door closed, the section of wall slid away, and a man stepped through.

His suit frosted over instantly, blanking the thick glass of his helmet and turning him into a mound of white. Cold radiated from him. Biron elevated the heaters and the gush of air that entered was warm and dry. For a moment the frost on the suit held its own, then began to thin and dissolve into a dew.

The Linganian's blunt metal fingers were fumbling at the clasps of the helmet as though he were impatient with his snowy blindness. It lifted off as a unit, the thick, soft insulation inside rumpling his hair as it passed.

Gillbret said, "Your Excellency!" In glad triumph, he said, "Biron, it is the Autarch himself."

But Biron, in a voice that struggled vainly against stupefaction, could only say, "Jonti!"

# 13. THE AUTARCH REMAINS

The Autarch gently toed the suit to one side and appropriated the larger of the padded chairs.

He said, "I haven't had that sort of exercise in quite awhile. But they say it never leaves you once you've learned, and, apparently, it hasn't in my case. Hello, Farrill! My Lord Gillbret, good day. And this, if I remember, is the Director's daughter, the Lady Artemisia!"

He placed a long cigarette carefully between his lips and brought it to life with a single intake of breath. The scented tobacco filled the air with its pleasant odor. "I did not expect to see you quite so soon, Farrill," he said.

"Or at all, perhaps?" said Biron acidly.

"One never knows," agreed the Autarch. "Of course, with a message that read only 'Gillbret'; with the knowledge that Gillbret could not pilot a space ship; with the further knowledge that I had myself sent a young man to Rhodia who *could* pilot a space ship and who was quite capable of stealing a Tyrannian cruiser in his desperation to escape; and with the knowledge that one of the men on the cruiser was reported to be young and of aristocratic bearing, the conclusion was obvious. I am not surprised to see you."

"I think you are," said Biron. "I think you're as surprised as hell to see me. As an assassin, you should be. Do you think I am worse at deduction than you are?"

"I think only highly of you, Farrill."

The Autarch was completely unperturbed, and Biron felt awkward and stupid in his resentment. He turned furiously to the others. "This man is Sander Jonti—the Sander Jonti I've told you of. He may be the Autarch of Lingane besides, or fifty Autarchs. It makes no difference. To me he is Sander Jonti."

Artemisia said, "*He* is the man who——"

Gillbret put a thin and shaking hand to his brow. "Control yourself, Biron. Are you mad?"

"This *is* the man! I am *not* mad!" shouted Biron. He controlled himself with an effort. "All right. There's no point yelling, I suppose. Get off my ship, Jonti. Now that's said quietly enough. Get off my ship."

"My dear Farrill. For what reason?"

Gillbret made incoherent sounds in his throat, but Biron pushed him aside roughly and faced the seated Autarch. "You made one mistake, Jonti. Just one. You couldn't tell in advance that when I got out of my dormitory room back on Earth I would leave my wrist watch inside. You see, my wrist-watch strap happened to be a radiation indicator."

The Autarch blew a smoke ring and smiled pleasantly.

Biron said, "And that strap never turned blue, Jonti. There was no bomb in my room that night. There was only a deliberately planted dud! If you deny it, you are a liar, Jonti, or Autarch, or whatever you please to call yourself.

"What is more, *you* planted that dud. *You* knocked me out with Hypnite and arranged the rest of that night's comedy. It makes quite obvious sense, you know. If I had been left to myself, I would have slept through the night and would never have known that anything was out of the way. So who rang me on the visiphone until he was sure I had awakened? Awakened, that is, to discover the bomb, which had been deliberately placed near a counter so that I couldn't miss it. Who blasted my door in so that I might leave the room before I found out that the bomb was only a dud after all? You must have enjoyed yourself that night, Jonti."

Biron waited for effect, but the Autarch merely nodded in polite interest. Biron felt the fury mount. It was like punching pillows, whipping water, kicking air.

He said harshly, "My father was about to be executed. I would have learned of it soon enough. I would have gone to Nephelos, or not gone. I would have followed my own good sense in the matter, confronted the Tyranni openly or not as I decided. I would have known my chances. I would have been prepared for eventualities.

"But you wanted me to go to Rhodia, to see Hinrik. But, ordinarily, you couldn't expect me to do what *you* wanted. I wasn't likely to go to *you* for advice. Unless, that is, you could stage an appropriate situation. You did!

"I thought I was being bombed and I could think of no reason. You could. You seemed to have saved my life. You seemed to know everything; what I ought to do next, for instance. I was off balance, confused. I followed your advice."

Biron ran out of breath and waited for an answer. There was none. He shouted. "You did not explain that the ship on which I left Earth was a Rhodian ship and that you had seen to it that the captain had been informed of my true identity. You did not explain that you intended me to be in the hands of the Tyranni the instant I landed on Rhodia. Do you deny that?"

There was a long pause. Jonti stubbed out his cigarette.

Gillbret chafed one hand in the other. "Biron, you are being ridiculous. The Autarch wouldn't——"

Then Jonti looked up and said quietly, "But the Autarch would. I admit it all. You are quite right, Biron, and I congratulate you on your penetration. The bomb *was* a dud planted by myself, and I sent you to Rhodia with the intention of having you arrested by the Tyranni."

Biron's face cleared. Some of the futility of life vanished.

He said, "Someday, Jonti, I will settle that matter. At the moment, it seems you are Autarch of Lingane with three ships waiting for you out there. That hampers me a bit more than I would like. However, the *Remorseless* is my ship. I am its pilot. Put on your suit and get out. The space line is still in place."

"It is not your ship. You are a pirate rather than a pilot."

"Possession is all the law here. You have five minutes to get into your suit." ·

"Please. Let's avoid dramatics. We need one another and I have no intention of leaving."

"I don't need *you*. I wouldn't need you if the Tyrannian home fleet were closing in right now and you could blast them out of space for me."

"Farrill," said Jonti, "you are talking and acting like an adolescent. I've let you have your say. May I have mine?"

"No. I see no reason to listen to you."

"Do you see one now?"

Artemisia screamed. Biron made one movement, then stopped. Red with frustration, he remained tense but helpless.

Jonti said, "I do take certain precautions. I am sorry to be so crude as to use a weapon as a threat. But I imagine it will help me force you to hear me."

The weapon he held was a pocket blaster. It was not designed to pain or stun. It killed!

He said, "For years I have been organizing Lingane against the Tyranni. Do you know what that means? It has not been easy. It has been almost impossible. The Inner Kingdoms will offer no help. We've known that from long experience. There is no salvation for the Nebular Kingdoms but what they work out for themselves. But to convince our native leaders of this is no friendly game. Your father was active in the matter and was killed. Not a friendly game at all. Remember that.

"And your father's capture was a crisis to us. It was life and horrible death to us. He was in our inner circles and the Tyranni were obviously not far behind us. They had to be thrown off stride. To do so, I could scarcely temper my dealings with honor and integrity. They fry no eggs.

"I couldn't come to you and say, 'Farrill, we've got to put the Tyranni on a false scent. You're the son of the Rancher and therefore suspicious. Get out there and be friendly with Hinrik of Rhodia so that the Tyranni may look in the wrong direction. Lead them away from Lingane. It may be dangerous; you may lose your life, but the ideals for which your father died come first.'

"Maybe you would have done it, but I couldn't afford to experiment. I maneuvered you into doing it without your knowledge. It was hard, I'll grant you. Still, I had no choice. I thought you might not survive; I tell you that frankly. But you were expendable; and I tell you *that* frankly. As it turned out, you did survive, and I am pleased with that.

"And there was one more thing, a matter of a document——"

Biron said, "What document?"

"You jump quickly. I said your father was working for me. So I know what he knew. You were to obtain that document and you were a good choice, at first. You were on Earth legitimately. You were young and not likely to be suspected. I say, *at first*!

"But then, with your father arrested, you became dangerous. You would be an object of prime suspicion to the Tyranni; and we could not allow the document to fall into your possession, since it would then almost inevitably fall into theirs. We had to get you off Earth before you could complete your mission. You see, it all hangs together."

"Then *you* have it now?" asked Biron.

The Autarch said, "No, I have not. A document which might have been the right one has been missing from Earth for years. If it *is* the right one, I don't know who has it. May I put away the blaster now? It grows heavy."

Biron said, "Put it away."

The Autarch did so. He said, "What has your father told you about the document?"

"Nothing that you don't know, since he worked for you."

The Autarch smiled. "Quite so!" but the smile had little of real amusement in it.

"Are you quite through with your explanation now?"

"Quite through."

"Then," said Biron, "get off the ship."

Gillbret said, "Now wait, Biron. There's more than private pique to be considered here. There's Artemisia and myself, too, you know. We have *something* to say. As far as I'm concerned, what the Autarch says makes sense. I'll remind you that on Rhodia I saved your life, so I think my views are to be considered."

"All right. You saved my life," shouted Biron. He pointed a finger towards the air lock. "Go with him, then. Go on. You get out of here too. You wanted to find the Autarch. There he is! I agreed to pilot you to him, and my responsibility is over. Don't try to tell *me* what to do."

He turned to Artemisia, some of his anger still brimming over. "And what about you? You saved my life too. Everyone went around saving my life. Do you want to go with him too?"

She said calmly, "Don't put words into my mouth, Biron. If I wanted to go with him, I'd say so."

"Don't feel any obligations. You can leave any time."

She looked hurt and he turned away. As usual, some cooler part of himself knew that he was acting childishly. He had been made to look foolish by Jonti and he was helpless in the face of the resentment he felt. And besides, why should they all take so calmly the thesis that it was perfectly right to have Biron Farrill thrown to the Tyranni, like a bone to the dogs, in order to keep them off Jonti's neck. Damn it, what did they think he was?

He thought of the dud bomb, the Rhodian liner, the Tyranni, the wild night on Rhodia, and he could feel the stinging of self-pity inside himself.

The Autarch said, "Well, Farrill?"

And Gillbret said, "Well, Biron?"

Biron turned to Artemisia. "What do *you* think?"

Artemisia said calmly, "I think he has three ships out there still, and is Autarch of Lingane, besides. I don't think you really have a choice."

The Autarch looked at her, and he nodded his admiration. "You are an intelligent girl, my lady. It is good that such a mind should be in such a pleasant exterior." For a measurable moment his eyes lingered.

Biron said, "What's the deal?"

"Lend me the use of your names and your abilities, and I will take you to what my Lord Gillbret called the rebellion world."

Biron said sourly, "You think there *is* one?"

And Gillbret said simultaneously, "Then it *is* yours."

The Autarch smiled. "I think there is a world such as my lord described, but it is not mine."

"It's *not* yours," said Gillbret despondently.

"Does that matter, if I can find it?"

"How?" demanded Biron.

The Autarch said, "It is not so difficult as you might think. If we accept the story as it has been told us, we must believe that there exists a world in rebellion against the Tyranni. We must believe that it is located somewhere in the Nebular Sector and that in twenty years it has remained undiscovered by the Tyranni. If such a situation is to remain possible, there is only one place in the Sector where such a planet can exist."

"And where is that?"

"You do not find the solution obvious? Doesn't it seem inevitable that the world could exist only within the Nebula itself?"

"*Inside* the Nebula!"

Gillbret said, "Great Galaxy, of course."

And, at the moment, the solution did indeed seem obvious and inescapable.

Artemisia said timidly, "Can people live on worlds inside the Nebula?"

"Why not?" said the Autarch. "Don't mistake the Nebula. It is a dark mist in space, but it is not a poison gas. It is an incredibly attenuated mass of dust that absorb and obscure the light of the stars within it, and, of course, those on the side directly opposite the observer. Otherwise, it is harmless, and, in the direct neighborhood of a star, virtually undetectable.

"I apologize if I seem pedantic, but I have spent the last several months at the University of Earth collecting astronomical data on the Nebula."

"Why there?" said Biron. "It is a matter of little importance, but I met you there and I am curious."

"There's no mystery to it. I left Lingane originally on my own business. The exact nature is of no importance. About six months ago I visited Rhodia. My agent, Widemos—your father, Biron—had been unsuccessful in his negotiations with the Director, whom we had hoped to swing to our side. I tried to improve matters and failed, since Hinrik, with apologies to the lady, is not the type of material for our sort of work."

"Hear, hear," muttered Biron.

The Autarch continued. "But I did meet Gillbret, as he may have told you. So I went to Earth, because Earth is the original home of humanity. It was from Earth that most of the original explorations of the Galaxy set out. It is upon Earth that most of the records exist. The Horsehead Nebula was explored quite thoroughly; at least, it was passed through a number of times. It was never settled, since the difficulties of traveling through a volume of space where stellar observations could not be made were too great. The explorations themselves, however, were all I needed.

"Now listen carefully. The Tyrannian ship upon which my Lord Gillbret was marooned was struck by a meteor after its first Jump. Assuming that the trip from Tyrann to Rhodia was along the usual trade route—and there is no reason to suppose anything else—the point in space at which the ship left its route is established. It would scarcely have traveled more than half a million miles in ordinary space between the first two Jumps. We can consider such a length as a point in space.

"It is possible to make another assumption. In damaging the control panels, it was quite possible that the meteor might have altered the direction of the Jumps, since that would require only an interference with the motion of the ship's gyroscope. This would be difficult but not impossible. To change the *power* of the hyperatomic thrusts, however, would require complete smashing of the engines, which, of course, were not touched by the meteor.

"With unchanged power of thrust, the length of the four remaining Jumps would not be changed, nor, for that matter, would their relative directions. It would be analogous to having a long, crooked wire bent at a single point in an unknown direction through an unknown angle. The final position of the ship would lie somewhere on the surface of an imaginary sphere, the center of which would be that point in space where the meteor struck, and the radius of which would be the vector sum of the remaining Jumps.

"I plotted such a sphere, and that surface intersects a thick extension of the Horsehead Nebula. Some six thousand square degrees of the sphere's surface, one fourth of the total surface, lies in the Nebula. It remains, therefore, only to find a star lying within the Nebula and within one million miles or so of the imaginary surface we are discussing. You will remember that when Gillbret's ship came to rest, it was within reach of a star.

"Now how many stars within the Nebula do you suppose we can find that close to the sphere's surface? Remember there are one hundred billion radiating stars in the Galaxy."

Biron found himself absorbed in the matter almost against his will. "Hundreds, I suppose."

"Five!" replied the Autarch. "Just five. Don't be fooled by the one hundred billion figure. The Galaxy is about seven trillion cubic light-years in volume, so that there are seventy cubic light-years per star on the average. It is a pity that I do not know which of those five have habitable planets. We might reduce the number of possibles to one. Unfortunately, the early explorers had no time for detailed observations. They plotted the positions of the stars, the proper motions, and the spectral types."

"So that in one of those five stellar systems," said Biron, "is located the rebellion world?"

"Only that conclusion would fit the facts we know."

"Assuming Gil's story can be accepted."

"I make that assumption."

"My story is true," interrupted Gillbret intensely. "I swear it."

"I am about to leave," said the Autarch, "to investigate each of the five worlds. My motives in doing so are obvious. As Autarch of Lingane I can take an equal part in their efforts."

"And with two Hinriads and a Widemos on your side, your bid for an equal part, and, presumably, a strong and secure position in the new, free worlds to come, would be so much the better," said Biron.

"Your cynicism doesn't frighten me, Farrill. The answer is obviously yes. If there is to be a successful rebellion, it would, again obviously, be desirable to have your fist on the winning side."

"Otherwise some successful privateer or rebel captain might be rewarded with the Autarchy of Lingane."

"Or the Ranchy of Widemos. Exactly."

"And if the rebellion is not successful?"

"There will be time to judge of that when we find what we look for."

Biron said slowly, "I'll go with you."

"Good! Then suppose we make arrangements for your transfer from this ship."

"Why that?"

"It would be better for you. This ship is a toy."

"It is a Tyrannian warship. We would be wrong in abandoning it."

"As a Tyrannian warship, it would be dangerously conspicious."

"Not in the Nebula. I'm sorry, Jonti. I'm joining you out of expedience. I can be frank too. I want to find the rebellion world. But there's no friendship between us. I stay at my own controls."

"Biron," said Artemisia gently, "the ship *is* too small for the three of us."

"As it stands, yes, Arta. But it can be fitted with a trailer. Jonti knows that as well as I do. We'd have all the space we needed then, and still be masters at our own controls. And, for that matter, it would effectively disguise the nature of the ship."

The Autarch considered. "If there is to be neither friendship nor trust, Farrill, I must protect myself. You may have your own ship and a trailer to boot, outfitted as you may wish. But I must have some guarantee for your proper behavior. The Lady Artemisia, at least, must come with me."

"*No!*" said Biron.

The Autarch lifted his eyebrows. "No? Let the lady speak."

He turned toward Artemisia, and his nostrils flared slightly. "I dare say you would find the situation very comfortable, my lady."

"You, at least, would *not* find it comfortable, my lord. Be assured of that," she retorted. "I would spare you the discomfort and remain here."

"I think you might reconsider if——" began the Autarch, as two little wrinkles at the bridge of his nose marred the serenity of his expression.

"I think not," interrupted Biron. "The Lady Artemisia has made her choice."

"And you back her choice then, Farrill?" The Autarch was smiling again.

"Entirely! All three of us will remain on the *Remorseless*. There will be no compromise on that."

"You choose your company oddly."

"Do I?"

"I think so." The Autarch seemed idly absorbed in his fingernails. "You seem so annoyed with me because I deceived you and placed your life in danger. It is strange, then, is it not, that you should seem on such friendly terms with the daughter of a man such as Hinrik, who in deception is certainly my master."

"I know Hinrik. Your opinions of him change nothing."

"You know everything about Hinrik?"

"I know enough."

"Do you know that he killed your father?" The Autarch's finger stabbed toward Artemisia. "Do you know that the girl you are so deeply concerned to keep under your protection is the daughter of your father's murderer?"

# 14. THE AUTARCH LEAVES

The tableau remained unbroken for a moment. The Autarch had lit another cigarette. He was quite relaxed, his face untroubled. Gillbret had folded into the pilot's seat, his face screwed up as though he were going to burst into tears. The limp straps of the pilot's stress-absorbing outfit dangled about him and increased the lugubrious effect.

Biron, paper-white, fists clenched, faced the Autarch. Artemisia, her thin nostrils flaring, kept her eyes not on the Autarch, but on Biron only.

The radio signaled, the soft clickings crashing with the effect of cymbals in the small pilot room.

Gillbret jerked upright, then whirled on the seat.

The Autarch said lazily, "I'm afraid we've been more talkative than I'd anticipated. I told Rizzett to come get me if I had not returned in an hour."

The visual screen was alive now with Rizzett's grizzled head.

And then Gillbret said to the Autarch, "He would like to speak to you." He made room.

The Autarch rose from his chair and advanced so that his own head was within the zone of visual transmission.

He said, "I am perfectly safe, Rizzett."

The other's question was heard clearly: "Who are the crew members on the cruiser, sir?"

And suddenly Biron stood next to the Autarch. "I am Rancher of Widemos," he said proudly.

Rizzett smiled gladly and broadly. A hand appeared on the screen in sharp salute. "Greetings, sir."

The Autarch interrupted. "I will be returning soon with a young lady. Prepare to maneuver for contact air locks." And he broke the visual connection between the two ships.

He turned to Biron. "I assured them it was you on board ship. There was some objection to my coming here alone otherwise. Your father was extremely popular with my men."

"Which is why you can use my name."

The Autarch shrugged.

Biron said, "It is all you can use. Your last statement to your officer was inaccurate."

"In what way?"

"Artemisia oth Hinriad stays with me."

"Still? After what I have told you?"

Biron said sharply, "You have told me nothing. You have made a bare statement, but I am not likely to take your unsupported word for anything. I tell you this without any attempt at tact. I hope you understand me."

"Is your knowledge of Hinrik such that my statement seems inherently inplausible to you?"

Biron was staggered. Visibly and apparently, the remark had struck home. He made no answer.

Artemisia said, "I say it's not so. *Do* you have proof?"

"No direct proof, of course. I was not present at any conferences between your father and the Tyranni. But I can present certain known facts and allow you to make your own inferences. First, the old Rancher of Widemos visited Hinrik six months ago. I've said that already. I can add here that he was somewhat overenthusiastic in his efforts, or perhaps he overestimated Hinrik's discretion. At any rate, he talked more than he should have. My Lord Gillbret can verify that."

Gillbret nodded miserably. He turned to Artemisia, who had turned to him with moist and angry eyes. "I'm sorry, Arta, but it's true. I've told you this. It was from Widemos that I heard about the Autarch."

The Autarch said, "And it was fortunate for myself that my lord had developed such long mechanical ears with which to sate his lively curiosity concerning the Director's meetings of state. I was warned of the danger, quite unwittingly, by Gillbret when he first approached me. I left as soon as I could, but the damage, of course, had been done.

"Now, to our knowledge, it was Widemos's only slip, and Hinrik, certainly, has no enviable reputation as a man of any greater independence and courage. Your father, Farrill, was arrested within half a year. If not through Hinrik, through this girl's father, then how?"

Biron said, "You did not warn him?"

"In our business we take our chances, Farrill, but he *was* warned. After that he made no contact, however indirect, with any of us, and destroyed whatever proof he had of connection with us. Some among us believed that he should leave the Sector, or, at the very least, go into hiding. He refused to do this.

"I think I can understand why. To alter his way of life would prove the truth of what the Tyranni must have learned, endanger the entire movement. He decided to risk his own life only. He remained in the open.

"For nearly half a year the Tyranni waited for a betraying gesture. They are patient, the Tyranni. None came, so that when they could wait no longer, they found nothing in their net but him."

"It's a lie," cried Artemisia. "It's all a lie. It's a smug, sanctimonious, lying story with no truth in it. If all you said were true, they would be watching you too. You would be in danger yourself. You wouldn't be sitting here, smiling and wasting time."

"My lady, I do not waste my time. I have already tried

to do what I could toward discrediting your father as a source of information. I think I have succeeded somewhat. The Tyranni will wonder if they ought to listen further to a man whose daughter and cousin are obvious traitors. And then again, if they are still disposed to believe him, why, I am on the point of vanishing into the Nebula where they will not find me. I should think my actions tend to prove my story rather than otherwise."

Biron drew a deep breath and said, "Let us consider the interview at an end, Jonti. We have agreed to the extent that we will accompany you and that you will grant us needed supplies. That is enough. Granting that all you have just said is truth, it is still beside the point. The crimes of the Director of Rhodia are not inherited by his daughter. Artemisia oth Hinriad stays here with me, provided she herself agrees."

"I do," said Artemisia.

"Good. I think that covers everything. I warn you, by the way. You are armed; so am I. Your ships are fighters, perhaps; mine is a Tryannian cruiser."

"Don't be silly, Farrill. My intentions are quite friendly. You wish to keep the girl here? So be it. May I leave by contact air lock?"

Biron nodded. "We will trust you so far."

The two ships maneuvered ever closer, until the flexible airlock extensions pouted outward toward one another. Carefully, they edged about, trying for the perfect fit. Gillbret hung upon the raido.

"They'll be trying to contact again in two minutes," he said.

Three times already the magnetic field had been triggered, and each time the extending tubes had stretched toward one another and met off-center, gaping crescents of space between them.

"Two minutes," repeated Biron, and waited tensely.

The second hand moved and the magnetic field clicked into existence a fourth time, the lights dimming as the motors adjusted to the sudden drain of power. Again the airlock extensions reached out, hovered on the brink of instability, and then, with a noiseless jar, the vibration of which hummed its way into the pilot room, settled into place properly, clamps automatically locking in position. An air-tight seal had been formed.

Biron drew the back of his hand slowly across his forehead and some of the tension oozed out of him.

"There it is," he said.

The Autarch lifted his space suit. There was still a thin film of moisture under it.

"Thanks," he said pleasantly. "An officer of mine will be right back. You will arrange the details of the supplies necessary with him."

The Autarch left.

Biron said, "Take care of Jonti's officer for me for a while, will you, Gil. When he comes in, break the air-lock contact. All you'll have to do is remove the magnetic field. This is the photonic switch you'll flash."

He turned and stepped out of the pilot room. Right now he needed time for himself. Time to think, mostly.

But there was the hurried footstep behind him, and the soft voice. He stopped.

"Biron," said Artemisia, "I want to speak to you."

He faced her. "Later, if you don't mind, Arta."

She was looking up at him intently. "No, now."

Her arms were poised as though she would have liked to embrace him but was not sure of her reception. She said, "You didn't believe what he said about my father?"

"It has no bearing," said Biron.

"Biron," she began, and stopped. It was hard for her to say it. She tried again, "Biron, I know that part of what has been going on between us has been because we've been alone and together and in danger, but——" She stopped again.

Biron said, "If you're trying to say you're a Hinriad, Arta, there's no need. I know it. I won't hold you to anything afterward."

"No. Oh no." She caught his arm and placed her cheek against his hard shoulder. She was speaking rapidly. "That's not it at all. It doesn't matter about Hinriad and Widemos at all. I—I love you, Biron."

Her eyes went up, meeting his. "I think you love me too. I think you would admit it if you could forget that I am a Hinriad. Maybe you will now that I've said it first. You told the Autarch you would not hold my father's deeds against me. Don't hold his rank against me, either."

Her arms were around his neck now. Biron could feel the softness of her breasts against him and the warmth of her breath on his lips. Slowly his own hands went upward and gently grasped her forearms. As gently, he disengaged her arms and, still as gently, stepped back from her.

He said, "I am not quits with the Hinriads, my lady."

She was startled. "You told the Autarch that——"

He looked away. "Sorry, Arta. Don't go by what I told the Autarch."

She wanted to cry out that it wasn't true, that her father had not done this thing, that in any case——

But he turned into the cabin and left her standing in the corridor, her eyes filling with hurt and shame.

# 15. THE HOLE IN SPACE

Tedor Rizzett turned as Biron entered the pilot room again. His hair was gray, but his body was still vigorous and his face was broad, red, and smiling.

He covered the distance between himself and Biron in a stride and seized the young man's hand heartily.

"By the stars," he said, "I'd need no word from you to tell me that you are your father's son. It is the old Rancher alive again."

"I wish it were," said Biron, somberly.

Rizzett's smile faltered. "So do we all. Every one of us. I'm Ted Rizzett, by the way. I'm a colonel in the regular Linganian forces, but we don't use titles in our own little game. We even say 'sir' to the Autarch. That reminds me!" He looked grave. "We don't have lords and ladies or even Ranchers on Lingane. I hope I won't offend if I forget to throw in the proper title sometimes."

Biron shrugged. "As you said, no titles in our little game. But what about the trailer? I'm to make arrangements with you, I take it."

For a flickering moment he looked across the room.

Gillbret was seated, quietly listening. Artemisia had her back to him. Her slim, pale fingers wove an abstracted pattern on the photocontacts of the computer. Rizzett's voice brought him back.

The Linganian had cast an all-inclusive glance about the room. "First time I've ever seen a Tyrannian vessel from the inside. Don't care much for it. Now you've got the emergency air lock due stern, haven't you? It seems to me the power thrusters girdle the midsection."

"That's right."

"Good. Then there won't be any trouble. Some of the old model ships had power thrusters due stern, so that trailers had to be set off at an angle. This makes the gravity adjustment difficult and the maneuverability in atmospheres just about nil."

"How long will it take, Rizzett?"

"Not long. How big would you want it?"

"How big could you get it?"

"Super de luxe? Sure. If the Autarch says so, there's no higher priority. We can get one that's practically a space ship in itself. It would even have auxiliary motors."

"It would have living quarters, I suppose."

"For Miss Hinriad? It would be considerably better than you have here——" He stopped abruptly.

At the mention of her name, Artemisia had drifted past coldly and slowly, moving out of the pilot room. Biron's eyes followed her.

Rizzett said, "I shouldn't have said Miss Hinriad, I suppose."

"No, no. It's nothing. Pay no attention. You were saying?"

"Oh, about the rooms. At least two sizable ones, with a communicating shower. It's got the usual closet room and plumbing arrangements of the big liners. She would be comfortable."

"Good. We'll need food and water."

"Sure. Water tank will hold a two months' supply; a little less if you want to arrange for a swimming pool aboard ship. And you would have frozen whole meats. You're eating Tyrannian concentrate now, aren't you?"

Biron nodded and Rizzett grimaced.

"It tastes like chopped sawdust, doesn't it? What else?"

"A supply of clothes for the lady," said Biron.

Rizzet wrinkled his forehead. "Yes, of course. Well, that will be her job."

"No, sir, it won't. We'll supply you with all the necessary measurements and you can supply us with whatever we ask for in whatever the current styles happen to be."

Rizzett laughed shortly and shook his head. "Rancher, she won't like that. She wouldn't be satisfied with any clothes she didn't pick. Not even if they were the identical items she would have picked if she had been given the chance. This isn't a guess now. I've had experience with the creatures."

Biron said, "I'm sure you're right, Rizzett. But that's the way it will have to be."

"All right, but I've warned you. It will be your argument. What else?"

"Little things. Little things. A supply of detergents. Oh yes, cosmetics, perfume—the things women need. We'll make the arrangements in time. Let's get the trailer started."

And now Gillbret was leaving without speaking. Biron's eyes followed him, too, and he felt his jaw muscles tighten. Hinriads! They were Hinriads! There was nothing he could do about it. They were Hinriads! Gillbret was one and *she* was another.

He said, "And, of course, there'll be clothes for Mr. Hinriad and myself. That won't be very important."

"Right. Mind if I use your radio? I'd better stay on this ship till the adjustments are made."

Biron waited while the initial orders went out. Then Rizzett turned on the seat and said, "I can't get used to seeing you here, moving, talking, alive. You're so like him. The Rancher used to speak about you every once in a while. You went to school on Earth, didn't you?"

"I did. I would have graduated a little over a week ago, if things hadn't been interrupted."

Rizzett looked uncomfortable. "Look, about your being sent to Rhodia the way you were. You mustn't hold it against us. We didn't like it. I mean, this is strictly between us, but some of the boys didn't like it at all. The Autarch didn't consult us, of course. Naturally, he wouldn't. Frankly, it was a risk on his part. Some of us—I'm not mentioning names—even wondered if we shouldn't stop the liner you were on and pull you off. Naturally that would have been the worst thing we could possibly have done. Still, we might have done it, except that in the last analysis, we knew that the Autarch must have known what he was doing."

"It's nice to be able to inspire that kind of confidence."

"We know him. There's no denying it. He's got it here." A finger slowly tapped his forehead. "Nobody knows exactly what makes him take a certain course sometimes. But it always seems the right one. At least he's outsmarted the Tyranni so far and others don't."

"Like my father, for instance."

"I wasn't thinking of him, exactly, but in a sense, you're right. Even the Rancher was caught. But then he was a different kind of man. His way of thinking was straight. He would never allow for crookedness. He would always underestimate the worthlessness of the next man. But then again, that was what we liked best, somehow. He was the same to everyone, you know.

"I'm a commoner for all I'm a colonel. My father was a metalworker, you see. It didn't make any difference to him. And it wasn't that I was a colonel, either. If he met the engineer's 'prentice walking down the corridor, he'd step aside and say a pleasant word or two, and for the rest of the day, the 'prentice would feel like a master engineman. It was the way he had.

"Not that he was soft. If you needed disciplining, you got it, but no more than your share. What you got, you deserved, and you knew it. When he was through, he was through. He didn't keep throwing it at you at odd moments for a week or so. That was the Rancher.

"Now the Autarch, he's different. He's just brains. You can't get next to him, no matter who you are. For instance. He doesn't really have a sense of humor. I can't speak to him the way I'm speaking to you right now. Right now, I'm just talking. I'm relaxed. It's almost free association. With him, you say exactly what's on your mind with no spare words. *And* you use formal phraseology, or he'll tell you you're slovenly. But then, the Autarch's the Autarch, and that's that."

Biron said, "I'll have to agree with you as far as the Autarch's brains are concerned. Did you know that he had deduced my presence aboard this ship before he ever got on?"

"He *did?* We didn't know that. Now, there, that's what I mean. He was going to go aboard the Tyrannian cruiser alone. To us, it seemed suicide. We didn't like it. But we assumed he knew what he was doing, and he did. He could have told us you were probably aboard ship. He must have known it would be great news that the Rancher's son had escaped. But it's typical. He wouldn't."

Artemisia sat on one of the lower bunks in the cabin. She had to bend into an uncomfortable position to avoid having the frame of the second bunk pry into her first thoracic vertebra, but that was a small item to her at the moment.

Almost automatically, she kept passing the palms of her hands down the side of her dress. She felt frayed and dirty, and very tired.

She was tired of dabbing at her hands and face with damp napkins. She was tired of wearing the same clothes for a week. She was tired of hair which seemed dank and stringy by now.

And then she was almost on her feet again, ready to turn about sharply; she wasn't going to see him; she wouldn't look at him.

But it was only Gillbret. She sank down again. "Hello, Uncle Gil."

Gillbret sat down opposite her. For a moment his thin face seemed anxious and then it started wrinkling into a smile. "I think a week of this ship is very unamusing too. I was hoping you could cheer *me* up."

But she said, "Now, Uncle Gil, don't start using psychology on me. If you think you're going to cajole me into feeling a responsibility for you, you're wrong. I'm much more likely to hit you."

"If it will make you feel better——"

"I warn you again. If you hold out your arm for me to hit, I'll do it, and if you say 'Does that make you feel better?' I'll do it again."

"In any case, it's obvious you've quarreled with Biron. What about?"

"I don't see why there's any necessity for discussion. Just leave me alone." Then, after a pause, "He thinks Father did what the Autarch said he did. I hate him for that."

"Your father?"

"No! That stupid, childish, sanctimonious fool!"

"Presumably Biron. Good. You hate him. You couldn't put a knife edge between the kind of hate that has you sitting here like this and something that would seem to my own bachelor mind to be a rather ridiculous excess of love."

"Uncle Gil," she said, "could he really have done it?"

"Biron? Done what?"

"No! Father. Could Father have done it? Could he have informed against the Rancher?"

Gillbret looked thoughtful and very sober. "I don't know." He looked at her out of the corner of his eyes. "You know, he *did* give Biron up to the Tyranni."

"Because he knew it was a trap," she said vehemently. "And it *was*. That horrible Autarch meant it as such. He said so. The Tyranni knew who Biron was and sent him to Father on purpose. Father did the only thing he could do. That should be obvious to anybody."

"Even if we accept that"—and again that sideways look—

"he did try to argue you into a rather unamusing kind of marriage. If Hinrik could bring himself to do that——"

She interrupted. "He had no way out there, either."

"My dear, if you're going to excuse every act of subservience to the Tyranni as something he had to do, why, then, how do you know he didn't have to hint something about the Rancher to the Tyranni?"

"Because I'm sure he wouldn't. You don't know Father the way I do. He hates the Tyranni. He *does*. I know it. He wouldn't go out of his way to help them. I admit that he's afraid of them and doesn't dare oppose them openly, but if he could avoid it somehow, he would never help them."

"How do you know he could avoid it?"

But she shook her head violently, so that her hair tumbled about and hid her eyes. It hid the tears a bit too.

Gillbret watched a moment, then spread his hands helplessly and left.

The trailer was joined to the *Remorseless* by a wasp-waist corridor attached to the emergency air lock in the rear of the ship. It was several dozen times larger than the Tyranni vessel in capacity, almost humorously outsized.

The Autarch joined Biron in a last inspection. He said, "Do you find anything lacking?"

Biron said. "No. I think we'll be quite comfortable."

"Good. And by the way, Rizzett tells me the Lady Artemisia is not well, or at least that she looks unwell. If she requires medical attention, it might be wise to send her to my ship."

"She is quite well," said Biron curtly.

"If you say so. Would you be ready to leave in twelve hours?"

"In two hours, if you wish."

Biron passed through the connecting corridor (he had to stoop a little) into the *Remorseless* proper.

He said with a careful evenness of tone, "You've got a

private suite back there, Artemisia. I won't bother you. I'll stay here most of the time."

And she replied coldly, "You don't bother me, Rancher. It doesn't matter to me where you are."

And then the ships blasted off, and after a single Jump they found themselves at the edge of the Nebula. They waited for a few hours while the final calculations were made on Jonti's ship. Inside the Nebula it would be almost blind navigation.

Biron stared glumly at the visiplate. There was nothing there! One entire half of the celestial sphere was taken up with blackness, unrelieved by a spark of light. For the first time, Biron realized how warm and friendly the stars were, how they filled space.

"It's like dropping through a hole in space," he muttered to Gillbret.

And then they Jumped again, into the Nebula.

Almost simultaneously Simok Aratap, Commissioner of the Great Khan, at the head of ten armed cruisers, listened to his navigator and said, "That doesn't matter. Follow them anyway."

And not one light light-year from the point at which the *Remorseless* entered the Nebula, ten Tyranni vessels did likewise.

# 16. HOUNDS!

Simok Aratap was a little uncomfortable in his uniform. Tyrannian uniforms were made of moderately coarse materials and fit only indifferently well. It was not soldierlike to complain of such inconveniences. In fact, it was part of the Tyrannian military tradition that a little discomfort on the part of the soldier was good for discipline.

But still Aratap could bring himself to rebel against that tradition to the extent of saying, ruefully, "The tight collar irritates my neck."

Major Andros, whose collar was as tight, and who had been seen in no other than military dress in the memory of man, said, "When alone, it would be quite within regulations to open it. Before any of the officers or men, any deviation from regulation dress would be disturbing influence."

Aratap sniffed. It was the second change induced by the quasi-military nature of the expedition. In addition to being forced into uniform, he had to listen to an increasingly self-assertive military aide. That had begun even before they left Rhodia.

Andros had put it to him baldly.

He had said, "Commissioner, we will need ten ships."

Aratap had looked up, definitely annoyed. At the moment he was getting ready to follow the young Widemos in a single vessel. He laid aside the capsules in which he was preparing his report for the Khan's Colonial Bureau, to be forwarded in the unhappy case that he did not return from the expedition.

"Ten ships, Major?"

"Yes, sir. Less will not do."

"Why not?"

"I intend to maintain a reasonable security. The young man is going somewhere. You say there is a well-developed conspiracy in existence. Presumably, the two fit together."

"And therefore?"

"And therefore we must be prepared for a possibly well-developed conspiracy. One that might be able to handle a single ship."

"Or ten. Or a hundred. Where does security cease?"

"One must make a decision. In cases of military action, it is my responsibility. I suggest ten."

Aratap's contact lenses gleamed unnaturally in the wall light as he raised his eyebrows. The military carried weight. Theoretically, in times of peace, the civilian made the decisions, but here again, military tradition was a difficult thing to set aside.

He said cautiously, "I will consider the matter."

"Thank you. If you do not choose to accept my recommendations, and my suggestions have only been advanced as such, I assure you"—the major's heels clicked sharply, but the ceremonial deference was rather empty, and Aratap knew it—"that would be your privilege. You would leave me, however, no choice but to resign my commission."

It was up to Aratap to retrieve what he could from that position. He said, "It is not my intention to hamper you in any decision you may make on a purely military question, Major. I wonder if you might be as amenable to my decisions in matters of purely political importance."

"What matters are these?"

"There is the problem of Hinrik. You objected yesterday to my suggestion that he accompany us."

The major said dryly, "I consider it unnecessary. With our forces in action, the presence of outlanders would be bad for morale."

Aratap sighed softly, just below the limits of hearing. Yet Andros was a competent man in his way. There would be no use in displaying impatience.

He said, "Again, I agree with you. I merely ask you to consider the political aspects of the situation. As you know, the execution of the old Rancher of Widemos was politically uncomfortable. It stirred up the Kingdoms unnecessarily. However necessary the execution was, it makes it desirable to refrain from having the death of the son attributed to us. As far as the people of Rhodia know, the young Widemos has kidnaped the daughter of the Director, the girl, by the way, being a popular and much publicized member of the Hinriads. It would be quite fitting, quite understandable, to have the Director head the punitive expedition.

"It would be a dramatic move, very gratifying to Rhodian patriotism. Naturally, he would ask for Tyrannian assistance, and receive it, but that can be played down. It would be easy, and necessary, to fix this expedition in the popular mind as a Rhodian one. If the inner workings of the conspiracy are uncovered, it will have been a Rhodian discovery. If the young Widemos is executed, it would be a Rhodian execution, as far as the other Kingdoms are concerned."

The major said, "It would still be a bad precedent to allow Rhodian vessels to accompany a Tyrannian military expedition. They would hamper us in a fight. In that way, the question becomes a military one."

"I did not say, my dear Major, that Hinrik would command a ship. Surely you know him better than to think him capable of commanding or even anxious to try. He will stay with us. There will be no other Rhodian aboard ship."

"In that case, I waive my objection, Commissioner," said the major.

\* \* \*

The Tyrannian fleet had maintained their position two light-years off Lingane for the better part of a week and the situation was becoming increasingly unstable.

Major Andros advocated an immediate landing on Lingane. "The Autarch of Lingane," he said, "has gone to considerable lengths to have us think him a friend of the Khan, but I do not trust these men who travel abroad. They gain unsettling notions. It is strange that just as he returns, the young Widemos travels to meet him."

"He has not tried to hide either his travels or his return, Major. And we do not know that Windemos goes to meet him. He maintains an orbit about Lingane. Why does he not land?"

"Why does he maintain an orbit? Let us question what he does and not what he does not do."

"I can propose something which will fit the pattern."

"I would be glad to hear it."

Aratap placed a finger inside his collar and tried futilely to stretch it. He said, "Since the young man is waiting, we can presume he is waiting for something or somebody. It would be ridiculous to think that, having gone to Lingane by so direct and rapid a route—a single Jump, in fact—that he is merely waiting out of indecision. I say, then, that he is waiting for a friend or friends to reach him. Thus reinforced, he will proceed elsewhere. The fact that he is not landing on Lingane directly would indicate that he does not consider such an action safe. That would indicate that Lingane in general—the Autarch in particular—is not concerned in the conspiracy, although individual Linganians may be."

"I don't know if we can always trust the obvious solution to be the correct one."

"My dear Major, this is not merely an obvious solution. It is a logical one. It fits a pattern."

"Maybe it does. But just the same, if there are no further developments in twenty-four hours, I will have no choice but to order an advance Linganeward."

\* \* \*

Aratap frowned at the door through which the major had left. It was disturbing to have to control at once the restless conquered and the short-sighted conquerors. Twenty-four hours. Something might happen; otherwise he might have to find some way of stopping Andros.

The door signal sounded and Aratap looked up with irritation. Surely it could not be Andros returning. It wasn't. The tall, stooped form of Hinrik of Rhodia was in the doorway, behind him a glimpse of the guard who accompanied him everywhere on the ship. Theoretically, Hinrik had complete freedom of movement. Probably he himself thought he had. At least, he never paid any attention to the guard at his elbow.

Hinrik smiled mistily. "Am I disturbing you, Commissioner?"

"Not at all. Take a seat, Director." Aratap remained standing. Hinrik seemed not to notice that.

Hinrik said, "I have something of importance to discuss with you." He paused, and some of the intentness passed out of his eyes. He added in quite a different tone, "What a large, fine ship this is!"

"Thank you, Director." Aratap smiled tightly. The nine accompanying ships were typically minute in size, but the flagship on which they stood was an outsized model adapted from the designs of the defunct Rhodian navy. It was perhaps the first sign of the gradual softening of the Tyrannian military spirit that more and more of such ships were being added to the navy. The fighting unit was still the tiny two-to three-man cruiser, but increasingly the top brass found reasons for requiring large ships for their own headquarters.

It did not bother Aratap. To some of the older soldiers such increasing softness seemed a degeneration; to himself it seemed increasing civilization. In the end—in centuries, perhaps—it might even happen that the Tyranni would melt away as a single people, fusing with the present conquered societies of the Nebular Kingdoms—and perhaps even that might be a good thing.

Naturally, he never expressed such an opinion aloud.

"I came to tell you something," said Hinrik. He puzzled over it awhile, then added, "I have sent a message home today to my people. I have told them I am well and that the criminal will be shortly seized and my daughter returned to safety."

"Good," said Aratap. It was not news to him. He himself had written the message, though it was not impossible that Hinrik by now had persuaded himself that he was the writer, or even that he actually headed the expedition. Aratap felt a twinge of pity. The man was disintegrating visibly.

Hinrik said, "My people, I believe, are quite disturbed over this daring raid upon the Palace by these well-organized bandits. I think they will be proud of their Director now that I have taken such rapid action in response, eh, Commissioner? They will see that there is still force among the Hinriads." He seemed filled with a feeble triumph.

"I think they will," said Aratap.

"Are we within range of the enemy yet?"

"No, Director, the enemy remains where he was, just off Lingane."

"Still? I remember what I came to tell you." He grew excited, so that the words tumbled out. "It is very important, Commissioner. I have something to tell you. There is treachery on board. I have discovered it. We must take quick action. Treachery——" He was whispering.

Aratap felt impatient. It was necessary to humor the poor idiot of course, but this was becoming a waste of time. At this rate he would become so obviously mad that he would be useless even as a puppet, which would be a pity.

He said, "No treachery, Director. Our men are stanch and true. Someone has been misleading you. You are tired."

"No, no." Hinrik put aside Aratap's arm which, for a moment, had rested upon his shoulder. "Where are we?"

"Why, here!"

"The ship, I mean. I have watched the visiplate. We are near no star. We are in deep space. Did you know that?"

"Why, certainly."

"Lingane is nowhere near. Did you know that?"

"It is two light-years off."

"Ah! Ah! Ah! Commissioner, no one is listening? Are you sure?" He leaned closely, while Aratap allowed his ear to be approached. "Then how do we know the enemy is near Lingane? He is too far to detect. We are being misinformed, and this signifies treachery."

Well, the man might be mad, but the point was a good one. Aratap said, "This is something fit for technical men, Director, and not for men of rank to concern themselves with. I scarcely know myself."

"But as head of the expedition I should know. I am head, am I not?" He looked about carefully. "Actually, I have a feeling that Major Andros does not always carry out my orders. Is he trustworthy? Of course, I rarely give him orders. It would seem strange to order a Tyrannian officer. But then, I must find my daughter. My daughter's name is Artemisia. She has been taken from me, and I am taking all this fleet to get her back. So you see, I must know. I mean, I must know how it is known the enemy is at Lingane. My daughter would be there too. Do you know my daughter? Her name is Artemisia."

His eyes looked up at the Tyranni Commissioner in appeal. Then he covered them with his hand and mumbled something that sounded like "I'm sorry."

Aratap felt his jaw muscles clench. It was difficult to remember that the man before him was a bereaved father and that even the idiot Director of Rhodia might have a father's feelings. He could not let the man suffer.

He said gently, "I will try to explain. You know there is such a thing as a massometer which will detect ships in space."

"Yes, yes."

"It is sensitive to gravitational effects. You know what I mean?"

"Oh yes. Everything has gravity." Hinrik was leaning toward Aratap, his hands gripping one another nervously.

"That's good enough. Now naturally the massometer can

only be used when the ship is close, your know. Less than a million miles away or so. Also, it has to be a reasonable distance from any planet, because if it isn't, all you can detect is the planet, which is much bigger."

"And has much more gravity."

"Exactly," said Aratap, and Hinrik looked pleased.

Aratap went on. "We Tyranni have another device. It is a transmitter which radiates through hyperspace in all directions, and what it radiates is a particular type of distortion of the space fabric which is not electromagnetic in character. In other words, it isn't like light or radio or even sub-etheric radio. See?"

Hinrik didn't answer. He looked confused.

Aratap proceeded quickly. "Well, it's different. It doesn't matter how. We can detect that something which is radiated, so that we can always know where any Tyrannian ship is, even if it's halfway across the Galaxy, or on the other side of a star."

Hinrik nodded solemnly.

"Now," said Aratap, "if the young Widemos had escaped in an ordinary ship, it would have been very difficult to locate him. As it is, since he took a Tyrannian cruiser, we know where he is at all times, although he doesn't realize that. That is how we know he is near Lingane, you see. And, what's more, he can't get away, so that we will certainly rescue your daughter."

Hinrik smiled. "That is well done. I congratulate you, Commissioner. A very clever ruse."

Aratap did not delude himself. Hinrik understood very little of what he had said, but that did not matter. It had ended with the assurance of his daughter's rescue, and somewhere in his dim understanding there must be the realization that this, somehow, was made possible by Tyrannian science.

He told himself that he had not gone to this trouble entirely because the Rhodian appealed to his sense of the pathetic. He had to keep the man from breaking down altogether for obvious political reasons. Perhaps the return of his daughter would improve matters. He hoped so.

There was the door signal again and this time it was Major Andros who entered. Hinrik's arm stiffened on the armrest of his chair and his face assumed a hunted expression. He lifted himself and began, "Major Andro——"

But Andros was already speaking quickly, disregarding the Rhodian.

"Commissioner," he said, "the *Remorseless* has changed position."

"Surely he has not landed on Lingane," said Aratap sharply.

"No," said the major. "He has Jumped quite away from Lingane."

"Ah. Good. He has been joined by another ship, perhaps."

"By many ships, perhaps. We can detect only his, as you are quite aware."

"In any case, we follow again."

"The order has already been given. I would merely like to point out that his Jump has taken him to the edge of the Horsehead Nebula."

"What?"

"No major planetary system exists in the indicated direction. There is only one logical conclusion."

Aratap moistened his lips and left hurriedly for the pilot room, the major with him.

Hinrik remained standing in the middle of the suddenly empty room, looking at the door for a minute or so. Then, with a little shrug of the shoulders, he sat down again. His expression was blank, and for a long while he simply sat.

The navigator said, "The space co-ordinates of the *Remorseless* have been checked, sir. They are definitely inside the Nebula."

"That doesn't matter," said Aratap. "Follow them anyway."

He turned to Major Andros. "So you see the virtues of

waiting. There is a good deal that is obvious now. Wherever else could the conspirators' headquarters be but in the Nebula itself? Where else could we have failed to locate them? A *very* pretty pattern."

And so the squadron entered the Nebula.

For the twentieth time Aratap glanced automatically at the visiplate. Actually, the glances were useless, since the visiplate remained quite black. There was no star in sight.

Andros said, "That's their third stop without landing. I don't understand it. What is their purpose? What are they after? Each stop of theirs is several days long. Yet they do not land."

"It may take them that long," said Aratap, "to calculate their next Jump. Visibility is nonexistent."

"You think so?"

"No. Their Jumps are too good. Each time they land very near a star. They couldn't do as well by massometer data alone, unless they actually knew the locations of the stars in advance."

"Then why don't they land?"

"I think," said Aratap, "they must be looking for habitable planets. Maybe they themselves do not know the location of the center of conspiracy. Or, at least, not entirely." He smiled. "We need only follow."

The navigator clicked heels. "Sir!"

"Yes?" Aratap looked up.

"The enemy has landed on a planet."

Aratap signaled for Major Andros.

"Andros," said Aratap, as the major entered, "have you been told?"

"Yes. I've ordered a descent and pursuit."

"Wait. You may be again premature, as when you wanted to lunge toward Lingane. I think this ship only ought to go."

"Your reasoning?"

"If we need reinforcements, you will be there, in command of the cruisers. If it is indeed a powerful rebel center, they may think only one ship has stumbled upon them. I will get word to you somehow and you can retire to Tyrann."

"Retire!"

"And return with a full fleet."

Andros considered. "Very well. This is our least useful ship in any case. Too large."

The planet filled the visiplate as they spiraled down.

"The surface seems quite barren, sir," said the navigator.

"Have you determined the exact location of the *Remorseless*?"

"Yes, sir."

"Then land as closely as you can without being sighted."

They were entering the atmosphere now. The sky as they flashed along the day half of the planet was tinged with a brightening purple. Aratap watched the nearing surface. The long chase was almost over!

# 17. AND HARES!

To those who have not actually been in space, the investigation of a stellar system and the search for habitable planets may seem rather exciting, at the least, interesting. To the spaceman, it is the most boring of jobs.

Locating a star, which is a huge glowing mass of hydrogen fusing into helium, is almost too easy. It advertises itself. Even in the blackness of the Nebula, it is only a question of distance. Approach within five billion miles, and it will still advertise itself.

But a planet, a relatively small mass of rock, shining only by reflected light, is another matter. One could pass through a stellar system a hundred thousand times at all sorts of odd angles without ever coming close enough to a planet to see it for what it is, barring the oddest of coincidences.

Rather, one adopts a system. A position is taken up in space at a distance from the star being investigated of some ten thousand times the star's diameter. From Galactic statistics it is known that not one time in fifty thousand is a planet located farther from its primary than that. Furthermore, practically never is a *habitable* planet located farther from its primary than one thousand times its sun's diameter.

This means that from the position in space assumed by the ship, any habitable planet must be within six degrees of the star. This represents an area only 1/3600th of the entire sky. That area can be handled in detail with relatively few observations.

The movement of the tele-camera can be so adjusted as to counteract the motion of the ship in its orbit. Under those conditions a time exposure will pinpoint the constellations in the star's neighborhood; provided, of course, that the blaze of the sun itself is blocked out, which is easily done. Planets, however, will have perceptible proper motions and therefore show up as tiny streaks on the film.

When no streaks appear, there is always the possibility that the planets are behind their primary. The maneuver is therefore repeated from another position in space and, usually, at a point closer to the star.

It is a very dull procedure indeed, and when it has been repeated three times for three different stars, each time with completely negative results, a certain depression of morale is bound to occur.

Gillbret's morale, for instance, had been suffering for quite a while. Longer and longer intervals took place between the moments when he found something "amusing."

They were readying for the Jump to the fourth star on the Autarch's list, and Biron said, "We hit a star each time, anyway. At least Jonti's figures are correct."

Gillbret said, "Statistics show that one out of three stars has a planetary system."

Biron nodded. It was a well-worn statistic. Every child was taught that in elementary Galactography.

Gillbret went on, "That means that the chances of finding three stars at random without a single planet—without one single planet—is two thirds cubed, which is eight twenty-sevenths, or less than one in three."

"So?"

"And we haven't found any. There must be a mistake."

"You saw the plates yourself. And, besides, what price statistics? For all we know, conditions are different inside a Nebula. Maybe the particle fog prevents planets from forming, or maybe the fog is the result of planets that didn't coalesce."

"You don't mean that?" said Gillbret, stricken.

"You're right. I'm just talking to hear myself. I don't know anything about cosmogony. Why the hell are planets formed, anyway? Never heard of one that wasn't filled with trouble." Biron looked haggard himself. He was still printing and pasting up little stickers on the control panels.

He said, "Anyway, we've got the blasters all worked out, range finders, power control—all that."

It was very difficult not to look at the visiplate. They'd be Jumping again soon, through that ink.

Biron said absently, "You know why they call it the Horsehead Nebula, Gil?"

"The first man to enter it was Horace Hedd. Are you going to tell me that's wrong?"

"It may be. They have a different explanation on Earth."

"Oh?"

"They claim it's called that because it looks like a horse's head."

"What's a horse?"

"It's an animal on Earth."

"It's an amusing thought, but the Nebula doesn't look like any animal to me, Biron."

"It depends on the angle you look at it. Now from Nephelos it looks like a man's arm with three fingers, but I looked at it once from the observatory at the University of Earth. It *does* look a little like a horse's head. Maybe that is how the name started. Maybe there never was any Horace Hedd. Who knows?" Biron felt bored with the matter, already. He was still talking simply to hear himself talk.

There was a pause, a pause that lasted too long, because it gave Gillbret a chance to bring up a subject which Biron did not wish to dicuss and could not force himself to stop thinking about.

Gillbret said, "Where's Arta?"

Biron looked at him quickly and said, "Somewhere in the trailer. I don't follow her about."

"The Autarch does. He might as well be living here."

"How lucky for her."

Gillbret's wrinkles became more pronounced and his small features seemed to screw together. "Oh, don't be a fool, Biron. Artemisia is a Hinriad. She can't take what you've been giving her."

Biron said, "Drop it."

"I won't. I've been spoiling to say this. Why are you doing this to her? Because Hinrik might have been responsible for your father's death? Hinrik is my cousin! You haven't changed toward me."

"All right," Biron said. "I haven't changed toward you. I speak to you as I always have. I speak to Artemisia as well."

"As you always have?"

Biron was silent.

Gillbret said, "You're throwing her at the Autarch."

"It's her choice."

"It isn't. It's your choice. Listen, Biron"—Gillbret grew confidential; he put a hand on Biron's knee—"this isn't a thing I like to interfere with, you understand. It's just that she's the only good thing in the Hinriad family just now. Would you be amused if I said I loved her? I have no children of my own."

"I don't question your love."

"Then I advise you for her good. Stop the Autarch, Biron."

"I thought you trusted him, Gil."

"As the Autarch, yes. As an anti-Tyrannian leader, yes. But as a man for a woman, as a man for Artemisia, no."

"Tell her that."

"She wouldn't listen."

"Do you think she would listen if I told her?"

"If you told her properly."

For a moment Biron seemed to hesitate, his tongue dabbing slightly at dry lips. Then he turned away, saying harshly, "I don't want to talk about it."

Gillbret said sadly, "You'll regret this."

Biron said nothing. Why didn't Gillbret leave him alone? It had occurred to him many times that he might regret all this. It wasn't easy. But what could he do? There was no safe way of backing out.

He tried breathing through his mouth to get rid, somehow, of the choking sensation in his chest.

The outlook was different after the next Jump. Biron had set the controls in accordance with the instructions from the Autarch's pilot, and left the manuals to Gillbret. He was going to sleep through this one. And then Gillbret was shaking his shoulder.

"Biron! Biron!"

Biron rolled over in his bunk and out, landing in a crouch, fists balled. "What is it?"

Gillbret stepped back hastily. "Now, take it easy. We've got an F-2 this time."

It sank in. Gillbret drew a deep breath and relaxed. "Don't ever wake me that way, Gillbret. An F-2, you say? I suppose you're referring to the new star."

"I surely am. It looks most amusing, I think."

In a way, it did. Approximately 95 per cent of habitable planets in the Galaxy circled stars of spectral types F or G; diameter from 750 to 1500 thousand miles, surface temperature from five to ten thousand centigrade. Earth's sun was G-0, Rhodia's F-8, Lingane's G-2, as was that of Nephelos. F-2 was a little warm, but not too warm.

The first three stars they had stopped at were of spectral type K, rather small and ruddy. Planets would probably not have been decent even if they had had any.

A good star is a good star! In the first day of photography, five planets were located, the nearest being one hundred and fifty million miles from the primary.

Tedor Rizzett brought the news personally. He visited the *Remorseless* as frequently as the Autarch, lighting the ship with his heartiness. He was whoofing and panting this time from the hand-over-hand exercises along the metal line.

He said, "I don't know how the Autarch does it. He never seems to mind. Comes from being younger, I guess." He added abruptly, "Five planets!"

Gillbret said, "For this star? You're sure?"

"It's definite. Four of them are J-type, though."

"And the fifth?"

"The fifth may be all right. Oxygen in the atmosphere, anyway."

Gillbret set up a thin sort of yell of triumph, but Biron said, "Four are J-type. Oh well, we only need one."

He realized it was a reasonable distribution. The large majority of sizable planets in the Galaxy possessed hydrogenated atmospheres. After all, stars are mostly hydrogen, and they are the source material of planetary building blocks. J-type planets had atmospheres of methane or ammonia, with molecular hydrogen in addition sometimes, and also considerable helium. Such atmospheres were usually deep and extremely dense. The planets themselves were almost invariably thirty thousand miles in diameter and up, with a mean temperature of rarely more than fifty below zero, centigrade. They were quite uninhabitable.

Back on Earth they used to tell him that these planets were called J-type because the J stood for Jupiter, the planet in Earth's solar system which was the best example of the type. Maybe they were right. Certainly, the other planet classification was the E-type and E did stand for Earth. E-types were usually small, comparatively, and their weaker gravity could not retain hydrogen or the hydrogen-containing gases, particularly since they were usually closer to the sun and warmer. Their atmospheres were thin and, if life-bearing, contained oxygen and nitrogen usually, with, occasionally, an admixture of chlorine, which would be bad.

"Any chlorine?" asked Biron. "How well have they gone over the atmosphere?"

Rizzett shrugged. "We can only judge the upper reaches

from out in space. If there were any chlorine, it would concentrate toward ground level. We'll see."

He clapped a hand on Biron's large shoulder. "How about inviting me to a small drink in your room, boy?"

Gillbret looked after them uneasily. With the Autarch courting Artemisia, and his right-hand man becoming a drinking companion of Biron, the *Remorseless* was becoming more Linganian than not. He wondered if Biron knew what he was doing, then thought of the new planet and let the rest go.

Artemisia was in the pilot room when they penetrated the atmosphere. There was a little smile on her face and she seemed quite contented. Biron looked in her direction occasionally. He had said, "Good day, Artemisia," when she came in (she hardly ever did come in; he had been caught by surprise), but she hadn't answered.

She had merely said, "Uncle Gil," very brightly; then, "Is it true we're landing?"

And Gil had rubbed his hands. "It seems so, my dear. We may be getting out of the ship in a few hours, walking on solid surface. How's that for an amusing thought?"

"I hope it's the right planet. If it isn't, it won't be so amusing."

"There's still another star," said Gil, but his brow furrowed and contracted as he said so.

And then Artemisia turned to Biron and said, coolly, "Did you speak, Mr. Farrill?"

Biron, caught by surprise again, started and said, "No, not really."

"I beg your pardon, then. I thought you had."

She passed by him so closely that the plastic flair of her dress brushed his knee and her perfume momentarily surrounded him. His jaw muscles knotted.

Rizzett was still with them. One of the advantages of the trailer was that they could put up a guest overnight. He said, "They're getting details on the atmosphere now. Lots of oxygen, almost 30 per cent, and nitrogen and inert gases.

It's quite normal. No chlorine." Then he paused and said, "Hmm."

Gillbret said, "What the matter?"

"No carbon dioxide. That's not so good."

"Why not?" demanded Artemisia from her vantage point near the visiplate, where she watched the distant surface of the planet blur past at two thousand miles an hour.

Biron said curtly, "No carbon dioxide—no plant life."

"Oh?" She looked at him, and smiled warmly.

Biron, against his will, smiled back, and somehow, with scarcely a visible change in her countenance, she was smiling through him, past him, obviously unaware of his existence; and he was left there, caught in a foolish smile. He let it fade.

It was just as well he avoided her. Certainly, when he was with her, he couldn't keep it up. When he could actually see her, the anesthetic of his will didn't work. It began hurting.

Gillbret was doleful. They were coasting now. In the thick lower reaches of the atmosphere, the *Remorseless*, with its aerodynamically undesirable addition of a trailer, was difficult to handle. Biron fought the bucking controls stubbornly.

He said, "Cheer up, Gil!"

He felt not exactly jubilant himself. Radio signals had brought no response as yet, and if this were *not* the rebellion world, there would be no point in waiting longer. His line of action was set!

Gillbret said, "It doesn't look like the rebellion world. It's rocky and dead, and not much water, either." He turned. "Did they try for carbon dioxide again, Rizzett?"

Rizzett's ruddy face was long. "Yes. Just a trace. About a thousandth of a per cent or so."

Biron said, "You can't tell. They might pick a world like this, just because it would look so hopeless."

"But I saw farms," said Gillbret.

"All right. How much do you suppose we can see of a

planet this size by circling it a few times? You know damn well, Gil, that whoever they are, they can't have enough people to fill a whole planet. They may have picked themselves a valley somewhere where the carbon dioxide of the air has been built up, say, by volcanic action, and where there's plenty of nearby water. We could whiz within twenty miles of them and never know it. Naturally, they wouldn't be ready to answer radio calls without considerable investigation."

"You can't build up a concentration of carbon dioxide that easily," muttered Gillbret. But he watched the visiplate intently.

Biron suddenly hoped that it *was* the wrong world. He decided that he could wait no longer. It would have to be settled, *now*!

It was a queer feeling.

The artificial lights had been turned off and sunlight was coming in unhindered at the ports. Actually, it was the less efficient method of lighting the ship, but there was a sudden desirable novelty to it. The ports were open, in fact, and a native atmosphere could be breathed.

Rizzett advised against it on the grounds that lack of carbon dioxide would upset the respiratory regulation of the body, but Biron thought it might be bearable for a short time.

Gillbret had come upon them, heads together. They looked up and leaned away from each other.

Gillbret laughed. Then he looked out of the open port, sighed, and said, "Rocks!"

Biron said mildly, "We're going to set up a radio transmitter at the top of the high ground. We'll get more range that way. At any rate, we ought to be able to contact all of this hemisphere. And if it's negative, we can try the other side of the planet."

"Is that what you and Rizzett were discussing?"

"Exactly. The Autarch and I will do the job. It's his suggestion, which is fortunate, since otherwise I would have had to make the same suggestion myself." He looked fleetingly at Rizzett as he spoke. Rizzett was expressionless.

Biron stood up. "I think it would be best if I unzipped my space-suit lining and wore that."

Rizzett was in agreement. It was sunny on this planet; there was little water vapor in the air and no clouds, but it was briskly cold.

The Autarch was at the main lock of the *Remorseless*. His overcoat was of thin foamite that weighed a fraction of an ounce, yet did a nearly perfect job of insulation. A small carbon-dioxide cylinder was strapped to his chest, adjusted to a slow leak that would maintain a perceptible $CO_2$ vapor tension in his immediate vicinity.

He said, "Would you care to search me, Farrill?" He raised his hands and waited, his lean face quietly amused.

"No," said Biron. "Do you want to check *me* for weapons?"

"I wouldn't think of it."

The courtesies were as frigid as the weather.

Biron stepped out into the hard sunlight and tugged at the handle of the two-handled suitcase in which the radio equipment was stowed. The Autarch caught the other.

"Not too heavy," said Biron. He turned, and Artemisia was standing just within the ship, silent.

Her dress was a smooth, unfigured white which folded in a smooth drape that fled before the wind. The semi-transparent sleeves whipped back against her arms, turning them to silver.

For a moment Biron melted dangerously. He wanted to return quickly; to run, leap into the ship, grasp her so that his fingers would leave bruises on her shoulders, feel his lips meet hers——

But he nodded briefly instead, and her returning smile, the light flutter of her fingers was for the Autarch.

Five minutes later he turned and there was still that glimmer of white at the open door, and then the rise in the ground cut off the view of the ship. The horizon was free of everything but broken and bare rock now.

Biron thought of what lay ahead, and wondered if he would ever see Artemisia again—and if she would care if he never returned.

# 18. OUT OF THE JAWS OF DEFEAT!

Artemisia watched them as they became tiny figures, trudging up the bare granite, then dipping below and out of sight. For a moment, just before they disappeared, one of them had turned. She couldn't be sure which one, and, for a moment, her heart hardened.

He had not said a word on parting. Not one word. She turned away from the sun and rock toward the confined metal interior of the ship. She felt alone, terribly alone; she had never felt so alone in her life.

It was that, perhaps, that made her shiver, but it would have been an intolerable confession of weakness to admit that it wasn't simply the cold.

She said peevishly, "Uncle Gil! Why don't you close the ports? It's enough to freeze a person to death." The thermometer dial read plus seven centigrade with the ship's heaters on high.

"My dear Arta," said Gillbret mildly, "if you will persist in your ridiculous habit of wearing nothing but a little fog here and there, you must expect to be cold." But he closed certain contacts, and, with little clicks, the air lock slid shut, the ports sunk inward and molded themselves into the smooth, gleaming hull. As they did so, the thick glass polarized and became nontransparent. The lights of the ship went on and the shadows disappeared.

Artemisia sat down in the heavily padded pilot's seat and fingered the arms aimlessly. *His* hands had often rested there, and the slight warmth that flooded her as she thought that (she told herself) was only the result of the heaters making themselves felt decently, now that the outer winds were excluded.

The long minutes passed, and it became impossible to sit quietly. She might have gone with him! She corrected the rebellious thought instantly as it passed through her mind, and changed the singular "him" to the plural "them."

She said, "Why do they have to set up a radio transmitter anyway, Uncle Gil?"

He looked up from the visiplate, the controls of which he was fingering delicately, and said, "Eh?"

"We've been trying to contact them from out in space," she said, "and we haven't reached anyone. What special good would a transmitter on the planet's surface do?"

Gillbret was troubled. "Why, we must keep trying, my dear. We must find the rebellion world." And, between his teeth, he added to himself, "We must!"

A moment passed, and he said, "I can't find them."

"Find whom?"

"Biron and the Autarch. The ridge cuts me off no matter how I arrange the external mirrors. See?"

She saw nothing but the sunny rock flashing past.

Then Gillbret brought the little gears to rest and said, "Anyway, that's the Autarch's ship."

Artemisia accorded it the briefest of glances. It lay deeper in the valley, perhaps a mile away. It glistened unbearably in the sun. It seemed to her, at the moment, to be the real enemy. *It* was, not the Tyranni. She wished suddenly, sharply, and very strongly that they had never gone to Lingane; that they had remained in space, the three of them only. Those had been funny days, so uncomfortable and yet so warm, somehow. And now she could only try to hurt him. Something *made* her hurt him, though she would have liked——

Gillbret said, "Now what does *he* want?"

Artemisia looked at him, seeing him through a watery mist, so that she had to blink rapidly to put him into normal focus. "Who?"

"Rizzett. I *think* that's Rizzett. But he's certainly not coming this way."

Artemisia was at the visiplate. "Make it larger," she ordered.

"At this short distance?" objected Gillbret. "You won't see anything. It will be impossible to keep it centered."

"Larger, Uncle Gil."

Muttering, he threw in the telescopic attachment and searched the bloated nubbles of rock that resulted. They jumped faster than the eye could follow at the lightest touch on the controls. For one moment, Rizzett, a large, hazy figure, flashed past, and in that moment his identity was unmistakable. Gillbret backtracked wildly, caught him again, hung on for a moment, and Artemisia said, "He's armed. Did you see that?"

"No."

"He's got a long-range blasting rifle, I tell you!"

She was up, tearing away at the locker.

"Arta! What are you doing?"

She was unzipping the lining from another space suit. "I'm going out there. Rizzett's following them. Don't you understand? The Autarch hasn't gone out to set up a radio. It's a trap for Biron." She was gasping as she forced herself into the thick, coarse lining.

"Stop it! You're imagining things."

But she was staring at Gillbret without seeing him, her face pinched and white. She should have seen it before, the way Rizzett had been coddling that fool. That emotional fool! Rizzett had praised his father, told him what a great man the Rancher of Widemos had been, and Biron had melted immediately. His every action was dictated by the thought of his father. How could a man let himself be so ruled by a monomania?

She said, "I don't know what controls the air lock. Open it."

"Arta, you're not leaving the ship. You don't know where they are."

"I'll find them. Open the air lock."

Gillbret shook his head.

But the space suit she had stripped had borne a holster. She said, "Uncle Gil, I'll use this. I swear I will."

And Gillbret found himself staring at the wicked muzzle of a neuronic whip. He forced a smile. "Don't now!"

"Open the lock!" she gasped.

He did and she went out, running into the wind, slipping across the rocks and up the ridge. The blood pounded in her ears. She had been as bad as he, dangling the Autarch before him for no purpose other than her silly pride. It seemed silly now, and the Autarch's personality sharpened in her mind, a man so studiedly cold as to be bloodless and tasteless. She quivered with repulsion.

She had topped the ridge, and there was nothing ahead of her. Stolidly she walked onward, holding the neuronic whip before her.


Biron and the Autarch had not exchanged a word during their walk, and now they came to a halt where the ground leveled off. The rock was fissured by the action of sun and wind through the millennia. Ahead of them there was an ancient fault, the farther lip of which had crumbled downward, leaving a sheer precipice of a hundred feet.

Biron approached cautiously and looked over it. It slanted outward past the drop, the ground riddled with craggy boulders which, with time and infrequent rains, had scattered out as far as he could see.

"It looks," he said, "like a hopeless world, Jonti."

The Autarch displayed none of Biron's curiosity in his surroundings. He did not approach the drop. He said, "This is the place we found before landing. It's ideal for our purposes."

It's ideal for your purposes, at least, thought Biron. He stepped away from the edge and sat down. He listened to the tiny hiss from his carbon-dioxide cylinder, and waited a moment.

Then he said, very quietly, "What will you tell them when you get back to your ship, Jonti? Or shall I guess?"

The Autarch paused in the act of opening the two-handled suitcase they had carried. He straightened and said, "What are you talking about?"

Biron felt the wind numb his face and rubbed his nose with his gloved hand. Yet he unbuttoned the foamite lining that wrapped him, so that it flapped wide as the gusts hit it.

He said, "I'm talking about your purpose in coming here."

"I would like to set up the radio rather than waste my time discussing the matter, Farrill."

"You won't set up a radio. Why should you? We tried reaching them from space, without a response. There's no reason to expect more of a transmitter on the surface. It's not a question of ionized radio-opaque layers in the upper atmosphere, either, because we tried the sub-ether as well and drew a blank. Nor are we particularly the radio experts in our party. So why did you really come up here, Jonti?"

The Autarch sat down opposite Biron. A hand patted the suitcase idly. "If you are troubled by these doubts, why did *you* come?"

"To discover the truth. Your man, Rizzett, told me you were planning this trip, and advised me to join you. I believe that your instructions to him were to tell me that by joining you I might make certain you received no messages that I remained unaware of. It was a reasonable point, except that I don't think you will receive any message. But I allowed it to persuade me, and I've come with you."

"To discover truth?" said Jonti mockingly.

"Exactly that. I can guess truth already."

"Tell *me* then. Let me discover truth as well."

"You came to kill me. I am here alone with you, and there is a cliff before us over which it would be certain death to fall. There would be no signs of deliberate violence. There would be no blasted limbs or any thought of weapon play. It would make a nice, sad story to take back to your ship. I had slipped and fallen. You might bring back a party to gather me up and give me a decent burial. It would all be very touching and I would be out of your way."

"You believe this, and yet you came?"

"I expect it, so you won't catch me by surprise. We are unarmed and I doubt that you could force me over by muscular power alone." For a moment Biron's nostrils flared. He half flexed his right arm, slowly and hungrily.

But Jonti laughed. "Shall we concern ourselves with our radio transmitter, then, since your death is now impossible?"

"Not yet. I am not done. I want your admission that you were going to try to kill me."

"Oh? Do you insist that I play my proper role in this impromptu drama you have developed? How do you expect to force me to do so? Do you intend to beat a confession out of me? Now understand, Farrill, you are a young man and I am disposed to make allowances because of that and because of the convenience of your name and rank. However, I must admit you have until now been more trouble than help to me."

"So I have been. By keeping alive, despite you!"

"If you refer to the risks you ran on Rhodia, I have explained it; I will not explain it again."

Biron rose. "Your explanation was not accurate. It has a flaw in it which was obvious from the beginning."

"Really?"

"Really! Stand up and listen to me, or I'll drag you to your feet."

The Autarch's eyes narrowed to slits as he rose. "I would not advise you to attempt violence, youngster."

"Listen." Biron's voice was loud and his cloak still bellied open in the breeze, disregarded. "You said that you sent me to a possible death on Rhodia only to implicate the Director in an anti-Tyrannian plot."

"That remains true."

"That remains a lie. Your prime object was to have me killed. You informed the captain of the Rhodian ship of my identity at the very beginning. You had no real reason for believing that I would ever be allowed to reach Hinrik."

"If I had wanted to kill you, Farrill, I might have planted a real radiation bomb in your room."

"It would have been obviously more convenient to have the Tyranni maneuvered into doing the killing for you."

"I might have killed you in space when I first boarded the *Remorseless*."

"So you might. You came equipped with a blaster and you had it leveled at me at one point. You had expected me on board, but you hadn't told your crew that. When Rizzett called and saw me, it was no longer possible to blast me. You made a mistake then. You told me you *had* told your men I was probably on board, and awhile later Rizzett told me you had not. Don't you brief your men concerning your exact lies as you tell them, Jonti?"

Jonti's face had been white in the cold, but it seemed to whiten further. "I should kill you now for giving me the lie, certainly. But what held back my trigger finger before Rizzett got on the visiplate and saw you?"

"Politics, Jonti. Artemisia oth Hinriad was aboard, and for the moment she was a more important object than myself. I'll give you credit for a quick change of plans. To have killed me in her presence would have ruined a bigger game."

"I had fallen in love so rapidly, then?"

"Love! When the girl concerned is a Hinriad, why not? You lost no time. You tried first to have her transferred to your ship, and when that failed, you told me that Hinrik had betrayed my father." He was silent for a moment, then said, "So I lost her and left you the field undisputed. Now, I presume, she is no longer a factor. She is firmly on your side and you may proceed with your plan to kill me without any fear that by doing it you may lose your chance at the Hinriad succession."

Jonti sighed and said, "Farrill, it is cold, and getting colder. I believe the sun is heading downward. You are unutterably foolish and you weary me. Before we end this farrago of nonsense, will you tell me why I should be in the least interested in killing you anyway? That is, if your obvious paranoia needs any reason."

"There is the same reason that caused you to kill my father."

*"What?"*

"Did you think I believed you for an instant when you said Hinrik had been the traitor? He might have been, were it not for the fact that his reputation as a wretched weakling is so well established. Do you suppose that my father was a complete fool? Could he possibly have mistaken Hinrik for anything but what he was? If he had not known his reputation, would not five minutes in his presence have revealed him completely as a hopeless puppet? Would my father have blabbed foolishly to Hinrik anything that might have been used to support a charge of treason against him? No, Jonti. The man who betrayed my father must have been one who was trusted by him."

Jonti took a step backward and kicked the suitcase aside. He poised himself to withstand a charge and said, "I see your vile implication. My only explanation for it is that you are criminally insane."

Biron was trembling, and not with cold. "My father was popular with your men, Jonti. Too popular. An Autarch cannot allow a competitor in the business of ruling. You saw to it that he did not remain a competitor. And it was your next job to see to it that I did not remain alive either to replace or to avenge him." His voice raised to a shout, which whipped away on the cold air. "Isn't this true?"

"No."

Jonti bent to the suitcase. "I can prove you are wrong!"

He flung it open. "Radio equipment. Inspect it. Take a good look at it." He tossed the items to the ground at Biron's feet.

Biron stared at them. "How does that prove anything?"

Jonti rose. "It doesn't. But now take a good look at this."

He had a blaster in his hand, and his knuckles were white with tension. The coolness had left his voice. He said, "I am tired of you. But I won't have to be tired much longer."

Biron said tonelessly, "You hid a blaster in the suitcase with the equipment?"

"Did you think I wouldn't? You honestly came here expecting to be thrown off a cliff and you thought I would try to do it with my hands as though I was a stevedor or a coal miner? I am Autarch of Lingane"—his face worked and his left hand made a flat, cutting gesture before him— "and I am tired of the cant and fatuous idealism of the Ranchers of Widemos." He whispered then, "Move on. Toward the cliff." He stepped forward.

Biron, hands raised, eyes on the blaster, stepped back. "You killed my father, then."

"I killed your father!" said the Autarch. "I tell you this so you may know in the last few moments of your life that the same man who saw to it that your father was blasted to bits in a disintegration chamber will see to it that you will follow him—and keep the Hinriad girl for himself thereafter, along with all that goes with her. Think of that! I will give you an extra minute to think of that! But keep your hands steady, or I will blast you and risk any questions my men may care to ask." It was as though his cold veneer, having cracked, left nothing but a burning passion exposed.

"You tried to kill me before this, as I said."

"I did. Your guesses were in every way correct. Does that help you now? Back!"

"No," said Biron. He brought his hands down and said, "If you're going to shoot, do so."

The Autarch said, "You think I will not dare?"

"I've asked you to shoot."

"And I will." The Autarch aimed deliberately at Biron's head and at a distance of four feet closed contact on his blaster.

# 19. DEFEAT!

Tedor Rizzett circled the little piece of tableland warily. He was not yet ready to be seen, but to remain hidden was difficult in this world of bare rock. In the patch of tumbled, crystalline boulders he felt safer. He threaded his way through them. Occasionally he paused to pass the soft back of the spongy gloves he wore over his face. The dry cold was deceptive.

He saw them now from between two granite monoliths that met in a V. He rested his blaster in the crotch. The sun was on his back. He felt its feeble warmth soak through, and he was satisfied. If they happened to look in his direction, the sun would be in their eyes and he himself would be that much less visible.

Their voices were sharp in his ear. Radio communication was in operation and he smiled at that. So far, according to plan. His own presence, of course, was not according to plan, but it would be better so. The plan was a rather overconfident one and the victim was not a complete fool, after all. His own blaster might yet be needed to decide the issue.

He waited. Stolidly he watched the Autarch lift his blaster as Biron stood there, unflinching.

Artemisia did not see the blaster lift. She did not see the two figures on the flat rock surface. Five minutes earlier she had seen Rizzett silhouetted for a moment against the sky, and since then she had followed him.

Somehow, he was moving too fast for her. Things dimmed and wavered before her and twice she found herself stretched on the ground. She did not recall falling. The second time, she staggered to her feet with one wrist oozing blood where a sharp edge had scraped her.

Rizzett had gained again and she had to reel after him. When he vanished in the glistening boulder forest, she sobbed in despair. She leaned against a rock, completely weary. Its beautiful flesh-pink tint, the glassy smoothness of its surface, the fact that it stood as an ancient reminder of a primeval volcanic age was lost upon her.

She could only try to fight the sensation of choking that pervaded her.

And then she saw him, dwarfed at the forked-rock formation, his back to her. She held the neuronic whip before her as she ran unevenly over the hard ground. He was sighting along the barrel of his rifle, intent upon the process, taking aim, getting ready.

She wouldn't make it in time.

She would have to distract his attention. She called, "Rizzett!" And again, "Rizzett, don't shoot!"

She stumbled again. The sun was blotting out, but consciousness lingered. It lingered long enough for her to feel the ground jar thuddingly against her, long enough to press her finger upon the whip's contact; and long enough for her to know that she was well out of range, even if her aim was accurate, which it could not be.

She felt arms about her, lifting. She tried to see, but her eyelids would not open.

"Biron?" It was a weak whisper.

The answer was a rough blur of words, but it was Rizzett's voice. She tried to speak further, then abruptly gave up. She had failed!

Everything was blotted out.

The Autarch remained motionless for the space it would take a man to count to ten slowly. Biron faced him as motionlessly, watching the barrel of the blaster that had just been fired point-blank at him. The barrel sank slowly as he watched.

Biron said, "Your blaster seems not to be in firing order. Examine it."

The Autarch's bloodless face turned alternately from Biron to his weapon. He had fired at a distance of four feet. It should have been all over. The congealed astonishment that held him broke suddenly and he disjoined the blaster in a quick movement.

The energy capsule was missing. Where it should have been, there was a useless cavity. The Autarch whimpered with rage as he hurled the lump of dead metal aside. It turned over and over, a black blot against the sun, smashing into the rock with a faint ringing sound.

"Man to man!" said Biron. There was a trembling eagerness in his voice.

The Autarch took a step backward. He said nothing.

Biron took a slow step forward. "There are many ways I could kill you, but not all would be satisfying. If I blasted you, it would mean that a millionth of a second would separate your life from your death. You would have no consciousness of dying. That would be bad. I think that instead there would be considerable satisfaction in using the somewhat slower method of human muscular effort."

His thigh muscles tensed, but the lunge they prepared was never completed. The cry that interrupted was thin and high, packed with panic.

"Rizzett!" it came. "Rizzett, don't shoot!"

Biron whirled in time to see the motion behind the rocks a hundred yards away and the glint of sun on metal. And then the hurled weight of a human body was upon his back. He bent under it, dropping to his knees.

The Autarch had landed fairly, his knees clasped hard about the other's waist, his fist thudding at the nape of Biron's neck. Biron's breath whooshed out in a whistling grunt.

Biron fought off the gathering blackness long enough to throw himself to one side. The Autarch jumped free, gaining clear footing while Biron sprawled on his back.

He had just time to double his legs up against himself as the Autarch lunged down upon him again. The Autarch bounced off. They were up together this time, perspiration turning icy upon their cheeks.

They circled slowly. Biron tossed his carbon-dioxide cylinder to one side. The Autarch likewise unstrapped his, held it suspended a moment by its mesh-metal hose, then stepped in rapidly and swung it. Biron dropped, and both heard and felt it whistle above his head.

He was up again, leaping on the other before the Autarch could regain his balance. One large fist clamped down on the other's wrist, while the other fist exploded in the Autarch's face. He let the Autarch drop and stepped back.

Biron said, "Stand up. I'll wait for you with more of the same. There's no hurry."

The Autarch touched his gloved hand to his face then stared sickly at the blood that smeared off upon it. His mouth twisted and his hand snaked out for the metal cylinder he had dropped. Biron's foot came heavily down upon it, and the Autarch yelled in agony.

Biron said, "You're too close to the edge of the cliff, Jonti. Mustn't reach in that direction. Stand up. I'll throw you the other way now."

But Rizzett's voice rang out: "Wait!"

The Autarch screamed, "Shoot this man, Rizzett! Shoot him now! His arms first, then his legs, and we'll leave him."

Rizzett brought his weapon up slowly against his shoulder.

Biron said, "Who saw to it that your own blaster was unloaded, Jonti?"

"What?" The Autarch stared blankly.

"It was not I who had access to your blaster, Jonti. Who did have? Who is pointing a blaster at you right now, Jonti? Not at me, Jonti, but at *you*!"

The Autarch turned to Rizzett and screamed, "Traitor!"

Rizzett said, in a low voice, "Not I, sir. That man is the traitor who betrayed the loyal Rancher of Widemos to his death."

"That is not I," cried the Autarch. "If he has told you I have, he lies."

"It is you yourself who have told us. I not only emptied your weapon, I also shorted your communicator switch, so that every word you said today was received by myself and by every member of the crew. We all know you for what you are."

"I am your Autarch."

"And also the greatest traitor alive."

For a moment the Autarch said nothing, but looked wildly from one to the other as they watched him with somber, angry faces. Then he wrenched to his feet, pulled together the parted seams of his self-control, and held them tightly by sheer nervous force.

His voice was almost cool as he said, "And if it were all true, what would it matter? You have no choice but to let matters stand as they are. One last intranebular planet remains to be visited. It *must* be the rebellion world, and only I know the co-ordinates."

He retained dignity somehow. One hand hung uselessly from a broken wrist; his upper lip had swollen ludicrously, and blood was caking his cheek, but he radiated the hauteur of one born to rule.

"You'll tell us," said Biron.

"Don't delude yourself that I will under any circumstances. I have told you already that there is an average of seventy cubic light-years per star. If you work by trial and error, without me, the odds are two hundred and fifty quadrillion to one against your coming within a billion miles of any star. *Any* star!"

Something went *click*! in Biron's mind.

He said, "Take him back to the *Remorseless*!"

Rizzett said in a low voice, "The Lady Artemisia——"

And Biron interrupted, "Then it *was* she. Where is she?"

"It's all right. She's safe. She came out without a carbon-dioxide cylinder. Naturally, as the $CO_2$ washed out of her blood stream, the automatic breathing mechanism of the body slowed. She was trying to run, didn't have the sense to breathe deeply voluntarily, and fainted."

Biron frowned. "Why was she trying to interfere with you, anyway? Making sure her boy friend didn't get hurt?"

Rizzett said, "Yes, she was! Only she thought I was the Autarch's man and was going to shoot *you*. I'll take back this rat now, and, Biron——"

"Yes?"

"Get back as soon as you can. He's still the Autarch, and the crew may need talking to. It's hard to break a lifetime habit of obedience. . . . She's behind that rock. Get to her before she freezes to death, will you? She won't leave."

Her face was almost buried in the hood that covered her head, and her body was formless in the thick, enveloping folds of the space-suit lining, but his steps quickened as he approached her.

He said, "How are you?"

She said, "Better, thank you. I am sorry if I caused any trouble."

They stood looking at each other, and the conversation seemed to have burned itself out in two lines.

Then Biron said, "I know we can't turn time backward, undo things that have been done, unsay things that have been said. But I do want you to understand."

"Why this stress on understanding?" Her eyes flashed. "I have done nothing but understand for weeks now. Will you tell me again about my father?"

"No. I knew your father was innocent. I suspected the

Autarch almost from the start, but I had to find out definitely. I could only prove it, Arta, by forcing him to confess. I thought I could get him to confess by trapping him into attempting to kill me, and there was only one way of doing that."

He felt wretched. He went on, "It was a bad thing to do. As bad, almost, as what he did to my father. I don't expect you to forgive me."

She said, "I don't follow you."

He said, "I knew he wanted you, Arta. Politically, you would be a perfect matrimonial object. The name of Hinriad would be more useful for his purposes than that of Widemos. So once he had you, he would need me no longer. I deliberately forced you on him, Arta. I acted as I did, hoping you would turn to him. When you did, he thought he was ready to rid himself of me, and Rizzett and I laid our trap."

"And you loved me all the time?"

Biron said, "Can't you bring yourself to believe that, Arta?"

"And of course you were ready to sacrifice your love to the memory of your father and the honor of your family. How does the old doggerel go? You could not love me, dear, so much, loved you not honor more!"

Biron said, miserably, "Please, Arta! I am not proud of myself but I could think of no other way."

"You might have told me your plan, made me your confederate rather than your tool."

"It was not your fight. If I had failed—and I might have—you would have remained out of it. If the Autarch had killed me and you were no longer on my side, you would be less hurt. You might even have married him, even been happy."

"Since you have won, it might be that I would be hurt at *his* loss."

"But you aren't."

"How do you know?"

Biron said desperately, "At least try to see my motives.

Granted that I was foolish—criminally foolish—can't you understand? Can't you try not to hate me?"

She said softly, "I have tried not to love you and, as you see, I have failed."

"Then you forgive me?"

"Why? Because I understand? No! If it were a matter of simply understanding, of seeing your motives, I would not forgive you your actions for anything I might have in life. If it were only that and nothing more! But I *will* forgive you, Biron, because I couldn't bear not to. How could I ask you to come back to me unless I forgave you?"

And she was in his arms, her weather-cold lips turning up to his. They were held apart by a double layer of thick garments. His gloved hands could not feel the body they embraced, but his lips were aware of her white, smooth face.

At last he said in concern, "The sun is getting lower. It's going to get colder."

But she said softly, "It's strange, then, that I seem to be getting warmer."

Together they walked back to the ship.

Biron faced them now with an appearance of easy confidence which he did not feel. The Linganian ship was large, and there were fifty in the crew. They sat now facing him. Fifty faces! Linganian faces bred from birth to unquestioning obedience to their Autarch.

Some had been convinced by Rizzett; others had been convinced by the arranged eavesdropping on the Autarch's statements to Biron earlier that day. But how many others were still uncertain or even definitely hostile?

So far Biron's talking had done little good. He leaned forward, let his voice grow confidential. "And what are you fighting for, men? What are you risking your lives for? A free Galaxy, I think. A Galaxy in which each world can decide what is best in its own way, produce its own wealth for its own good, be slave to none and master of none. Am I right?"

There was a low murmur of what might have been agreement, but it lacked enthusiasm.

Biron went on, "And what is the Autarch fighting for? For himself. He is the Autarch of Lingane. If he won, he would be Autarch of the Nebular Kingdoms. You would replace a Khan by an Autarch. Where would be the benefit of that? Is that worth dying for?"

One in the audience cried out, "He would be one of us, not a filthy Tyranni."

Another shouted, "The Autarch was looking for the rebellion world to offer his services. Was that ambition?"

"Ambition should be made of sterner stuff, eh?" Biron shouted back, ironically. "But he would come to the rebellion world with an organization at his back. He could offer them all of the Lingane; he could offer them, he thought, the prestige of an alliance with the Hinriads. In the end, he was pretty sure, the rebellion world would be his to do with what he pleased. Yes, this was ambition.

"And when the safety of the movement ran counter to his own plans, did he hesitate to risk your lives for the sake of his ambition? My father was a danger to him. My father was honest and a friend of liberty. But he was too popular, so he was betrayed. In that betrayal, the Autarch might have brought to ruins the entire cause and all of you with it. Which one of you is safe under a man who will deal with the Tyranni whenever it suits his purpose? Who can be safe serving a cowardly traitor?"

"Better," whispered Rizzett. "Stick to that. Give it to them."

Again the same voice called from the back rows. "The Autarch knows where the rebellion world is. Do *you* know?"

"We will discuss that later. Meanwhile, consider instead that under the Autarch we were all headed for complete ruin; that there is still time to save ourselves by turning from his guidance to a better and nobler way; that it is still possible from the jaws of defeat to snatch——"

"——only defeat, my dear young man," came a soft interrupting voice, and Biron turned in horror.

The fifty crewmen came babbling to their feet, and for a moment it seemed as though they might surge forward, but they had come to council unarmed; Rizzett had seen to that. And now a squad of Tyrannian guardsmen were filing through the various doors, weapons ready.

And Simok Aratap himself, a blaster in each hand, stood behind Biron and Rizzett.

# 20. WHERE?

Simok Aratap weighed carefully the personalities of each of the four who faced him and felt the stirring of a certain excitement within him. This would be the big gamble. The threads of the pattern were weaving toward a close. He was thankful that Major Andros was no longer with him; that the Tyrannian cruisers had gone as well.

He was left with his flagship, his crew and himself. They would be sufficient. He hated unwieldiness.

He spoke mildly, "Let me bring you up to date, my lady and gentlemen. The Autarch's ship has been boarded by a prize crew and is now being escorted back to Tyrann by Major Andros. The Autarch's men will be tried according to law and if convicted will receive the punishment for treason. They were routine conspirators and will be treated routinely. But what shall I do with you?"

Hinrik of Rhodia sat beside him, his face crumpled in utter misery. He said, "Consider that my daughter is a young girl. She was led into this unwillingly. Artemisia, tell them that you were——"

"Your daughter," interposed Aratap, "will probably be

released. She is, I believe, the matrimonial object of a highly placed Tyrannian nobleman. Obviously, that will be kept in mind."

Artemisia said, "I'll marry him, if you'll let the rest go."

Biron half rose, but Aratap waved him down. The Tyrannian Commissioner smiled and said, "My lady, please! I can strike bargains, I admit. However, I am not the Khan, but merely one of his servants. Therefore, any bargain I do make will have to be justified thoroughly at home. So what is it exactly that you offer?"

"My agreement to the marriage."

"That is not yours to offer. Your father has already agreed and that is sufficient. Do you have anything else?"

Aratap was waiting for the slow erosion of their wills to resist. The fact that he did not enjoy his role did not prevent him from filling it efficiently. The girl, for instance, might at this moment burst into tears and that would have a salutary effect on the young man. They had obviously been lovers. He wondered if old Pohang would want her under the circumstances, and decided that he probably would. The bargain would still be all in the ancient's favor. For the moment he thought distantly that the girl was very attractive.

And she was maintaining equilibrium. She was not breaking down. Very good, thought Aratap. She was strong willed as well. Pohang would not have joy of his bargain after all.

He said to Hinrik, "Do you wish to plead for your cousin too?"

Hinrik's lips moved soundlessly.

Gillbret cried, "No one pleads for me. I don't want anything of any Tyranni. Go ahead. Order me shot."

"You are hysterical," said Aratap. "You know that I cannot order you shot without trial."

"He is my cousin," whispered Hinrik.

"That will be considered too. You noblemen will someday have to learn that you cannot presume too far on your usefulness to us. I wonder if your cousin has learned that lesson yet."

He was satisfied with Gillbret's reactions. That fellow,

at least, sincerely wanted death. The frustration of life was too much for him. Keep him alive, then, and that alone would break him.

He paused thoughtfully before Rizzett. This was one of the Autarch's men. At the thought he felt a faint embarrassment. At the start of the chase, he had dismissed the Autarch as a factor on the basis of what seemed iron logic. Well, it was healthy to miss occasionally. It kept self-confidence balanced at a point safely short of arrogance.

He said, "You're the fool who served a traitor. You would have been better off with us."

Rizzett flushed.

Aratap went on, "If you ever had any military reputation, I am afraid this would destroy it. You are not a nobleman and considerations of state will play no part in your case. Your trial will be public and it will become known that you were a tool of a tool. Too bad."

Rizzett said, "But you are about to suggest a bargain, I suppose?"

"A bargain?"

"Khan's evidence, for instance? You have only a shipload. Wouldn't you want to know the rest of the machinery of revolt?"

Aratap shook his head slightly. "No. We have the Autarch. He will do as a source of information. Even without it, we need only make war on Lingane. There would be little left of revolt thereafter, I'm sure. There will be no bargain of that sort."

And this brought him to the young man. Aratap had left him for last because he was the cleverest of the lot. But he was young, and young people were often not dangerous. They lacked patience.

Biron spoke first, saying, "How did you follow us? Was he working with you?"

"The Autarch? Not in this case. I believe the poor fellow was trying to play both sides of the game, with the usual success of the unskillful."

Hinrik interrupted, with an incongruously childish eagerness, "The Tyranni have an invention that follows ships through hyperspace."

Aratap turned sharply. "If Your Excellency will refrain from interrupting, I would be obliged," and Hinrik cringed.

It really didn't matter. None of these four would be dangerous hereafter, but he had no desire to decrease by even one any of the uncertainties in the young man's mind.

Biron said, "Now, look, let's have facts, or nothing. You don't have us here because you love us. Why aren't we on the way back to Tyrann with the others? It's that you don't know how to go about killing us. Two of us are Hinriads. I am a Widemos. Rizzett is a well-known officer of the Linganian fleet. And that fifth one you have, your own pet coward and traitor, is still Autarch of Lingane. You can't kill any of us without stinking up the Kingdoms from Tyrann to the edge of the Nebula itself. You've *got* to try to make some sort of bargain with us, because there's nothing else you can do."

Aratap said, "You are not altogether wrong. Let me weave a pattern for you. We followed you, no matter how. You may disregard, I think, the Director's overactive imagination. You paused near three stars without landing on any planet. You came to a fourth and found a planet to land on. There we landed with you, watched, waited. We thought there might be something to wait for and we were right. You quarreled with the Autarch and both of you broadcast without limitation. That had been arranged by you for your own purposes, I know, but it suited our purpose as well. We overheard.

"The Autarch said that only one last intra-nebular planet remained to be visited and that it might be the rebellion world. This is interesting, you see. A rebellion world. You know, my curiosity is aroused. Where would that fifth and last planet be located?"

He let the silence last. He took a seat and watched them dispassionately—first one, then another.

Biron said, "There is no rebellion world."

"You were looking for nothing, then?"

"We were looking for nothing."

"You are being ridiculous."

Biron shrugged wearily. "You are yourself ridiculous if you expect more of an answer."

Aratap said, "Observe that this rebellion world must be the center of the octopus. To find it is my only purpose in keeping you alive. You each have something to gain. My lady, I might free you of your marriage. My Lord Gillbret, we might establish a laboratory for you, let you work undisturbed. Yes, we know more of you than you think." (Aratap turned away hastily. The man's face was working. He might weep and that would be unpleasant.) "Colonel Rizzett, you will be saved the humiliation of court-martial and the certainty of conviction and the ridicule and loss of reputation that would go with it. You, Biron Farrill, would be Rancher of Widemos again. In your case, we might even reverse the conviction of your father."

"And bring him back to life?"

"And restore his honor."

"His honor," said Biron, "rests in the very actions that led to his conviction and death. It is beyond your power to add to or detract from it."

Aratap said, "One of you four will tell me where to find this world you seek. One of you will be sensible. He will gain, whichever one it is, what I have promised. The rest of you will be married, imprisoned, executed—whatever will be worst for you. I warn you, I can be sadistic if I must be."

He waited a moment. "Which one will it be? If you don't speak, the one next to you will. You will have lost everything and I will still have the information I want."

Biron said, "It's no use. You're setting this up so carefully, and yet it won't help you. There is no rebellion world."

"The Autarch says there is."

"Then ask the Autarch your question."

Aratap frowned. The young man was carrying the bluff forward past the point of reason.

He said, "My own inclination is to deal with one of you."

"Yet you have dealt with the Autarch in the past. Do so

again. There is nothing you can sell to us that we are willing to buy from you." Biron looked about him. "Right?"

Artemisia crept closer to him and her hand folded slowly about his elbow. Rizzett nodded curtly and Gillbret muttered, "Right!" in a breathless manner.

"You have decided," said Aratap, and put his finger on the correct knob.

The Autarch's right wrist was immobilized in a light metal sheath, which was held magnetically tight to the metal band about his abdomen. The left side of his face was swollen and blue with bruise except for a ragged, force-healed scar that seamed it redly. He stood before them without moving after that first wrench which had freed his good arm from the grip of the armed guard at his side.

"What do you want?"

"I will tell you in a moment," said Aratap. "First, I want you to consider your audience. See whom we have here. There is the young man, for instance, whom you planned death for, yet who lived long enough to cripple you and destroy your plans, although you were an Autarch and he was an exile."

It was difficult to tell whether a flush had entered the Autarch's mangled face. There was no single muscle motion upon it.

Aratap did not look for one. He went on quietly, almost indifferently, "This is Gillbret oth Hinriad, who saved the young man's life and brought him to you. This is the Lady Artemisia, whom, I am told, you courted in your most charming manner and who betrayed you, nevertheless, for love of the youngster. This is Colonel Rizzett, your most trusted military aide, who also ended up betraying you. What do you owe these people, Autarch?"

The Autarch said again, "What do you want?"

"Information. Give it to me and you will be Autarch again. Your earlier dealings with us would be held in your favor at the Khan's court. Otherwise——"

"Otherwise?"

"Otherwise I will get it from these, you see. They will be saved and you will be executed. That is why I ask whether you owe them anything, that you should give them the opportunity of saving their lives by yourself being mistakenly stubborn."

The Autarch's face twisted painfully into a smile. "They cannot save their lives at my expense. They do not know the location of the world you seek. I do."

"I have not said what the information I want is, Autarch."

"There is only one thing you can want." His voice was hoarse—all but unrecognizable. "If my decision is to speak, then my Autarchy will be as before, you say."

"More closely guarded, of course," amended Aratap politely.

Rizzett cried out, "Believe him, and you'll but add treason to treason and be killed for it in the end."

The guard stepped forward, but Biron anticipated him. He flung himself upon Rizzett, struggling backward with him.

"Don't be a fool," he muttered. "There's nothing you can do."

The Autarch said, "I don't care about my Autarchy, or myself, Rizzett." He turned to Aratap. "Will these be killed? That, at least, you must promise." His horridly discolored face twisted savagely. "That one, above all." His finger stabbed toward Biron.

"If that is your price, it is met."

"If I could be his executioner, I would relieve you of all further obligation to me. If my finger could control the execution blast, it would be partial repayment. But if not that, at least I will tell you what he would have you not know. I give you rho, theta, and phi in parsecs and radians: 7352.43, 1.7836, 5.2112. Those three points will determine the position of the world in the Galaxy. You have them now."

"So I have," said Aratap, writing them down.

And Rizzett broke away, crying, "Traitor! Traitor!"

Biron, caught off balance, lost his grip on the Linganian and was thrown to one knee. "Rizzett," he yelled futilely.

Rizzett, face distorted, struggled briefly with the guard. Other guards were swarming in, but Rizzett had the blaster now. With hands and knees he struggled against the Tyrannian soldiers. Hurling himself through the huddle of bodies, Biron joined the fight. He caught Rizzett's throat, choking him, pulling him back.

"Traitor," Rizzett gasped, struggling to maintain aim as the Autarch tried desperately to squirm aside. He fired! And then they disarmed him and threw him on his back.

But the Autarch's right shoulder and half his chest had been blasted away. Grotesquely, the forearm dangled freely from its magnetized sheath. Fingers, wrist, and elbow ended in black ruin. For a long moment it seemed that the Autarch's eyes flickered as his body remained in crazy balance, and then they were glazed and he dropped and was a charred remnant upon the floor.

Artemisia choked and buried her face against Biron's chest. Biron forced himself to look once, firmly and without flinching, at the body of his father's murderer, then turned his eyes away. Hinrik, from a distant corner of the room, mumbled and giggled to himself.

Only Aratap was calm. He said, "Remove the body."

They did so, flaring the floor with a soft heat ray for a few moments to remove the blood. Only a few scattered char marks were left.

They helped Rizzett to his feet. He brushed at himself with both hands, then whirled fiercely toward Biron. "What were *you* doing? I almost missed the bastard."

Biron said wearily, "You fell into Aratap's trap, Rizzett."

"Trap? I killed the bastard, didn't I?"

"That was the trap. You did him a favor."

Rizzett made no answer, and Aratap did not interfere. He listened with a certain pleasure. The young fellow's brains worked smoothly.

Biron said, "If Aratap overheard what he claimed to have overheard, he would have known that only Jonti had the information he wanted. Jonti said that, with emphasis, when he faced us after the fight. It was obvious that Aratap was questioning us only to rattle us, to get us to act brainlessly at the proper time. I was ready for the irrational impulse he counted upon. You were not."

"I had thought," interposed Aratap softly, "that you would have done the job."

"I," said Biron, "would have aimed at you." He turned to Rizzett again. "Don't you see that he didn't want the Autarch alive? The Tyranni are snakes. He wanted the Autarch's information; he didn't want to pay for it; he couldn't risk killing him. You did it for him."

"Correct," said Aratap, "and I have my information."

Somewhere there was the sudden clamor of bells.

Rizzett began, "All right. If I did him a favor, I did myself one at the same time."

"Not quite," said the Commissioner, "since our young friend has not carried the analysis far enough. You see, a new crime has been committed. Where the only crime is treason against Tyrann, your disposal would be a delicate matter politically. But now that the Autarch of Lingane has been murdered, you may be tried, convicted, and executed by Linganian law and Tyrann need play no part in it. This will be convenient for——"

And then he frowned and interrupted himself. He heard the clanging, and stepped to the door. He kicked the release.

"What is happening?"

A soldier saluted. "General alarm, sir. Storage compartments."

"Fire?"

"It is not yet known, sir."

Aratap thought to himself, Great Galaxy! and stepped back into the room. "Where is Gillbret?"

And it was the first anyone knew of the latter's absence.

Aratap said, "We'll find him."

They found him in the engine room, cowering amid the giant structures, and half dragged, half carried him back to the Commissioner's room.

The Commissioner said dryly, "There is no escape on a ship, my lord. It did you no good to sound the general alarm. The time of confusion is even then limited."

He went on, "I think it is enough. We have kept the cruiser you stole, Farrill, my own cruiser, on board ship. It will be used to explore the rebellion world. We will make for the lamented Autarch's reference points as soon as the Jump can be calculated. This will be an adventure of a sort usually missing in this comfortable generation of ours."

There was the sudden thought in his mind of his father in command of a squadron, conquering worlds. He was *glad* Andros was gone. This adventure would be his alone.

They were separated after that. Artemisia was placed with her father, and Rizzett and Biron were marched off in separate directions. Gillbret struggled and screamed.

"I won't be left alone. I won't be in solitary."

Aratap sighed. This man's grandfather had been a great ruler, the history books said. It was degrading to have to watch such a scene. He said, with distaste, "Put my lord with one of the others."

And Gillbret was put with Biron. There was no speech between them till the coming of space-ship "night," when the lights turned a dim purple. It was bright enough to allow them to be watched through the tele-viewing system by the guards, shift and shift about, yet dim enough to allow sleep.

But Gillbret did not sleep.

"Biron," he whispered. "Biron."

And Biron, roused from a dull semi-drowse, said, "What do you want?"

"Biron, I have done it. It is all right, Biron."

Biron said, "Try to sleep, Gil."

But Gillbret went on, "But I've done it, Biron. Aratap may be smart, but I'm smarter. Isn't that amusing? You don't have to worry, Biron. Biron, don't worry. I've fixed it." He was shaking Biron again, feverishly.

Biron sat up. "What's the matter with you?"

"Nothing. Nothing. It's all right. But I fixed it." Gillbret was smiling. It was a sly smile, the smile of a little boy who has done something clever.

"What have you fixed?" Biron was on his feet. He seized the other by the shoulders and dragged him upright as well. "Answer me."

"They found me in the engine room." The words were jerked out. "They thought I was hiding. I wasn't. I sounded the general alarm for the storage room because I had to be alone for just a few minutes—a very few minutes. Biron, I shorted the hyperatomics."

"What?"

"It was easy. It took me a minute. And they won't know. I did it cleverly. They won't know until they try to Jump, and then all the fuel will be energy in one chain reaction and the ship and us and Aratap and all knowledge of the rebellion world will be a thin expansion of iron vapor."

Biron was backing away, eyes wide. "You did that?"

"Yes." Gillbret buried his head in his hands and rocked to and fro. "We'll be dead. Biron, I'm not afraid to die, but not alone. Not alone. I had to be with someone. I'm glad I'm with you. I want to be with someone when I die. But it won't hurt; it will be so quick. It won't hurt. It won't—hurt."

Biron said, "Fool! Madman! We might still have won out but for this."

Gillbret didn't hear him. His ears were filled with his own moans. Biron could only dash to the door.

"Guard," he yelled. *"Guard!"* Were there hours or merely minutes left?

# 21. HERE?

The soldier came clattering down the corridor. "Get back in there." His voice was sour and sharp.

They stood facing one another. There were no doors to the small bottom-level rooms which doubled as prison cells, but a force field stretched from side to side, top to bottom. Biron could feel it with his hand. There was a tiny resilience to it, like rubber stretched nearly to its extreme, and then it stopped giving, as though the first initial pressure turned it to steel.

It tingled Biron's hand, and he knew that though it would stop matter completely, it would be as transparent as space to the energy beam of a neuronic whip. And there was a whip in the guard's hand.

Biron said, "I've got to see Commissioner Aratap."

"Is that what you're making a noise about?" The guard was not in the best of humors. The night watch was unpopular and he was losing at cards. "I'll mention it after lights-on."

"It won't wait." Biron felt desperate. "It's important."

"It will have to wait. Will you get back, or do you want a bit of the whip?"

"Look," said Biron, "the man with me is Gillbret oth Hinriad. He is sick. He may be dying. If a Hinriad dies on a Tyrannian ship because you will not let me speak to the man in authority, you will not have a good time of it."

"What's wrong with him?"

"I don't know. Will you be quick or are you tired of life?"

The guard mumbled something and was off.

Biron watched him as far as he could see in the dim purple. He strained his ears in an attempt to catch the heightened throbbing of the engines as energy concentration climbed to a pre-Jump peak, but he heard nothing at all.

He strode to Gillbret, seized the man's hair, and pulled his head back gently. Eyes stared into his out of a contorted face. There was no recognition in them, only fear.

"Who are you?"

"It's only me—Biron. How do you feel?"

It took time for the words to penetrate. Gillbret said, blankly, "Biron?" Then, with a quiver of life, "Biron! Are they Jumping? Death won't hurt, Biron."

Biron let the head drop. No point in anger against Gillbret. On the information he had, or thought he had, it was a great gesture. All the more so, since it was breaking him.

But he was writhing in frustration. Why wouldn't they let him speak to Aratap? Why wouldn't they let him out? He found himself at a wall and beat upon it with his fists. If there were a door, he could break it down; if there were bars, he could pull them apart or drag them out of their sockets, by the Galaxy.

But there was a force field, which nothing could damage. He yelled again.

There were footsteps once more. He rushed to the open-yet-not-open door. He could not look out to see who was coming down the corridor. He could only wait.

It was the guard again. "Get back from the field," he

barked. "Step back with your hands in front of you." There
was an officer with him.

Biron retreated. The other's neuronic whip was on him,
unwaveringly. Biron said, "The man with you is not Aratap.
I want to speak to the Commissioner."

The officer said, "If Gillbret oth Hinriad is ill, you don't
want to see the Commissioner. You want to see a doctor."

The force field was down, with a dim blue spark showing
as contact broke. The officer entered, and Biron could see
the Medical Group insignia on his uniform.

Biron stepped in front of him. "All right. Now listen to
me. This ship mustn't Jump. The Commissioner is the only
one who can see to that, and I must see him. Do you
understand that? You're an officer. You can have him awakened."

The doctor put out an arm to brush Biron aside, and
Biron batted it away. The doctor cried out sharply and
called, "Guard, get this man out of here."

The guard stepped forward and Biron dived. They went
thumping down together, and Biron clawed up along the
guard's body, hand over hand, seizing first the shoulder and
then the wrist of the arm that was trying to bring its whip
down upon him.

For a moment they remained frozen, straining against
one another, and then Biron caught motion at the corner of
his eye. The medical officer was rushing past them to sound
the alarm.

Biron's hand, the one not holding the other's whip wrist,
shot out and seized the officer's ankle. The guard writhed
nearly free, and the officer kicked out wildly at him, but,
with the veins standing out on his neck and temples, Biron
pulled desperately with each hand.

The officer went down, shouting hoarsely. The guard's
whip clattered to the floor with a harsh sound.

Biron fell upon it, rolled with it, and came up on his
knees and one hand. In his other was the whip.

"Not a sound," he gasped. "Not one sound. Drop anything else you've got."

The guard, staggering to his feet, his tunic ripped, glared hatred and tossed a short, metal-weighted, plastic club away from himself. The doctor was unarmed.

Biron picked up the club. He said, "Sorry. I have nothing to tie and gag you with and no time anyway."

The whip flashed dimly once, twice. First the guard and the doctor stiffened in agonized immobility and dropped solidly, in one piece, legs and arms bent grotesquely out from their bodies as they lay, in the attitude they had last assumed before the whip struck.

Biron turned to Gillbret, who was watching with dull, soundless vacuity.

"Sorry," said Biron, "but you, too, Gillbret," and the whip flashed a third time.

The vacuous expression was frozen solid as Gillbret lay there on his side.

The force field was still down and Biron stepped out into the corridor. It was empty. This was space-ship "night" and only the watch and the night details would be up.

There would be no time to try to locate Aratap. It would have to be straight for the engine room. He set off. It would be toward the bow, of course.

A man in engineer's work clothes hurried past him.

"When's the next Jump?" called out Biron.

"About half an hour," the engineer returned over his shoulder.

"Engine room straight ahead?"

"And up the ramp." The man turned suddenly. "Who are you?"

Biron did not answer. The whip flared a fourth time. He stepped over the body and went on. Half an hour left.

He heard the noise of men as he sped up the ramp. The light ahead was white, not purple. He hesitated. Then he put the whip into his pocket. They would be busy. There would be no reason for them to suspect him.

He stepped in quickly. The men were pygmies scurrying about the huge matter-energy converters. The room glared with dials, a hundred thousand eyes staring their information out to all who would look. A ship this size, one almost in the class of a large passenger liner, was considerably different from the tiny Tyrannian cruiser he had been used to. There, the engines had been all but automatic. Here they were large enough to power a city, and required considerable supervision.

He was on a railed balcony that circled the engine room. In one corner there was a small room in which two men handled computers with flying fingers.

He hurried in that direction, while engineers passed him without looking at him, and stepped through the door.

The two at the computers looked at him.

"What's up?" one asked. "What are you doing up here? Get back to your post." He had a lieutenant's stripes.

Biron said, "Listen to me. The hyperatomics have been shorted. They've got to be repaired."

"Hold on," said the second man. "I've seen this man. He's one of the prisoners. Hold him, Lancy."

He jumped up and was making his way out the other door. Biron hurdled the desk and the computer, seized the belt of the controlman's tunic and pulled him backward.

"Correct," he said. "I'm one of the prisoners. I'm Biron of Widemos. But what I say is true. The hyperatomics are shorted. Have them inspected, if you don't believe me."

The lieutenant found himself staring at a neuronic whip. He said, carefully, "It can't be done, sir, without orders from Officer of the Day, or from the Commissioner. It would mean changing the Jump calculations and delaying us hours."

"Get the authority, then. Get the Commissioner."

"May I use the communicator?"

"Hurry."

The lieutenant's arm reached out for the flaring mouthpiece of the communicator, and halfway there plummeted down hard upon the row of knobs at one end of his desk. Bells clamored in every corner of the ship.

Biron's club was too late. It came down hard upon the lieutenant's wrist. The lieutenant snatched it away, nursing it and moaning over it, but the warning signals were sounding.

Guards were rocketing in upon the balcony through every entrance. Biron slammed out of the control room, looked in either direction, then hopped the railing.

He plummeted down, landing knees bent, and rolled. He rolled as rapidly as he could to prevent setting himself up as a target. He heard the soft hissing of a needle gun near his ear, and then he was in the shadow of one of the engines.

He stood up in a crouch, huddling beneath its curve. His right leg was a stabbing pain. Gravity was high so near the ship's hull and the drop had been a long one. He had sprained his knee badly. It meant that there would be no more chase. If he won out, it was to be from where he stood.

He called out, "Hold your fire! I am unarmed." First the club and then the whip he had taken from the guard went spinning out toward the center of the engine room. They lay there in stark impotence and plain view.

Biron shouted, "I have come to warn you. The hyperatomics are shorted. A Jump will mean the death of us all. I ask only that you check the motors. You will lose a few hours, perhaps, if I am wrong. You will save your lives, if I am right."

Someone called, "Go down there and get him."

Biron yelled, "Will you sell your lives rather than listen?"

He heard the cautious sound of many feet, and shrank backward. Then there was a sound above. A soldier was sliding down the engine toward him, hugging its faintly warm skin as though it were a bride. Biron waited. He could still use his arms.

And then the voice came from above, unnaturally loud, penetrating every corner of the huge room. It said, "Back to your places. Halt preparations for the Jump. Check the hyperatomics."

It was Aratap, speaking through the public-address system. The order then came, "Bring the young man to me."

Biron allowed himself to be taken. There were two soldiers on each side, holding him as though they expected him to explode. He tried to force himself to walk naturally, but he was limping badly.

Aratap was in semidress. His eyes seemed different: faded, peering, unfocused. It occurred to Biron that the man wore contact lenses.

Aratap said, "You have created quite a stir, Farrill."

"It was necessary to save the ship. Send these guards away. As long as the engines are being investigated, there's nothing more I intend doing."

"They will stay just awhile. At least, until I hear from my engine men."

They waited, silently, as the minutes dragged on, and then there was a flash of red upon the frosted-glass circle above the glowing lettering that read "Engine Room."

Aratap opened contact. "Make your report!"

The words that came were crisp and hurried: "Hyper-atomics on the C Bank completely shorted. Repairs under way."

Aratap said, "Have Jump recalculated for plus six hours."

He turned to Biron and said coolly, "You were right."

He gestured. The guards saluted, turned on their heels, and left one by one with a smooth precision.

Aratap said, "The details, please."

"Gillbret oth Hinriad during his stay in the engine room thought the shorting would be a good idea. The man is not responsible for his actions and must not be punished for it."

Aratap nodded. "He has not been considered responsible for years. That portion of the events will remain between you and me only. However, my interest and curiosity are aroused by your reasons for preventing the destruction of the ship. You are surely not afraid to die in a good cause?"

"There is no cause," said Biron. "There is no rebellion world. I have told you so already and I repeat it. Lingane was the center of revolt, and that has been checked. I was interested only in tracking down my father's murderer, the Lady Artemisia only in escaping an unwanted marriage. As for Gillbret, he is mad."

"Yet the Autarch believed in the existence of this mysterious planet. Surely he gave me the co-ordinates of something!"

"His belief is based on a madman's dream. Gillbret dreamed something twenty years ago. Using that as a basis, the Autarch calculated five possible planets as the site of this dream world. It is all nonsense."

The Commissioner said, "And yet something disturbs me."

"What?"

"You are working so hard to persuade me. Surely I will find all this out for myself once I have made the Jump. Consider that it is not impossible that in desperation one of you might endanger the ship and the other save it as a complicated method for convincing me that I need look no further for the rebellion world. I would say to myself: If there were really such a world, young Farrill would have let the ship vaporize, for he is a young man and romantically capable of dying what he would consider a hero's death. Since he has risked his life to prevent that happening, Gillbret is mad, there is no rebellion world, and I will return without searching further. Am I too complicated for you?"

"No. I understand you."

"And since you have saved our lives, you will receive appropriate consideration in the Khan's court. You will have saved your life and your cause. No, young sir, I am not quite so ready to believe the obvious. We will still make the Jump."

"I have no objections," said Biron.

"You are cool," said Aratap. "It is a pity you were not born one of us."

He meant it as a compliment. He went on, "We'll take you back to your cell now, and replace the force field. A simple precaution."

Biron nodded.

The guard that Biron had knocked out was no longer there when they returned to the prison room, but the doctor was. He was bending over the still-unconscious form of Gillbret.

Aratap said, "Is he still under?"

At his voice the doctor jumped up. "The effects of the whip have worn off, Commissioner, but the man is not young and has been under a strain. I don't know if he will recover."

Biron felt horror fill him. He dropped to his knees, disregarding the wrenching pain, and reached out a hand to touch Gillbret's shoulder gently.

"Gil," he whispered. He watched the damp, white face anxiously.

"Out of the way, man." The medical officer was scowling at him. He removed his black doctor's wallet from an inner pocket.

"At least the hypodermics aren't broken," he grumbled. He leaned over Gillbret, the hypodermic, filled with its colorless fluid, poised. It sank deep, and the plunger pressed inward automatically. The doctor tossed it aside and they waited.

Gillbret's eyes flickered, then opened. For a while they stared unseeingly. When he spoke finally, his voice was a whisper. "I can't see, Biron. I can't see."

Biron leaned close again. "It's all right, Gil. Just rest."

"I don't want to." He tried to struggle upright. "Biron, when are they Jumping?"

"Soon, soon!"

"Stay with me, then. I don't want to die alone." His fingers clutched feebly, and then relaxed. His head lolled backward.

The doctor stooped, then straightened. "We were too late. He's dead."

Tears stung at Biron's eyelids. "I'm sorry, Gil," he said, "but you didn't know. You didn't understand." They didn't hear him.

They were hard hours for Biron. Aratap had refused to allow him to attend the ceremonies involved in the burial of a body at space. Somewhere in the ship, he knew, Gillbret's body would be blasted in an atomic furnace and then exhausted into space, where its atoms might mingle forever with the thin wisps of interstellar matter.

Artemisia and Hinrik would be there. Would they understand? Would *she* understand that he had done only what he had to do?

The doctor had injected the cartilaginous extract that would hasten the healing of Biron's torn ligaments, and already the pain in his knee was barely noticeable, but then that was only physical pain, anyway. It could be ignored.

He felt the inner disturbance that meant the ship had Jumped and then the worst time came.

Earlier he had felt his own analysis to be correct. It *had* to be. But what if he were wrong? What if they were now at the very heart of rebellion? The information would go streaking back to Tyrann and the armada would gather. And he himself would die knowing that he might have saved the rebellion, but had risked death to ruin it.

It was during that dark time that he thought of the document again. The document he had once failed to get.

Strange the way the notion of the document came and went. It would be mentioned, and then forgotten. There was a mad, intensive search for the rebellion world and yet no search at all for the mysterious vanished document.

Was the emphasis being misplaced?

It occurred to Biron then that Aratap was willing to come upon the rebellion world with a single ship. What was that confidence he had? Could he dare a planet with a ship?

The Autarch had said the document had vanished years before, but then who had it?

The Tyranni, perhaps. They might have a document the secret of which would allow one ship to destroy a world.

If that were true, what did it matter where the rebellion world was, or if it existed at all.

Time passed and then Aratap entered. Biron rose to his feet.

Aratap said, "We have reached the star in question. There *is* a star there. The co-ordinates given us by the Autarch were correct."

"Well?"

"But there is no need to inspect it for planets. The star, I am told by my astrogators, was a nova less than a million years ago. If it had planets then, they were destroyed. It is a white dwarf now. It can have no planets."

Biron stared. "Then——"

Aratap said, "So you are right. There is no rebellion world."

# 22. THERE!

All of Aratap's philosophy could not completely wipe out the feeling of regret within him. For a while he had not been himself, but his father over again. He, too, these last weeks had been leading a squadron of ships against the enemies of the Khan.

But these were degenerate days, and where there might have been a rebellion world, there was none. There were no enemies of the Khan after all; no worlds to gain. He remained only a Commissioner, still condemned to the soothing of little troubles. No more.

Yet regret was a useless emotion. It accomplished nothing.

He said, "So you are right. There is no rebellion world."

He sat down and motioned Biron into a seat as well. "I want to talk to you."

The young man was staring solemnly at him, and Aratap found himself gently amazed that they had met first less than a month ago. The boy was older now, far more than a month older, and he had lost his fear. Aratap thought to himself, I am growing completely decadent. How many of

221

us are beginning to like individuals among our subjects? How many of us wish them well?

He said, "I am going to release the Director and his daughter. Naturally, it is the politically intelligent thing to do. In fact, it is the politically inevitable. I think, though, that I will release them now and send them back on the *Remorseless*. Would you care to pilot them?"

Biron said, "Are you freeing me?"

"Yes."

"Why?"

"You saved my ship, and my life as well."

"I doubt that personal gratitude would influence your actions in matters of state."

Aratap was within a hair of laughing outright. He *did* like the boy. "Then I'll give you another reason. As long as I was tracking a giant conspiracy against the Khan, you were dangerous. When that giant conspiracy failed to materialize, when all I had was a Linganian cabal of which the leader is dead, you were no longer dangerous. In fact, it would be dangerous to try either you or the Linganian captives.

"The trials would be in Linganian courts and therefore not under our full control. They would inevitably involve discussion of the so-called rebellion world. And though there is none, half the subjects of Tyrann would think there might be one after all, that where there was such a deal of drumming, there must be a drum. We would have given them a concept to rally round, a reason for revolt, a hope for the future. The Tyrannian realm would not be free of rebellion this side of a century."

"Then you free us all?"

"It will not be exactly freedom, since none of you is exactly loyal. We will deal with Lingane in our own way, and the next Autarch will find himself bound by closer ties to the Khanate. It will be no longer an Associated State, and trials involving Linganians will not necessarily be tried in Linganian courts hereafter. Those involved in the conspiracy, including those in our hands now, will be exiled to worlds nearer Tyrann, where they will be fairly harmless. You yourself cannot return to Nephelos and need not expect to be restored to your Ranch. You will stay on Rhodia, along with Colonel Rizzett."

"Good enough," said Biron, "but what of the Lady Artemisia's marriage?"

"You wish it stopped?"

"You must know that we would like to marry each other. You said once there might be some way of stopping the Tyrannian affair."

"At the time I had said that I was trying to accomplish something. What is the old saying? 'The lies of lovers and diplomats shall be forgiven them.'"

"But there *is* a way, Commissioner. It need only be pointed out to the Khan that when a powerful courtier would marry into an important subject family, it may be motives of ambition that lead him on. A subject revolt may be led by an ambitious Tyrannian as easily as by an ambitious Linganian."

Aratap did laugh this time. "You reason like one of us. But it wouldn't work. Would you want my advice?"

"What would it be?"

"Marry her yourself, quickly. A thing once done would be difficult to undo under the circumstances. We would find another woman for Pohang."

Biron hesitated. Then he put out a hand. "Thank you, sir."

Aratap took it. "I don't like Pohang particularly, anyway. Still, there is one thing further for you to remember. Don't let ambition mislead you. Though you marry the Director's daughter, you will never yourself be Director. You are not the type we want."

Aratap watched the shrinking *Remorseless* in the visiplate and was glad the decision had been made. The young man was free; a message was already on its way to Tyrann through the sub-ether. Major Andros would undoubtedly swell into apoplexy, and there would not be wanting men at court to demand his recall as Commissioner.

If necessary, he would travel to Tyrann. Somehow he would see the Khan and make him listen. Given all the facts, the King of Kings would see plainly that no other course of action was possible, and thereafter he could defy any possible combination of enemies.

The *Remorseless* was only a gleaming dot now, scarcely distinguishable from the stars that were beginning to surround it now that they were emerging from the Nebula.

Rizzett watched the shrinking Tyrannian flagship in the visiplate. He said, "So the man let us go! You know, if the Tyranni were all like him, damned if I wouldn't join their fleet. It upsets me in a way. I have definite notions of what Tyranni are like, and he doesn't fit. Do you suppose he can hear what we say?"

Biron set the automatic controls and swiveled in the pilot's seat. "No. Of course not. He can follow us through hyperspace as he did before, but I don't think he can put a spy beam on us. You remember that when he first captured us all he knew about us was what he overheard on the fourth planet. No more."

Artemisia stepped into the pilot room, her finger on her lips. "Not too loudly," she said. "I think he's sleeping now. It won't be long before we reach Rhodia, will it, Biron?"

"We can do it in one Jump, Arta. Aratap had it calculated for us."

Rizzett said, "I've got to wash my hands."

They watched him leave, and then she was in Biron's arms. He kissed her lightly on forehead and eyes, then found her lips as his arms tensed about her. The kiss came to a lingering and breathless end. She said, "I love you very much," and he said, "I love you more than I can say." The conversation that followed was both as unoriginal as that and as satisfying.

Biron said after a while, "Will he marry us before we land?"

Artemisia frowned a little. "I tried to explain that he's Director and captain of the ship and that there are no Tyranni here. I don't know though. He's quite upset. He's not himself at all, Biron. After he's rested, I'll try again."

Biron laughed softly. "Don't worry. He'll be persuaded."

Rizzett's footsteps were noisy as he returned. He said, "I wish we still had the trailer. There isn't room here to take a deep breath."

Biron said, "We'll be on Rhodia in a matter of hours. We'll be Jumping soon."

"I know." Rizzett scowled. "And we'll stay on Rhodia till we die. Not that I'm complaining overloud; I'm glad I'm alive. But it's a silly end to it all."

"There hasn't been any ending," said Biron softly.

Rizzett looked up. "You mean we can start all over? No, I don't think so. You can, perhaps, but not I. I'm too old and there's nothing left for me. Lingane will be dragged into line and I'll never see it again. That bothers me most of all, I think. I was born there and lived there all my life. I won't be but half a man anywhere else. You're young; you'll forget Nephelos."

"There's more to life than a home planet, Tedor. It's been our great shortcoming in the past centuries that we've been unable to recognize that fact. *All* planets are our home planets."

"Maybe. Maybe. If there *had* been a rebellion world, why, then, it might have been so."

"There *is* a rebellion world, Tedor."

Rizzett said sharply, "I'm in no mood for that, Biron."

"I'm not telling a lie. There *is* such a world and I know its location. I might have known it weeks ago, and so might anyone in our party. The facts were all there. They were knocking at my mind without being able to get in until that moment on the fourth planet when you and I had beat down Jonti. Do you remember him standing there, saying that we would never find the fifth planet without his help? Do you remember his words?"

"Exactly? No."

"I think I do. He said, 'There is an average of seventy cubic light-years per star. If you work by trial and error, without me, the odds are two hundred and fifty quadrillion to one against your coming within a billion miles of any star. *Any* star!' It was at that moment, I think, that the facts got into my mind. I could feel the click."

"Nothing clicks in my mind," said Rizzett. "Suppose you explain a bit."

Artemisia said, "I don't see what you can mean, Biron."

Biron said, "Don't you see that it is exactly those odds which Gillbret is supposed to have defeated? You remember his story. The meteor hit, deflected his ship's course, and at the end of its Jumps, it was actually *within* a stellar system. That could have happened only by a coincidence so incredible as to be not worth any belief."

"Then it *was* a madman's story and there is no rebellion world."

"Unless there is a condition under which the odds against landing within a stellar system are less incredible, and there is such a condition. In fact, there is one set of circumstances, and only one, under which he *must* have reached a system. It would have been inevitable."

"Well?"

"You remember the Autarch's reasoning. The engines of Gillbret's ship were not interfered with, so the power of the hyperatomic thrusts, in other words, the lengths of the Jumps, were not changed. Only their direction was changed in such a way that one of the five stars in an incredibly vast area of the Nebula was reached. It was an interpretation which, on the very face of it, was improbable."

"But the alternatives?"

"Why, that neither power *nor* direction was altered. There is no real reason to suppose the direction of drive to have been interfered with. That was only assumption. What if the ship had simply followed its original course? It had been aimed at a stellar system, therefore it ended in a stellar system. The matter of odds doesn't enter."

"But the stellar system it was aimed at——"

"—was that of Rhodia. So he went to Rhodia. Is that so obvious that it's difficult to grasp?"

Artemisia said, "But then the rebellion world must be at home! That's impossible."

"Why impossible? It is somewhere in the Rhodian System. There are two ways of hiding an object. You can put it where no one can find it, as, for instance, within the Horsehead Nebula. Or else you can put it where no one would ever think of looking, right in front of their eyes in plain view.

"Consider what happened to Gillbret after landing on the rebellion world. He was returned to Rhodia alive. His theory was that this was in order to prevent a Tyrannian search for the ship which might come dangerously close to the world itself. But then why was he kept alive? If the ship had been returned with Gillbret dead, the same purpose would have been accomplished and there would have been no chance of Gillbret's talking, as, eventually, he did.

"Again, that can only be explained by supposing the rebellion world to be within the Rhodian System. Gillbret was a Hinriad, and where else would there be such respect for the life of a Hinriad but in Rhodia?"

Artemisia's hands clenched spasmodically. "But if what you say is true, Biron, then Father is in terrible danger."

"And has been for twenty years," agreed Biron, "but perhaps not in the manner you think. Gillbret once told me how difficult it was to pretend to be a dilettante and a good-for-nothing, to pretend so hard that one had to live the part even with friends and even when alone. Of course, with him, poor fellow, it was largely self-dramatization. He didn't really live the part. His real self came out easily enough with you, Arta. It showed to the Autarch. He even found it necessary to show it to me on fairly short acquaintance.

"But it is possible, I suppose, to really live such a life completely, if your reasons are sufficiently important. A man might live a lie even to his daughter, be willing to see her terribly married rather than risk a lifework that depended on complete Tyrannian trust, be willing to seem half a madman——"

Artemisia found her voice. She said huskily, "You can't mean what you're saying!"

"There is no other meaning possible, Arta. He has been Director over twenty years. In that time Rhodia has been continually strengthened by territory granted it by the Tyranni, because they felt it would be safe with him. For twenty years she has organized rebellion without interference from them, because he was so obviously harmless."

"You're guessing, Biron," said Rizzett, "and this kind of a guess is as dangerous as the ones we've made before."

Biron said, "This is no guess. I told Jonti in that last discussion of ours that he, not the Director, must have been the traitor who murdered my father, because my father would never have been foolish enough to trust the Director with any incriminating information. But the point is—and I knew it at the time—that this was just what my father did. Gillbret learned of Jonti's conspiratorial role through what he overheard in the discussions between my father and the Director. There is no other way in which he could have learned it.

"But a stick points both ways. We thought my father was working for Jonti and trying to enlist the support of the Director. Why is it not equally probable, or even more probable, that he was working for the Director and that his role within Jonti's organization was as an agent of the rebellion world attempting to prevent a premature explosion on Lingane that would ruin two decades of careful planning?

"Why do you suppose it seemed so important to me to save Aratap's ship when Gillbret shorted the motors? It wasn't for myself. I didn't, at the time, think Aratap would free me, no matter what. It wasn't even so much for you, Arta. It was to save the Director. He was the important man among us. Poor Gillbret didn't understand that."

Rizzett shook his head. "I'm sorry. I just can't make myself believe all that."

It was a new voice that spoke. "You may as well. It is

true." The Director was standing just outside the door, tall and somber-eyed. It was his voice and yet not quite his voice. It was crisp and sure of itself.

Artemisia ran to him. "Father! Biron says——"

"I heard what Biron said." He was stroking her hair with long, gentle motions of the hand. "And it is true. I would even have let your marriage take place."

She stepped back from him, almost in embarrassment. "You sound so different. You sound almost as if——"

"As if I weren't your father." He said it sadly. "It will not be for long, Arta. When we are back on Rhodia, I will be as you knew me, and you must accept me so."

Rizzett stared at him, his usually ruddy complexion as gray as his hair. Biron was holding his breath.

Hinrik said, "Come here, Biron."

He placed a hand on Biron's shoulder. "There was a time, young man, when I was ready to sacrifice your life. The time may come again in the future. Until a certain day I can protect neither of you. I can be nothing but what I have always seemed. Do you understand that?"

Each nodded.

"Unfortunately," said Hinrik, "damage has been done. Twenty years ago I was not as hardened to my role as I am today. I should have ordered Gillbret killed, but I could not. Because I did not, it is now known that there is a rebellion world and that I am its leader."

"Only we know that," said Biron.

Hinrik smiled bitterly. "You think that because you are young. Do you think Aratap is less intelligent than yourself? The reasoning by which you determined the location and leadership of the rebellion world is based on facts known to him, and he can reason as well as you. It is merely that he is older, more cautious; that he has grave responsibilities. He must be certain.

"Do you think he released you out of sentiment? I believe that you have been freed now for the same reason you were freed once before—simply that you might lead him farther along the path that leads to me."

Biron was pale. "Then I must leave Rhodia?"

"No. That would be fatal. There would seem no reason for you to leave, save the true one. Stay with me and they will remain uncertain. My plans are nearly completed. One more year, perhaps, or less."

"But Director, there are factors you may not be aware of. There is the matter of the document——"

"For which your father was searching?"

"Yes."

"Your father, my dear boy, did not know all there was to know. It is not safe to have anyone in possession of all the facts. The old Rancher discovered the existence of the document independently in the references to it in my library. I'll give him credit. He recognized its significance. But if he had consulted me, I would have told him it was no longer on Earth."

"That's exactly it, sir. I am certain the Tyranni have it."

"But of course not. *I* have it. I've had it for twenty years. It was what started the rebellion world, for it was only when I had it that I knew we could hold our winnings once we had won."

"It is a weapon, then?"

"It is the strongest weapon in the universe. It will destroy the Tyranni and us alike, but will save the Nebular Kingdoms. Without it, we could perhaps defeat the Tyranni, but we would only have exchanged one feudal despotism for another, and as the Tyranni are plotted against, we would be plotted against. We and they must both be delivered into the ashcan of outmoded political systems. The time for maturity has come as it once came on the planet Earth, and there will be a new kind of government, a kind that has never yet been tried in the Galaxy. There will be no Khans, no Autarchs, Directors, or Ranchers."

"In the name of Space," roared Rizzett suddenly, "what will there be?"

"People."

"People? How can they govern? There must be some one person to make decisions."

"There is a way. The blueprint I have, dealt with a small section of one planet, but it can be adapted to all the Galaxy."

The Director smiled. "Come, children, I may as well marry you. It can do little more harm now."

Biron's hand tightly enclosed Artemisia's and she was smiling at him. They felt the queer inward twinge as the *Remorseless* made its single precalculated Jump.

Biron said, "Before you start, sir, will you tell me something about the blueprint you mention, so that my curiosity will be satisfied and I can keep my mind on Arta?"

Artemisia laughed and said, "You had better do it, Father. I couldn't bear an abstracted groom."

Hinrik smiled. "I know the document by heart. Listen."

And with Rhodia's sun bright on the visiplate, Hinrik began with those words that were older—far older—than any of the planets in the Galaxy save one:

"'We the people of the United States, in order to form a more perfect Union, establish justice, insure domestic tranquillity, provide for the common defense, promote the general welfare, and secure the blessings of liberty to ourselves and our posterity, do ordain and establish this Constitution for the United States of America. . . .'"

# AFTERWORD

*The Stars, Like Dust*—was written and first published in 1950. At that time, we did not know as much about planetary atmospheres as we do now. In Chapter 17, I speak of a lifeless world as possessing nitrogen and oxygen, but no carbon dioxide. It seems now quite certain, that a lifeless "E-type" world (a small and rocky one, like Earth, that is relatively close to its star) would, if it possessed an atmosphere, have one that was made up of nitrogen and carbon dioxide, but no oxygen.

I can't change Chapter 17 appropriately without having to rewrite a great deal of the book, so I will ask you to suspend your disbelief in this respect and enjoy the book (assuming you do) on its own terms.

Isaac Asimov
November, 1982

# ABOUT THE AUTHOR

Isaac Asimov was born in the Soviet Union to his great surprise. He moved quickly to correct the situation. When his parents emigrated to the United States, Isaac (three years old at the time) stowed away in their baggage. He has been an American citizen since the age of eight.

Brought up in Brooklyn, and educated in its public schools, he eventually found his way to Columbia University and, over the protests of the school administration, managed to annex a series of degrees in chemistry, up to and including a Ph.D. He then infiltrated Boston University and climbed the academic ladder, ignoring all cries of outrage, until he found himself Professor of Biochemistry.

Meanwhile, at the age of nine, he found the love of his life (in the inanimate sense) when he discovered his first science-fiction magazine. By the time he was eleven, he began to write stories, and at eighteen, he actually worked up the nerve to submit one. It was rejected. After four long months of tribulation and suffering, he sold his first story and, thereafter, he never looked back.

In 1941, when he was twenty-one years old, he wrote the classic short story "Nightfall" and his future was assured. Shortly before that he had begun writing his robot stories, and shortly after that he had begun his Foundation series.

What was left except quantity? At the present time, he has published over 260 books, distributed through every major division of the Dewey system of library classification, and shows no signs of slowing up. He remains as youthful, as lively, and as lovable as ever, and grows more handsome with each year. You can be sure that this is so since he has written this little essay himself and his devotion to absolute objectivity is notorious.

He is married to Janet Jeppson, psychiatrist and writer, has two children by a previous marriage, and lives in New York City.